AMERICA LOVES

Johanna Lindsey

"First rate romance."
New York Daily News

"Johanna Lindsey has a sure touch where
historical romance is concerned."
Newport News Daily Press

"She manages to etch memorable characters
in every novel she writes."
Chicago Sun-Times

"Johanna Lindsey transports us. . . . We
have no choice but to respond to the
humor and the intensity."
San Diego Union-Tribune

"The charm and appeal of her characters
are infectious."
Publishers Weekly

"Long may she continue to write."
CompuServe Romance Reviews

Johanna Lindsey

JOINING

AVON BOOKS
An Imprint of HarperCollinsPublishers

AVON BOOKS
An Imprint of HarperCollins*Publishers*
10 East 53rd Street
New York, New York 10022-5299

Copyright © 1999 by Johanna Lindsey
ISBN-13: 978-0-06-113114-1
ISBN-10: 0-06-113114-8
www.avonbooks.com

First Avon Books special printing: September 2006
First Avon Books paperback printing: April 2000
First Avon Books hardcover printing: May 1999

Avon Trademark Reg. U.S. Pat. Off. and in Other Countries, Marca Registrada, Hecho en U.S.A.
HarperCollins® is a registered trademark of HarperCollins Publishers Inc.

Printed in the U.S.A.

10 9 8 7 6 5 4 3 2 1

JOINING

One

England, 1214

Walter de Roghton sat in the antechamber outside the king's chamber, where he had been left
to wait. He was still hopeful that he was to have
the audience that he had been promised, but as
minutes turned to hours and still he was not
summoned, it was doubtful that it would be tonight. Other lords had gathered, other hopefuls
like himself who wanted something of King
John. Walter was the only one among them who
didn't appear nervous. He was; he just managed
to conceal it much better than the others.

And there was much to be nervous about.
John Plantagenet was one of the most hated
kings in all of Christendom, one of the most
treacherous and deceitful. A king who thought
nothing of hanging innocent children who'd
been held as hostages when he needed to set an

example for his enemies. As an example, it had failed. As a heinous act, it had served to turn John's barons even more against him, in fear and disgust.

This was a king who twice tried to wrest the crown from his own brother, Richard Lionheart, and had twice been forgiven that treason due to their mother's intervention. And once the crown was his upon Richard's death, he'd had the only other claimant to it, his young nephew Arthur, killed, and Arthur's sister Eleanor imprisoned for more than half her life.

Some had pitied John as the youngest of King Henry's four sons. There had been nothing left of Henry's kingdom to give to John after it had been divided among his older brothers. Thus the name that had long followed him of John Lackland. But there was little to pity about the man who had become king. There was nothing to pity about the man who had put his country under excommunication for many years because of his war with the church, a ban that had only just been lifted. No, there was much to hate about this king, and much to fear.

Walter was making himself more nervous thinking about John's many misdeeds, though he still managed to appear calm to any who might glance his way. For the thousandth time he wondered, was it worth it? And what if his proposed plan went awry?

Walter could, in truth, live out the rest of his days without ever coming under the king's notice. He was a minor baron, after all, one who had no need to frequent the king's court. But there was the rub. He was of little import . . . yet he would have it otherwise.

It should have been otherwise years ago, when he had discovered the perfect heiress and diligently courted her, only to have her stolen from him by a lord with a greater title. The woman who should have been his wife, Lady Anne of Lydshire, would have brought him great wealth and power with her dower lands. Instead she had been given to Guy de Thorpe, the Earl of Shefford, more than doubling de Thorpe's holdings, thereby making *his* one of the more powerful families in England.

The wife Walter did finally end up with had been a bad choice all around, as it turned out, which only added salt to the wound of his resentment. The property she had brought him had been acceptable at the time, but was unfortunately located in La Marche, and so lost when John lost most of his French holdings. Walter could have retained the land if he'd been willing to swear allegiance to the French king, but then he would have lost his keep in England. And his property in England was the larger.

Additionally, his wife had given him no sons, and only one daughter. Useless, that woman was. His daughter, Claire, however, he finally had a use for, now she'd reached the marriageable age of ten and two.

Thus Walter's visit to King John was twofold, revenge for that long-ago slight, when he had been overlooked as a suitor for Anne, and to finally wrest her property and more from Shefford by marrying Claire to Shefford's only son and heir.

It was a brilliant plan and the timing for it was ideal. Rumors were flying that John was soon going to make another attempt to seize the Angevin lands he had lost so long ago. And Walter had a carrot to dangle in front of John—if only he could lay the plan before him.

Finally the door to John's chamber opened and Chester, one of the few earls whom John still trusted completely, ushered Walter in. He made haste to kneel before the king, was impatiently waved to his feet.

The chamber was not empty as Walter had hoped. John's wife Isabelle was there, with one of her ladies-in-waiting. Walter had never seen the queen this close before, and spent several bemused moments in awe when he did glance at her. Verily, the rumors of her were indeed true. If she was not the most beautiful woman in the world, she was surely the most beautiful in England.

John was more than twice her age—he had married Isabelle when she was just ten and two. And although that was an age to marry, most nobles who took brides that young chose to wait a few years before they actually consummated the marriages. Not so John, for Isabelle had been ripe for her age, and too beautiful to resist for a man whose wenching had been notorious prior to this marriage.

Not as tall as his brother Richard, but still handsome at two score and six, John was the dark one of the family, with black hair now liberally laced with gray, and his father's green eyes and somewhat stocky build.

John smiled indulgently when he noted the

direction of Walter's gaze and his incredulity, a reaction he was most used to and pleased with. His young wife's beauty did him proud. But his smile was brief, the hour late, and he did not recognize Walter, had only been told by his clerk that one of his barons had urgent news for him.

So his question was bald and to the point. "Do I know you?"

Walter blushed to have been distracted from his cause for even a few moments. "Nay, Your Grace, we have never met, for 'tis rarely I come to court. I am Walter de Roghton. I hold a small keep from the Earl of Pembroke."

"Then mayhap your news should have been given to Pembroke, who could have relayed it to me?"

" 'Tis not of a nature to entrust to any other, m'lord, and—and 'tis not exactly news," Walter was forced to admit. "I knew no other way to explain to your clerk when he did ask me for the reason I was here."

John was piqued by the cryptic reply. He was himself a man who dealt much in subtleties and innuendos. "Not news, but something I should know, and not entrusted even to your liege lord?" John smiled now. "Verily, keep me in suspense no longer."

"If we could speak in privacy?" Walter whispered, again looking toward the queen.

John made a moue, but still directed Walter toward the window seat on the far side of the room from the ladies. He spoke of many things with his lovely young wife, but he allowed some things were best not discussed with a woman known to love gossip.

John carried a glass of wine with him. He had not offered Walter the same. And his impatience was palpable.

Walter got right to the point as soon as they sat facing each other in the deep window embrasure. "You are likely aware of the betrothal, contracted years ago with your brother Richard's blessing, of Shefford's heir and the Crispin girl?"

"Aye, I believe I have heard mention of it ere now, a match foolishly made due more to friendship than gain."

"Not exactly, Your Grace," Walter said carefully. "Mayhap you are not aware, then, that Nigel Crispin returned from the Holy Land with a veritable fortune, and a good portion of it comes with the bride to the marriage?"

"A fortune?"

John's interest was thoroughly aroused now. He had always lacked the funds to run his kingdom properly, since Richard had drained the realm coffers for his bloody crusading. But a fortune to a minor baron such as Walter likely would not be anywhere near a fortune a king would take note of.

So he wanted clarified, "What mean you a fortune? A few hundred marks and some gold cups?"

"Nay, Your Grace, more like a king's ransom several times over."

John shot to his feet, incredulous. Any king's ransom that was mentioned in his day could only refer to the one demanded in ransom for his brother Richard when he had been captured by one of his enemies on his return home from the Holy Lands.

"More than a hundred thousand marks?"

"Easily double that," Walter replied.

"How is it you know this, when it has never reached my ears ere now?"

" 'Tis no secret among Lord Nigel's close acquaintances, aye, even a heroic tale of how he came by this fortune in the saving of your brother's life. 'Tis just not something he would want spread far and wide, and rightly so, with so many thieves rife in the lands. I only heard mention of it by accident myself, when I heard how much of that fortune comes with Shefford's bride-to-be."

"And how much would that be?"

"Seventy-five thousand marks."

"Unheard-of!" John exclaimed.

"But understandable, since Crispin is not land-rich, whereas Shefford is. Crispin could be land-rich did he choose to, but he is an unostentatious man, 'twould seem, who is happy with his little castle and only a few other small holdings. Verily, few realize it, just how powerful Crispin is with such wealth behind him, the immense army of mercenaries he could raise if need be."

John did not need to hear more. "And if those two families join in marriage, they would in truth be more powerful than even Pembroke and Chester."

What he didn't add was they could be even more powerful than he himself, especially when so many of his barons ignored his demands for aid, or turned outright rebel against him, but Walter understood that, as did John.

"Then you see the need to prevent this joining?" Walter ventured.

"What I see is that Guy de Thorpe has never denied me aid when requested, has continually supported my wars, ofttimes even sending his son and a well-supplied army of knights to fill my ranks. What I see is this nigh landless Nigel Crispin will now be taxed accordingly. What I *see* is if I did perforce forbid this joining, these two *friends*"—this was said with a full dose of disgust—"would then have cause to still join— but against me."

"But if something or someone other than yourself prevented that particular joining?" Walter asked slyly.

At that, John burst out laughing, drawing a brief, curious look from his wife across the room. "I would not be the least bit remorseful."

Walter smiled serenely, for this was what he had counted on. "It would be of even further benefit, Your Grace, if, when Shefford must look for a new bride, you were to suggest one with dower lands across the channel. 'Tis known he sends knights for your wars in England and Wales, but he sends scutage for your French wars, since he has no personal interest there. But did his son's wife have dower lands in, say, La Marche, then he would have a personal interest in seeing that the Count of La Marche troubles you no more. And three hundred knights is worth more than the one thousand mercenaries their fees in scutage would bring you, you will agree."

John smiled as well, for that was indeed true. One loyal, well-trained knight was worth far more than a half dozen mercenaries. And three hundred well-trained knights, which was what Shefford could muster, could mean the difference in winning an important skirmish.

"I suppose you have just such a daughter with dower lands in La Marche?" John asked, as a mere formality. He already guessed the answer.

"Indeed, m'lord."

"Then I see no reason not to recommend her—if the Shefford whelp does go looking for a new bride."

It was not exactly a promise, but then King John was not known to keep promises. But Walter was satisfied.

Two

"*You know my* feelings on this, Father. 'Twould tax me little to name *many* heiresses more suitable for my wife, one or two I would even *like* to have, yet you have bound me to your friend's daughter who brings us naught but more coins, which we do not need."

Guy de Thorpe stared at his son and sighed. Wulfric had come late to his marriage, when he had despaired of ever having a son. His two eldest daughters were already wed ere he was even born. Guy even had grandchildren who were older than his son. But for an only son—at least his only legitimate son—Guy could not truly find fault with him, had much to be proud of—except for his stubbornness, and with it, his propensity to argue with his sire.

Like Guy, Wulfric was a large man, with muscles honed thick from training and warfare. They both also bore the thick black hair and blue eyes from Guy's father, though Guy's were a lighter blue, while Wulfric's a darker hue, and Guy's thick mane was now more gray than black. The square, unyielding jaw was more Anne's, though, and that straight, patrician nose came from her side of the family as well. Still, Wulfric much resembled Guy, was in fact a more handsome version; leastwise the ladies thought him fair to look upon.

"Is that why you have chased after wars since the girl came of age, Wulf? To avoid wedding her?"

Wulfric had the grace to blush, since that was exactly what he had done. But he defended himself. "The one time I met her, she had her falcon attack me. I still carry the scar."

Guy was incredulous. "*That* is why you have always refused to go again with me to Dunburh Castle? *Jesu*, Wulf, she was just a small child. You carry a grudge against a child?"

Wulfric flushed with remembered anger now, rather than embarrassment. "She was a veritable shrew, Father. Verily, she acted more the boy than the girl, challenging, swearing, attacking any who would gainsay her, no matter their size or age. But nay, that is not why I do not want her. I want Agnes of York instead."

"Why?"

Wulfric was given pause at the unexpected direct query. "Why?"

"Aye, why? Do you love her?"

"I know I would like to see her in my bed, but love her? Nay, I doubt me I do."

Guy chuckled at that, much relieved. "There is naught wrong with lust. 'Tis a healthy emotion—if you discount what pious priests say of it. A man is lucky if he finds it in his marriage, luckier still if he finds love there as well. But you know as well as I that a marriage is not needed to have either."

"So I am peculiar, to prefer to lust after my wife rather than her serving wenches," Wulfric maintained stubbornly.

It was Guy's turn to blush. 'Twas no secret that he bore no great love for his wife, Anne. But he was fond of her, and gave her every respect, including keeping his mistresses out of her domain. Unlike his friend Nigel, who had loved his wife dearly, and to this day continued to mourn her loss, Guy had never known that emotion with a woman, nor did he feel deprived to have never known it. But lust, on the other hand—he'd had many mistresses over the years, too many to count, and if Anne had not heard of them, his son certainly had.

Though there was no censure in Wulfric's look. He had been wenching himself from a young age, so was in no position to cast stones. Therefore, Guy saw no need to explain how easily lust could be satisfied, whether with one's wife or not. What a man would prefer was rarely the plate he was served. But then such was life.

He said instead, "I will not embarrass our family by asking to null the betrothal contract. You know that Nigel Crispin is my closest friend. You also know that he saved my life, when my horse had fallen on me, trapping me beneath it so I could not escape, and a Saracen scimitar was within inches of taking off my head. There was naught I could do to repay him—that he would accept—then. 'Twas mostly gratitude that had me offer what was dearest to me, you, when he at last sired daughters. The joining of our families was secondary. What he could contribute to that joining was of little import—at least at the time."

"At the time? Mean you to say 'tis important now?" Wulfric said in scoffing tones.

Guy again sighed. "If the king demanded only the forty days service due him, 'twould not be important, but he asks for more than that. If you had given him only the forty days due, 'twould not be important, but you gave him more. Even now you just return from fighting, yet already mention you mean to cross the channel with the king on his next campaign. Well, enough is enough, Wulf. We cannot continue to support our people and the king's army as well."

"You never said we were struggling," Wulfric replied almost accusingly.

"I would not have you worry, when you were off fighting John's battles. And 'tis not a dire circumstance, just a troublesome one, with too many things occurring in the last ten years to deplete our reserves. The king's visit here last year with his entire court hurt, but that is to be expected, occurs anywhere he goes, which is why he can never stay long in one place. Those campaigns in Wales hurt more, with not a farm there in sight to feed your men, and the Welsh gone into the hills a-hiding . . ."

Guy said no more on that account. Wulfric's expression had gone sour as he remembered how nigh futile was warfare against the Welsh, who would not meet an army on the field, but would whittle away at it from ambush. Wulfric had lost many of his own men in Wales.

"All I am saying, Wulf, is that what your wife will bring to us—"

Wulfric's stubbornness reared up again to interrupt, "She is *not* my wife yet."

And Guy continued as if he hadn't heard, though he likewise stressed, "Your *wife* brings us what is needful at this time. Powerful alliances we have aplenty. All five of your sisters were placed exceedingly well. Land we have aplenty, though once you wed, more can be bought if needful, more castles can be raised, improvements made . . . *Jesu*, Wulf, 'tis a fortune she brings us, and that is *naught* to scoff at, whether 'tis needful or not."

Guy took a long draft of his wine before he mentioned the worst of it. "Besides, you have kept her waiting so long that it would now be a serious insult to beg off, now she's so far past marriageable age—due to your delays. Well, no more. 'Tis time you collect her and have done with it. See that you leave for Dunburh within the week."

"Is that an order?" Wulfric asked stiffly.

"It is if it must be. I will not break the contract, Wulf. 'Tis too late for that when she is ten and eight now. Will you shame me by doing so?"

Wulfric could only reply, albeit furiously, "Nay, I'll fetch her. I'll even marry her. But whether I'll live with her remains to be seen."

So saying, he stalked from the hall. Guy watched him until he was gone from sight, then turned to stare into the fire in the Great Hearth.

The hour was late. He'd waited until Anne and her ladies had left the hall before he'd summoned Wulfric. Mayhap he should have enlisted Anne's support instead.

Wulfric never argued with his mother, not as he did with Guy. Verily, he seemed to enjoy ceding to her wishes, for he loved her dearly. And Anne was even more eager than Guy to have the marriage done. She was the one who had nagged him to speak with Wulfric ere he found himself another war to run off to. In anticipation of having her own coffers replenished, no doubt. But at least she could have got their son to agree, without seeing how much he hated doing so.

Guy sighed again, wondering now if he was doing Nigel's daughter a disservice, forcing his son to marry her.

Three

It was a day-and-a-half journey to Dunburh, even accompanied by a score of men-at-arms, as well as several knights. These were not for his own protection, but because they would be escorting a lady and likely her retinue of servants on the return journey. And brigands were rife in John's realm.

Some of John's own barons, having been exiled, had taken their war to the roads, attacking those still in John's favor. So even if Guy hadn't insisted on his taking precautions, Wulfric would have done so. He wasn't going to have his father accuse him of losing the bride-to-be by carelessness—whether he would like to or not.

The bride-to-be . . . Just the thought of that scrawny little she-devil had him growling low in his throat. Which made his half brother raise a brow at him in puzzlement.

They had just broken camp on the second day of the journey, were back on the road and making good time. With so many men to find lodgings for, no easy feat, he had deemed it best just to camp beside the road last eventide. Though he would have to find those lodgings on the return trip, since *she* was like to insist on sleeping in a bed.

"You *still* have not reconciled yourself to this marriage?" Raimund asked him as they rode side by side.

"Nay, and 'tis as like I never will," Wulfric admitted. "It feels as if I am bought with coin—an abhorrent feeling to say the least."

Raimund snorted. "When our father made the offering, not hers? If 'twere the other way around, then aye, I might agree. But—"

"Faugh, I would speak of it no more—"

"Nay, 'tis best you chew on it now, ere you must deal with her directly," Raimund cautioned. "What truly vexes you about this match, Wulf?"

Wulfric sighed. "There was naught to like about her when she was a child, but there was much to dislike. I am not hopeful that a few years will have changed her. I fear I will hate my wife."

"For certain, 'twould not be the first time that has happened," Raimund said with a chuckle. "You want to find an agreeable marriage, look to the villeins. They have the choice of mates. Nobles have not that luxury."

That was said with such obvious gloating, Wulfric threw a fist at his brother, who let out his laughter now as he dodged the blow. "You needn't remind me that you chose your own wife, *and* love her dearly," Wulfric snarled. "And you are no villein," he added, grumbling even louder.

Raimund smiled fondly at his brother, for not many would claim his nobility with the conviction that Wulfric did, since Raimund's mother had in fact been a villein, putting him in the unenviable position of not being accepted by either villein or noble. But Raimund had been more fortunate than most bastards, for Guy had acknowledged him, had even had him fostered and trained to knighthood, and once knighted, had bestowed on him a small keep that he could call his own.

Because of that property, he had been able to win the woman of his choice to wife, Sir Richard's daughter, Eloise. Richard was a landless knight himself in Guy's household, and so had had little hope of finding a man of property for his only child, and had been delighted by Raimund's interest. Nay, Raimund did not envy his brother being the earl's only legitimate son. His was a simple life and he liked it that way. Wulfric's life was ever like to be much more complicated.

"How much time has passed since you did first meet her?" Raimund ventured.

"Nigh a dozen years."

Raimund rolled his eyes. "Christ's Toes, think you she has not changed at all in that time? Not been taught proper behavior suitable to her rank? She'll be like to beg your forgiveness for whatever caused your dislike—and what *did* cause it?"

"She was six, I was ten and three—and aware of who she was to me, even if she was not. I sought her out to meet her, found her in the Dunburh mews with two young lads near her age. She was showing them a large gyrfalcon, claiming it was hers. Had even got the bird onto her arm. It was damn near as big as she was."

As he told the tale, it came back to him clearly, that day he'd met his betrothed. She was not clean, looked like she'd been rolling about in the dirt, had smudges all over her piquant face. And long legs she had for her small size, made glaringly apparent because she was not dressed as she should be, but was wearing cross-gartered leggings and a rough tunic very like those of the lads with her.

He had in fact been hard-pressed to figure out which of the three she was. He had been warned of her attire, though, by those he'd asked for her whereabouts. They thought it a grand joke, the Dunburh castlefolk, that their lord's daughter went about dressed as she did—by choice.

Some villeins might dress their daughters so, but only if they had extra male clothes and could not afford female ones. But what female, a lady at that, dressed like a male by choice? She did. And with her long brown hair clubbed back, and the dirt, Wulfric would never have figured out which of the three was she.

When someone called her name he realized she was holding a huge bird on her arm, and the falcon not even hooded, and his first inclination had been to protect her. She could not realize how dangerous hunting birds were. And she was far too young to be allowed near them. No doubt she had sneaked in there whilst the falconer was away.

And then he heard her brag to her young,

gullible friends, "She's mine now. She'll only take food from me."

Hers? Wulfric could not contain his snort of disbelief. The sound drew her attention, but no more than her curiosity. She was, after all, too young to realize he'd as much as called her a liar.

"Who are you?" was all she'd asked him.

"I am the man you will be wedded to once you are old enough for wedding."

He could not reason why she would take offense at those words, which were no more than the truth, but she did. Verily, the way her light green eyes had flared and then filled with golden heat, 'twas a powerful rage that had come upon her.

"She flew into a rage then and called *me* a liar and a half dozen of the foulest names I'd ever heard," he told Raimund. "Then ordered me, *ordered* me, to be gone from her sight."

Raimund tried to hold back his laughter, but couldn't quite manage it. "*Jesu*, all that from a child that young?"

"A she-devil that young," Wulfric replied. "When I did not leave—truly, I was too incredulous to move—her eyes narrowed on me and she lifted her arm just so, enough to send that falcon straight at me. I brought up my hand to hold it off. My mistake. Its beak sunk between my first two knuckles and wouldst not let go."

Raimund whistled softly. " 'Tis lucky you did not lose one of your fingers."

"I lost a big enough chunk of skin to leave a scar when I finally shook it off me, sending it into the wall. I know not if I killed it, but the little witch surely thought I did, for she attacked me immediately, literally pounding on me with her little fists, which would have availed her naught—I was big for my age as you know, and she barely reached my waist in height. But she bit me, and the moment I howled from that, one of her blows landed where I could have wished it had not, bringing me to my knees."

Raimund grinned. "Well, since I know you have left a long trail of satisfied wenches since then, I'd say that wound was not serious."

Wulfric gave him a fulminating glare. " 'Twas not the least humorous, brother. I was in pain, and she was still beating on me, and now I was down to her level, her blows rained about my head. She nigh poked my eye out. She left numerous scratches about my face."

'Twas worse than that, though he did not like to admit it. But he had been in severe pain from the blow to his groin, was dripping blood from the hole in his hand all over the floor, himself— and her. And she was so swift in her pummeling, a veritable whirlwind, that he could not manage to catch her hands to get her to stop, nor hold her back with his uninjured hand long enough to give him any relief, for she wiggled loose of any hold he got on her.

He should have clouted her smartly as she deserved, but he'd never hit a child or anyone so much smaller than he, much less a female. But trying to keep from hurting her had only got him injured further. At last he'd had to shove her away, forcefully enough to get her far back from him so he could stumble to his feet and make his escape, which he'd done right quickly.

Thankfully, he'd never seen her again. He'd made certain of that. He'd hid his wound from his father, but had made his excuses to return to Lord Edward, whom he had been fostered with since he was seven—and where he'd first met and befriended his brother Raimund, who had also been sent to Edward Fitzallen for training. And he'd always made sure he was gone from Shefford Castle whenever Nigel would come to visit with his family, and he never went again to Dunburh with his father.

"You do realize," Raimund offered, "that she will not be like that now, that someone would have taken her in hand and taught her how to be a proper lady?"

"Aye, I know it. She will not flail at me with her fists again—she would not dare. But how do you teach a wench not to be a shrew when she is born a shrew?"

"Mayhap with sweet words and giving her naught to be shrewish about?"

Wulfric snorted. "I meant not for me to teach her, but for her to have been taught, which is what I doubt was done. She will *appear* to be a lady now, I've no doubt, but 'twill just be a she-devil dressed up nicely is what I fear. And the first time she narrows those cattish green eyes at me . . ."

"You'll what?"

Wulfric sighed. "I wish I knew."

Four

"If I remember rightly, we should be at Dunburh Castle within the hour," Wulfric remarked as he gazed about his surroundings. "'Tis just over that knoll in the distance there. Actually, if we cut through these woods, we will make better time, for the road meanders a bit ere it veers back toward Dunburh."

There was a clear path through the woods, where others had no doubt taken the quicker route. This time of the year there were few leaves left on the trees to offer any obstructions, so even though it was a thick woods, the other side could still be seen, enough to note a meadow beyond, and farther, a village.

"For twelve years he avoids this place, but is now suddenly eager to get there," Raimund teased.

"Eager for a warm fire is all," Wulfric shot back with a quelling look.

Raimund ignored the look, but could certainly agree a fire would be appreciated. The sky was clear, but the weather had gotten decidedly more chilly about midmorning. They could all use a warm fire—or a little exercise.

"What say we stay to the road and race the last league?" Raimund suggested.

Wulfric all but rolled his eyes. "Quickest way to get a castle closed against you is to race toward it, when they know not who you are. Nay, that will not get us to that fire any time soon. We cut through the woods and come up the back side through their village."

He didn't wait for any other suggestions, but turned down the narrow path. The meadow was soon reached, then the village, which they skirted around so as not to cause alarm among the villeins. Though in truth not many were out on such a cold morning so there were no plots to tend this time of year.

The castle was still a ways off, through another stand of trees, though its towers could be seen above the treetops. There was thicker foliage along the new path, most of it shrubbery turned brown, though there were green pines aplenty, blocking most of the castle from view.

When they had reached halfway between the castle and village, they heard the clash of arms. It was a sound that made Wulfric smile. He was a man of war, had trained most of his life for it, excelled at it, and so enjoyed making use of what he had learned. Raimund shared the same sentiments, and they grinned at each other before they both spurred their horses forward to round the next bend in the path.

'Twas indeed a skirmish they came upon. At first they thought it could have been just practice, but not with so many involved, and a woman in the midst of it.

There were four mounted men, and about seven more on the ground, counting the woman, but they were all wearing thick winter cloaks, and so joined in the combat, 'twas hard to tell who were the Dunburh folks and who were the attackers. Which was why Wulfric could not just charge forward and start killing indiscriminately.

He halted his men, but they were not noticed, not soon enough to suit him, so he moved forward to shout, "Who needs help here?"

Wulfric had to shout it twice, there was so much noise in the clashing of blades. But the second shout got the attention of all, as did the score of men mounted behind him, and for a brief moment there was utter silence as everyone there stared at the new arrivals.

It was a very brief moment, though, for those four on horseback scattered posthaste, disappearing into the trees on either side of the path. They *could* have been from Dunburh and running for the castle, thinking the attackers were aided, but 'twas not likely, not when the woman was still there and coming forward to curtsy to him.

Her cloak opened in the curtsy, revealing rich apparel beneath—a lady then, and a comely one at that, who now had his full attention. She had been terrified, was only just now gaining color back in her face. Her wimple had fallen askew, showing dark sable brown hair, and when she looked up at him now, it was with green eyes so light a hue, they resembled crystal-clear peridots . . .

Green eyes? *Jesu*, was this her? His betrothed, demurely offering her gratitude? Nay, he could not be that lucky. She could not have changed this much, turned into this sweet morsel of womanhood.

Even her voice was soothingly soft as she said to him, "Your arrival could not have been more timely, my lord, and is much appre—"

His lady did not get to finish, was shoved rudely aside by a young lad who glared up at Wulfric and shouted, "Do not sit there like a sotted drunkard, go after them! They need capturing!"

Wulfric stiffened, about as offended as he could ever remember being. The audacious boy could not be more than ten and four, was dressed no better than the meanest villein, which was about all Wulfric noticed about him, since he was in the process of dismounting so he could throttle the fellow.

But before his leg cleared the saddle, he heard that same derogatory voice grumble, "Incompetents who call themselves knights. You offer help, then do not give it."

Wulfric resumed his seat to nudge his horse forward. The stupid boy had not sense enough to run before the horse reached him, waited there defiantly standing his ground, as much as daring Wulfric to do his worst. Wulfric admired bravery, but not stupidity, and the lad had to be a half-wit, to speak so to a mounted knight. Which was the only thing that stayed his hand at the moment—he did not beat children, women, nor idiots who knew no better.

So he said in a reasonable tone, "You would

have preferred to continue as you were—losing the battle? I ended the fray. I offered no more'n that."

"You let them escape!" he was accused.

"I am not a sheriff to chase down brigands, and if you say one more word to me, sirrah, I will have your tongue for my supper."

At which point the lady stepped in front of the lad and extended a placating hand toward Wulfric. "Please," she beseeched him, "no more violence."

The boy must be her servant, for her to try to protect him. And Wulfric was so pleased with how she had turned out that he would have deferred any matter to her just then.

"As you wish, my lady. May I return you to Dunburh? 'Tis my destination."

She nodded shyly, but asked, "You are here to see my father?"

Wulfric gave her a brilliant smile. If he had had any doubts left that she was his betrothed, she had just relieved them.

He was very careful in lifting her onto the saddle in front of him. She weighed no more than a child. She smelled of summer roses. *Jesu*, he was a happy man.

"I am indeed here to see Lord Nigel—and you," he said once she was settled.

She turned to look back at him, her lovely eyes rounded in surprise. "Me?"

"Mayhap I should have introduced myself sooner." He grinned. "I am Wulfric de Thorpe, and 'tis my greatest pleasure to meet you— again—my lady."

The gasp was not hers, came from someone

on the ground. He looked to see who was so disturbed by his identity, but saw only the half-wit lad running off toward the castle.

He was frowning after the boy, thinking he would speak with Lord Nigel about lessoning the fellow, when he heard his lady say, "But we have not met ere now."

Wulfric smiled to himself. Excellent. She did not remember their first unfortunate encounter all those years ago, and since he would as soon forget it as well, he was not going to remind her of it.

So he said, "My mistake, but no matter, the pleasure is still mine, demoiselle. And I am sure you would like to apprise your father of what happened here, as would I, so let us adjourn to the castle."

It took only a few minutes more to get there at a brisk clip. Where the attack had occurred had been just far enough away from village and castle for the clashing of weapons not to have been heard from either. Intentional? Likely. And Wulfric wished now that he had sent his men after the miscreants. They'd attacked his betrothed, after all, though he hadn't realized that until they were already long fled. But whether by design or by fluke, no one attacked what belonged to him without serious consequence.

As soon as he reached the compound, the lady was quick to make excuses and scurry into the keep, while he still had to speak with Nigel's seneschal about the quartering of his men before he joined her there. But several of his men he sent back to see if they could find and follow any tracks left by the attackers. 'Twouldn't hurt to aid Lord Nigel in their apprehension.

Dunburh was not as he remembered; indeed it was now much larger than it had been when Wulfric had last seen it. It was a grand stronghold for a minor baron such as Nigel Crispin was, but then few men could claim a fortune like Crispin's, even among the great earls of the land.

A thick curtain wall had been added to Dunburh's defense, more than doubling the size of the inner ward, but the old single defending wall was still standing as well, and many new buildings had gone up betwixt the two. Verily, there were more than enough buildings here to house a huge army with little crowding—and give them sport in two tilting yards, even an area set aside for the practice of archery.

Wulfric was eager to rejoin his betrothed and get to know her better, so he was not long in entering the towering keep himself. He still could not quite believe his good fortune, that she would have so changed. Someone had indeed taken her in hand to teach her the proper demeanor of a lady. He could not imagine a more ideal wife, softly spoken, shy, and comely!

She was much prettier than Agnes of York, her skin smoother, her piquant face mesmerizing. She had not stirred his lust the way Agnes could, but he had little doubt that she would. He had merely been so surprised and delighted by her that little room had been left for other emotions.

The inner stairs that led up to the Great Hall were well lit with torches. The chapel was up there, too, in the forebuilding, both reached from a rather large antechamber. Another set of stairs continued to the fourth floor of the keep.

Wulfric, in his hurry, still nearly collided with the small form just leaving the chapel. It took him only a second to realize who it was, less time than that to feel his hackles rise again. The servant might be lacking in wits—there was no other excuse for the way he had dared to speak to a knight of the realm—but clearly he had avoided punishment, which did not sit well with Wulfric.

Which was why he said in a sneering tone, "Praying for forgiveness for that wayward tongue?" hoping the lad would recognize his mistake and fear the consequences so it never happened again.

But the lad faced him boldly. "Praying you would go away, but I see my prayers were not answered."

It was too much. The fellow was a servant. *Any* servant would get cuffed for such insolence to a noble of the realm. Wulfric was reaching to do just that, but the boy had more or less dismissed him and turned away to enter the hall and move off to the side of it, obviously so used to saying whatever pleased him that he had no fear whatsoever that he might be taken to task.

Irate, Wulfric followed immediately after him, would have chased the lad down to the kitchens if needs be, but others in the hall sighted him and Nigel called out to him, forcing him to give his full attention to his host instead.

Seeing his betrothed with her father, however, took the edge off of his annoyance and he made

his way eagerly to the Great Hearth to join
them. This was another area that had seen improvements due to Nigel's wealth. There was
not one high-backed chair there, usually re-
served for the lord of the castle, but four, all
thickly draped with furs to add to their comfort.
A low carved table sat at the center of them, a
tray of refreshments on it. Other stools and
benches were set about, showing that this was
an area many made use of.

The fire roared softly, giving a welcome
warmth for those just coming in from outside,
yet the rest of the large hall was not cold. The
windows, which were letting in ample light,
were every one of them set with expensive glass,
keeping the biting weather at bay. Huge tapes-
tries covering the stone walls aided this as well.

It was a hall like any other, designed to accommodate most of the castle folk at one sitting,
yet it was much more luxurious and comfortable
than others he'd seen. The king himself would
be envious of this chamber, Wulfric thought,
and wondered if John had ever visited. Likely
not, or he would have found some reason to
confiscate it.

It did not sit well with Wulfric, that he faith-
fully served a king he did not like even a little.
But his sentiments were not far different from
every other noble in the lands. John had endeared himself to few, made enemies with
many, yet he was still their king, and men of
honor would keep their sworn oaths to him—
until they could tolerate him no longer.

Nigel met him halfway to lead him back to the

hearth. He seemed delighted that Wulfric was there, exceedingly so, effusive in his welcome.

"It gladdens my heart that you are finally here, Wulfric, for the joining of our families. Your father sent word that you were coming, but we did not expect you quite this soon, or I would have warned my daughter to prepare herself. But I see that you have met her already."

They had reached the hearth, where the lady mentioned was standing nervously awaiting them. Wulfric made haste to put her at ease, smiling at her warmly, taking her trembling hand to bring it to his lips.

"Aye, we have met, my lord," he said to Nigel, while he kept his eyes on the lady. "Though we have not been formally introduced."

"I am not your betrothed, Lord Wulfric."

She was blushing painfully as she said it, because she had not said it sooner, there in the woods when she should have. Her timidness had kept her silent, and her fear that he would be upset—he was simply too big a man for her to risk upsetting, when angry men terrified her.

Clearly he was confused now, and she was sorry for that, said quickly to explain, "I am her sister, Jhone."

Nigel was looking confused now as well. "But you did meet Milisant—did you not? You just entered the hall with her."

Wulfric looked back toward the entrance. He had entered with no one but that . . . boy. *Jesu*, no, please, no, that could not be her. 'Twould mean she had changed not one whit in all these years . . . 'twould mean he was saddled with the she-devil after all, just as he had feared.

Five

"*Fetch her down* here, Jhone, and see that she is dressed properly for once."

That was the order Nigel had given his daughter, the daughter Wulfric had mistakenly thought was to be his—several hours ago. 'Twas obvious that Milisant Crispin was not going to come down to the hall, dressed properly or not. For once? *Jesu*, did that mean the wench never dressed or behaved like the lady she was supposed to be?

Wulfric was holding his tongue so as not to insult his father's dearest friend, but it was not easy to keep quiet when he was furious that the woman he was being forced to wed was anything but womanly. *How* could this man have let his oldest daughter, his heir no less, run wild like this—and get away with it?

Nigel had tried to entertain him while they waited, with stories of King Richard, whom he had much admired, and many of the wars he had participated in. He was a much-scarred old knight who had seen many a battle. He was younger than Wulfric's father by some five years, had been young when they went on Crusade together. Guy had already married off two daughters before he went to the Holy Land, but Nigel had left only a wife behind. He had sired no children until he returned to England.

Wulfric vaguely recalled now that there was one other daughter. 'Twas not something he had paid much attention to when mentioned, his having no interest in Nigel's other children. He had also known that Nigel's wife had died not many years after Milisant was born, but just because the girl had had no mother to teach her the ways of a lady was no excuse for the way she had turned out. Many other ladies died in childbirth, yet their daughters were still reared properly.

They fell into an uncomfortable silence as they continued to wait. Servants came and went. The tressel tables were being set up as the dinner hour approached—and still the two women did not return to the hall.

Nigel at last sighed and said, albeit with an embarrassed smile, "Mayhap I should explain to you about my eldest daughter, Milisant. She is not what you would expect a young woman her age to be."

That was an understatement, but Wulfric said merely, "This I did notice."

Yet even that reply had Nigel wincing. "I have never understood why, but she has always wished she were my son, rather than my daughter. It makes no difference, she is still my heir, but she does not see it that way. She would pick up a sword and be a knight, if she could manage to wield one. It infuriates her that she lacks the strength to be as she would like. So she does other manly things instead that she can manage."

Wulfric was almost afraid to ask, but had to know. "Other things?"

"She hunts, not as a lady might, but as a hunter would. She has mastered the use of the bow. Verily, I know of no man more accurate with one. She had figured out for herself how to defend Dunburh, if it was ever required of her to do so. Though it will never be required, she still prides herself that she could do it. She befriends certain animals that she considers un-huntable—actually, she has an uncanny way with animals, always has been able to easily tame wild things since she was a small child."

Wulfric felt himself flushing, hearing that last. 'Twas possible, he had to admit now, that the young Milisant *had* owned the falcon as she had claimed all those years ago, that she'd done the taming of it herself.

"So she prefers manly endeavors. Does this mean she scoffs at womanly pursuits?"

"Not just scoffs, but refuses to have aught to do with," Nigel said with another sigh. "I am sure you noticed her attire. 'Tis not through lack of trying that I have been unable to get her to wear the clothes she was born to wear. I give her no coin to buy her own clothes, have them made for her instead. She trades them with the villeins for the clothes she prefers. I take those away, she barters fresh meat for more. I take those away as well—*Jesu*, my villeins ran out of clothes, were all nigh naked that summer I tried to curb her ways.''

It would have been rude to ask why the girl was not simply ordered to do as she was told. And Wulfric was afraid to find out that she had so little respect for her father that she would have disobeyed him. But he had a right to know the worst of it—faugh, how could it be any worse than this?

"She does not realize that she looks—ridiculous, dressed as a man?"

"Think you she cares? Nay, she cares naught about her appearance. She has not the vanity you would expect a woman to have."

Wulfric sighed now. There was no help for it, he had to ask, "Why was this allowed to happen? Why was her behavior not curbed long ago, ere it got to be so—unwomanly?"

As he had anticipated, the question caused Nigel no small bit of embarrassment. " 'Tis my fault, as you may suspect. My only excuse is that I did not know Mili was not behaving as she aught to until it was too late. When my wife died, I—I lost my own reasoning. Even when I was here, I was not—here. I am not sure you can understand, the depths I sunk to in my mourning, but I have very little remembrance of those first years after she died."

"My father has said you loved her dearly," Wulfric remarked uneasily, for Nigel looked now as if he were sinking down into that grief again.

"Aye, I loved her, but I was not aware of how much until she was gone. My brother, Albert, God keep him, lived with us at the time. I trusted him to see to my girls, but he was a widower himself, and—and he thought it amusing, Milisant's boyish ways, so made no effort to curb her."

"But you said you were here—"

"Aye, but rarely sober, lad," Nigel admitted. "And my girls would often pretend to be each other—'twas a game they played. So when I would see Jhone, I thought 'twas Milisant, and so was unaware that aught was amiss, until, as I said, it was too late. When I did finally see her as she had become, she was already set in her ways, and refused to be reined in."

Wulfric stiffened slightly. "Refused?"

"She has much fire, my Milisant, not like her sister, Jhone, who is somewhat timid. The fiery spirit and courage she gets from her mother. 'Tis one of the reasons I have been unable to use harsh measures against her. I am afraid she knows she reminds me much of her mother and thus uses it to her advantage."

'Twas not a father's duty to mold his daughters as he did his sons, and to be fair, Wulfric pointed out, "No one would expect you to have trained her, yet were there no ladies here to see to it?"

Nigel shook his head. "There have been none here of high enough rank since my wife's passing, other than those belonging to my household knights, but none of them have had the fortitude to butt heads with my daughter. When I finally came to my senses to realize Milisant was not getting the training she should have, I sent her to Fulbray Castle to be fostered there in the hopes that Lord Hugh's lady could take her in hand. But 'twas too late by then, she had already gone her own way for too long, and after several years of trying, they sent her back with the missive that 'twas hopeless. They had tried everything they could without seriously hurting her, and mild punishments had done no good."

Wulfric wondered if the older man realized he had described a woman who was not fit to be a wife, that no man in his right mind would want such an unnatural female . . . *Jesu*, that was the very thing that was going to get him out of this marriage. Nigel himself would feel obliged to release him from the betrothal contract. It just needed to be pointed out, and Wulfric did just that.

"I thank you for your honesty, Lord Nigel, but all things considered, think you she would make a good wife?"

To his utter disappointment, Nigel smiled now. "Aye, I have little doubt of it, that children, and a husband she loves, are all that is needful to soften her edges and make her see the error of her ways."

"*How* can you be so sure of that?"

"Because that is what happened with her mother, and she is her mother's daughter. I said my wife had a fiery spirit, yet truth be told, she was a harridan when we did first meet, full of rage and pride, with a vicious tongue that could and did slice deep. Yet love changed her completely."

It was hard, truly hard, to keep from scoffing, yet Wulfric still remarked, "You assume she will love me. What if she does not?"

Nigel chuckled at that, further confounding

him, until he said, "There is naught that I can see wrong with you—far from it. Or do you tell me that you have difficulty with women?" At Wulfric's flush, he added, "I thought not. And my daughter will be no different, given time, once you are the center of her life. Verily, I would trust no other than Guy's son to have the care of my eldest, for if you are at all like your father, I know you will do right by her."

And that ended Wulfric's last hope of getting Nigel to void the contract. He *was* going to be stuck with the she-devil, because he was his father's son, because he was not a churlish knight as some men were, because he did not beat those weaker than he as many men did, because his father had taught him differently.

He was understandably bitter, not wanting to be the trainer of his own wife, as it seemed he would have to be. Some of that came through in his next remark, if not in the tone, which he kept carefully neutral.

"Yet I must deal with her in the interim, Lord Nigel, before this hopeful change occurs. She ignores your orders. What makes you think she will obey mine?"

"Because she knows how far she can transgress with me and not suffer for it, yet with you she will not have that advantage. She is not foolish, my boy, far from it. She is merely . . . strange in her attitude, and in what she views as important—at this time. But what she finds important now will change once she settles into marriage."

The father was optimistic. Wulfric was not.

Six

Jhone had a devil of a time tracking her sister down. Milisant might have gone up the stairs leading to the north tower chamber they shared, but as Jhone had suspected, instead of going there she had traversed the corridor to the west tower stairs, which would bring her back down and out of the keep entirely. And Dunburh was no small place to find her easily when she cared not to be found.

She did find her finally, in the stable, making friends with Wulfric de Thorpe's black stallion. It was not one of the huge destriers bred and used in battle for their viciousness and willingness to trample anything in their path. Destriers did not make good traveling mounts specifically because of their lethal dispositions, and so any knight with access to a friendlier horse would reserve his destrier just for battle. But it was still a large animal, and being a stallion, had not looked very friendly—until now.

"You are not trying to turn him against his owner, are you?" Jhone asked her sister uneasily as she approached the stall.

"I thought about it."

That surly reply had Jhone smiling. "But changed your mind?"

"Aye. I would not see the stallion hurt, which is no doubt what would happen if that bastard suddenly could not control him. It *is* his tendency to lash out and cause pain, as I learned firsthand."

"That was long ago, Mili," Jhone reminded her gently. "He was only a boy then, not fully a man as he is now. Surely he has changed—"

Milisant's head snapped up, her eyes filling with golden heat as she cut in, "You saw for yourself out there on the path. He *would* have struck me if you had not stepped forward when you did."

"But he did not know 'twas you."

"How much smaller am I than he, no matter *what* he thought me?"

Jhone could hardly refute that, so she remarked instead, "I was there to see his horror when he did realize just who you were."

"Good," Milisant shot back. "Then when I return to the hall, 'twill be to hear that that silly contract has been set aside."

"I am not so sure of that," Jhone said, biting her lip. "Would he have that power? To break a contract made by his father?"

Milisant frowned. "Nay, I suppose not. Then I will just have to make sure that Papa breaks it. I was going to anyway, just did not think 'twould be necessary this soon." And then she snorted. "And why would I think so? He could have come to claim me at any time these last six years, but he did not. Truly, I had all but forgotten about *him*."

That was not exactly true, and they both knew it. Milisant had her heart set on another, yet could not wed him until the old contract that promised her to Wulfric de Thorpe was set aside. So she could not help but think about her long-standing betrothed, even if those thoughts had not been pleasant ones.

"He may be tardy in showing up, Mili, but he has shown up. What if you do still have to wed him?"

"I would sooner jump off yonder tower."

"Milisant!"

"I did not say I would, just that I would rather."

Jhone leaned against the plank of the stall, not knowing how to make this easier for her sister, yet agonizing over her turmoil. It was cruel of de Thorpe to wait this long, without any communication, without once coming to visit so the two of them could gain knowledge of each other and be more at ease with the notion of their joining. She did not count that time that he did come all those years ago that had left such a bitter mark on her sister.

With no word, and so much time passed, 'twas no wonder Milisant had turned her thoughts and heart to another young knight, one she approved of and greatly liked, one who did not mind that she was not like other girls. They were even good friends, and Jhone had learned firsthand that being friends with your husband-to-be made a great difference and alleviated much fear on the bride's part.

Jhone had been wed herself two years ago to a young man who *had* come often to visit since their betrothal when she reached her tenth year. So she'd had six years to get to know him and had been most pleased with him, and was still saddened over his loss, for he had died not long after.

But she was the younger, and she had felt strange marrying ere Milisant did, and felt that her sister might feel somewhat embarrassed over it as well—and have yet another mark to hold against her betrothed because of it. Though Milisant had never admitted to any embarrassment, and if she had felt it, hid it well.

"You really think Papa will agree to set the contract aside after the groom has shown up for you? You no longer have his absence to use as a weapon in your reasoning."

Milisant dropped her forehead to the stallion's in a dejected manner. "He will," she said so softly Jhone barely heard it and had to doubt the conviction of it, then louder as she looked back up. "He must. I *cannot* wed that—that brute, Jhone! He would smother me, try to break me. And once Papa knows that I love another, he will see reason. Just because Wulfric de Thorpe has finally shown up does not excuse the lateness of it, and 'twas the lateness of it that had me looking elsewhere."

That did sound reasonable and was in fact true. Up until two years ago, Milisant had not thought of breaking the contract that had been in existence since the year of her birth. She had hated it, and hated her betrothed, but she had been resigned to her fate—until even more time passed and Wulfric still had not made an appearance, nor sent any excuses. And their father did often concede to Milisant's wishes, or more to the point, he would eventually give up trying to make her conform to his.

But for some reason, Jhone had a sinking feeling that Milisant would not succeed with their father this time. Contracts were a sacred thing that men adhered to, that women could not begin to fathom the reasoning for, since they were never consulted on the making of such. And somehow she knew that her sister was just as aware of this, which was one of the reasons she was festering with so much anger. And Jhone sensed the anger.

The other reason was no doubt that attack on the path. Fear had been the first emotion there, but fear did tend to turn to anger once the fear was gone. And who would have expected an attack like that so close to Dunburh? Milisant had not even brought along her weapons, since they had only been going to the village.

"I told Papa what happened on the path," Jhone said. "He sent Sir Milo to see about tracking down those men."

"Good." Milisant nodded. "Milo is a competent knight—not like some," she added in a grumble.

Jhone refused to comment on those "some." "I cannot imagine who they were, though, or why they seemed intent on getting to you."

"You noticed that as well?" Milisant asked with a thoughtful frown. "I thought I had imagined it, that they seemed centered on me."

Jhone shook her head. " 'Tis true, but why?"

At that, Milisant shrugged. "Why else? Ransom. 'Tis hardly a secret, with all the improvements made in the last ten years to Dunburh's defenses, that Papa's coffers are nigh overflowing. And I am his heir."

Jhone chuckled. "Aye, but who would know that you are his heir, to look at you?"

Milisant grinned. "True. Yet Dunburh sees much traffic in the way of traveling merchants and minstrels, and more frequently, mercenaries seeking work, any of whom could have found out who I am. 'Twas likely some of those mercenaries who got turned down, who saw kidnapping me as an easy way to fill their pockets."

Jhone nodded thoughtfully. That did seem the most likely reason.

"But you will have to be more careful now," Jhone warned. "And that means you cannot go off hunting alone as has been your habit."

"If I'd had my bow with me, Jhone, they never would have gotten that close, and well you know it."

That was true as well, but did not convince Jhone that caution was not needed. "There were only four of them. Next time there may be more in number. 'Twould not hurt for you to abstain from hunting, or take a few guards with you—at least until they are caught."

"We will see," was all Milisant would promise, an unsatisfactory answer at best.

But Jhone knew better than to try to browbeat her sister to get her to do as she would like. With Milisant, much more subtle tactics were required. So she said no more on that subject—for now. And she still had the main subject to deal with, of why she had sought her sister out. And *that* she was not sure how to broach either, without having Milisant turn stubborn.

So for the moment, Jhone chose an unrelated topic, remarking, "Stomper will become jealous if you give much more care to that stallion in his presence."

Milisant smiled across the way at the much larger horse that was patiently waiting for a bit of her attention. "Nay, he knows that the sharing of my feelings does not mean there is less for him."

She did leave the stall, though, to visit the other horse, and the stallion attempted to follow. She stopped to speak a few soft words to him. When she turned to leave again, he was content to stay.

Jhone had seen the same thing happen many times before. From as far back as she could remember, Milisant had shown an affinity for animals. 'Twas almost as if they could understand her perfectly when she spoke to them. 'Twas almost as if she could feel their pain and fear as her own, and they could sense this and draw comfort from it. That was not the case, of course; she would be silly to suppose it was. She just empathized with animals. Those she befriended did not feel threatened. But even those she hunted were asked their forgiveness ere she killed them, and too frequently she gave them an opportunity to escape her arrows. Mayhap because she only hunted for food, never for sport.

Jhone had empathy as well, not for animals, but for people. At least, it seemed as if she could sense emotions much stronger than the average person could. That was one reason the anger that large men felt so terrified her. Because she felt that anger so intensely, almost as if it were her own, and that frightened her.

That was why she had loved her husband, William, so much, and had asked her father to decline any other offers that might be submitted for her, for she was not ready to embrace marriage again. William had never felt anger. His disposition had been too light and carefree for him to ever take anything so seriously that 'twould cause him anger. And he had loved her dearly, which she had also felt most strongly. It would be nigh impossible to find another like William, so she wanted no other.

After a few words and gentle touches to the other horse, Milisant turned to leave the stable. Jhone finally said, "Papa sent me to fetch you to the hall—properly dressed."

Milisant stopped with a snort. "Put on a bliaut for *him?* When you show me one made of nettles."

Jhone covered her mouth quickly, but not ere Milisant saw the grin. "Well, I do not have one like that, but I do have extras—since I know that you have already burned the last ones that Papa had made for you."

"Then you wear one and be me. I will not willingly go forth to speak with that churl."

It was not an absurd request. They had often, in the past, pretended to be each other. 'Twas a game they had played as children, and one Jhone had much enjoyed, since when she pretended to be Milisant, she also seemed to gain

Milisant's courage and daring, something she sadly lacked when she was herself. But they had not switched places for several years, and in this instance, to deal with de Thorpe, nay, she could not do it. He frightened her too much.

"Mili, I cannot. He would have me trembling, and you do not want him to have that impression of you, do you? Besides, Papa would know, will be looking for just that."

Milisant scowled. "Then tell Papa you could not find me, that I left the castle. There is no reason for me to deal at all with de Thorpe, when I mean to have that contract set aside—as soon as I can find Papa alone to speak with him."

"Papa will be angry if I return to the hall without you," Jhone predicted.

"Papa is ofttimes angry with me. It never lasts."

Jhone was not so sure that would be the case this time. Wulfric de Thorpe was no ordinary visitor, after all. Their father would want him shown the honor due him as an earl's son, the same as an earl would receive, nigh the same as was due the king. And *Jesu*, she had not even had a chamber readied for him yet!

Jhone paled with the thought, and said quickly to her sister, "I will tell him, but he will not like it. So do not delay too long in speaking with him, Mili, and soothing his temper."

She rushed out of the stable then, leaving Milisant frowning after her and mumbling, "Soothe it? Since when do I do other than flame it?" And then she yelled after her sister, "You are the one who can soothe him, not me!" but Jhone was already beyond hearing her.

Seven

Milisant went to the armory for a bow—she was not going to risk entering the keep to fetch her own—and sneaked out the side gate where she could quickly blend with the woods. She was still churning with emotion, and none of it pleasant.

A hare came forward to greet her and she stopped to scratch it beneath its chin. She had many friends in these woods and the meadows beyond that she had made over the years. Some she took into the castle, but most she could not. There were just too many.

The animal sensed her dark mood, though, and quickly scampered off. She sighed and continued on, her steps soundless. When she was deep in the wood she stopped again and climbed a tree to settle on a sturdy limb. She had a bird's-eye view of the surrounding area and what animals were nearby that had not found a warm hole to hibernate in for the winter. She was in a mood to kill something, which was why she would not. She never hunted when she was angry. She had brought the bow merely for her own protection, since she knew those attackers had fled into these woods.

She was fleeing as well, trying to escape a memory that had been brought back so clearly today, thanks to *him*. It had been a day she might not even have remembered, it being so long ago and she so young, if there had not been so much pain involved with the memory.

She had been proudly showing off her newest accomplishment to her friends, the taming of Rhiska. The falconer had given up on Rhiska, because she was a captured gyrfalcon, not raised from a baby, and had refused to adapt to human handling. He had in fact been ready to turn her over to the cooks, or so he'd said, something Milisant only realized much later had been a jest. So some of her pride had come from thinking she had saved the bird's life by taming it.

But then he had appeared, drawing her notice with a sound, and looking at her as if she had done something wrong. And since she had tamed Rhiska without the falconer knowing, entering his domain when she had been expressly forbidden access, she knew she *had* done something wrong, but she could not fathom how this stranger could know.

But what he said to her, "I am the man you will be wedded to, once you are old enough for wedding," had been the very worst thing he could have said. He had been handsome enough. Another girl might have been thrilled to hear him say such a thing. But Milisant had just that week decided she was never going to marry.

Several days earlier, one of the village villeins had beat his wife so severely that she had died from it by the next day. The whispers that followed the incident, however, made a frightful impression on Milisant at that young age.

"She deserved it," and " 'Twas his right to discipline his own wife," and "He could have been a bit less heavy-handed. Who's going to cook for him now, eh?" And "A wife should know better than to make her husband wroth with her."

To Milisant's young mind, the best way to avoid all of that was to simply never wed. Such an easy solution, she wondered why more women did not think of it. And she had yet to be told about Wulfric de Thorpe, had yet to learn that she was already contracted to marry him. So she thought herself safe from heavy-handed husbands—until *he* stood there, claiming with such confidence that she would be wedding him.

He was a liar, of course, and so she called him, but his words had frightened her too, because he sounded so sure of himself. It had been a bad year for her all the way around, the year she'd found out that most of the things she wanted to do, she'd never be able to do. It was also the year that she had discovered, or at least her friends had, that she had a terrible temper, and she'd yet to figure out how to control it.

The liar got a taste of it, but when she ordered him to leave, he just stood there, staring. That was the last straw. She was going to have him thrown out of the castle and the gate barred to him.

She moved to put Rhiska back on her perch so she could leave the mews to summon one of the men-at-arms to deal with the stranger. She was furious that she had been ignored. After all, she was the lord's daughter, and this man was a stranger. But Rhiska sensed her anger and reacted to it, flying straight at him.

Milisant was surprised, and even more surprised when the foolish boy put up a gloveless hand to ward off a falcon. The hawk had not been trained to hunt yet, so had not been trained yet to return at a call. But all hawks were hunters by nature; they just did not usually attack people. Rhiska did, though, clamped right on to the boy's hand. Milisant started forward to talk the bird off of him, but the boy was too swift in his own reaction and shook Rhiska off.

The bird died almost instantly. Milisant did not need to examine it to know it was dead, she had felt the life spirit flow out of it, and she went a little mad in that moment of loss, launching herself at the boy as Rhiska had done, wanting to kill him as he had killed her bird.

She had no awareness, really, of what she was doing, she was so mad with grief, no awareness until she flew back from his push and crashed into one of the bird perches. She collapsed on her foot, heard the snap of her ankle, felt the pain wash over her. But the horror of a broken foot was worse than any pain, for she knew such breaks did not mend, that anyone who suffered such would be lame for life. And lame folk were not pitied, they were ignored, considered so inferior they became less than villeins—they became beggars.

She did not scream, made no sound, mayhap because of the shock. And to this day, she never knew how she had withstood the pain to push that bone back where it ought to be, never knew why she had done it, except for that terrifying thought of being lame the rest of her life.

Her two friends had run quickly for help so she could be carried inside the keep. The stranger had gone as soon as he had done his damage. She had not seen him again. But ironically, because she still had not made a sound, her injury had not been thought serious, had been thought no more than a twisting that would mend right quickly.

Only Jhone had known otherwise and had shared her horror of the expected lameness. Even the castle leech had known no different, for his answer had been to break out his leeches for a bloodletting. He had not even glanced once toward her injury. But then that was his answer for any malady. His bloody leeches were kept well fed.

For three months Milisant would not walk on her foot. For three months she would not remove the boot she had laced tightly to her ankle either, for fear of what it would look like underneath. She had only tied the boot on because it had seemed to relieve the pain somewhat, and so she had left it on.

But even after the pain had gone away completely, she had been too afeared to take a single step on her foot, or examine it closely. 'Twas only because Jhone had finally complained of being kicked too often by that boot whilst they slept that Milisant had at last removed it, leading to the discovery that she was not going to be a cripple after all.

To this day, Milisant said a daily prayer of thanks that her foot had somehow mended itself correctly, without leaving her lame. 'Twas not until two years later that she'd finally learned who that stranger had been, and that she really was promised to wed him. He had not lied, but he had not endeared himself to her in killing her Rhiska and nigh crippling her, far from it. She despised him and despised the very thought of being forced to marry him.

For six years after she'd learned the truth, she had worried about it, then for another year, then another. But when she'd been ten and four she'd stopped worrying about it. Wulfric had not come to Dunburh again and it had begun to look like he never would. So she had determined to wed her friend Roland instead as soon as he was old enough.

Her father would just have to be reasonable about this. With Roland she could be happy, she was sure of it, for she admired him greatly and they were already close friends. With Wulfric— she did not care to think how miserable her life would be with a brute such as he.

He was handsome enough, had been so as a boy, was more so as a man. He still could not compare to Roland, who had the face of an angel and the body of a giant—like his father, whom Milisant had met one time when he'd come to visit Roland at Fulbray.

She and Roland had both been fostered at Ful- bray. Most all boys were fostered for their knight's training, since it was assumed that at home their retainers and parents might go easy on them. 'Twas hardening future knights needed. Many girls were fostered as well simply because it was the custom to do so. But not all girls were sent off, primarily those whose mothers had died, or were more often at court than at home to teach them.

She had been fascinated by Roland from the start, because she knew him to be near her age, which was eight at the time, yet he was so huge, heads above the other boys he trained with. And he learned so quickly, was adept at everything he did. She envied him at first, his ease with all the skills that she would have liked to learn herself.

That was how she met him. She would not stay in the keep with the ladies, learning sewing, embroidery, social graces, and the like, things that interested her not at all. What interested her occurred out in the tilting and practice yards, the beauty of a well-aimed arrow, the power of a lance held just right, the deadly precision of a well-timed sword thrust—seeing a true benefit and return for effort and practice, a life-and-death difference.

For two years she hid from Dame Margaret, whose thankless task of trying to track her down to drag her back to the ladies' solar was usually futile. She learned how to craft her own bows and arrows from a master bowman who thought her just another of the young pages eager to learn.

She and Roland had one thing greatly in common, which was why they had become such fast friends. They were both of them very different from others their own age, Milisant in her scorn of ladylike pursuits, Roland in his incredible size and exceptional abilities.

She had not seen Roland for several years now, not since he had last stopped to visit on his way home to Clydon for the holidays. Unlike her, he was still at Fulbray and would be until he was knighted.

That could have occurred already, though, and she would not know it. They corresponded, but infrequently, it being costly to have such missives written, much less delivered. And she had put off writing to him lately, since she wanted to propose that they join in marriage, yet she was not quite sure how to go about that.

She was pondering how her father could handle that matter, soon as she had his agreement to null her contract with de Thorpe, when she heard a horse approaching. She then saw it, and its rider, coming slowly toward the tree she was perched in. He would not notice her, though, had his eyes on the ground. It took her a moment to recognize him—one of the knights who had been with Wulfric.

She was surprised when he stopped directly beneath her tree. Then she heard, "You trust that limb to support you without breaking?"

Milisant stiffened. Never before had she been sighted, even by the falconer, who trained the hawks in these woods and so had reason to frequently look up. And the knight had not once glanced up toward her. He did so now, revealing blue eyes of a dark hue—not quite as dark as *his* eyes, yet set much the same.

"You would not be de Thorpe's brother," she

guessed, "for he is an only son. A cousin may-hap?"

He started now, but as quickly chuckled. "Most people who know us not do not discern a relationship. How is it that you did?"

It was true they did not look much alike. He was much smaller than Wulfric, much thinner, too. And he had light brown hair, where Wulfric's was darkest black. Their bones were set much differently as well, this man's jaw softer, his nose thicker, his brows straight and bushy rather than sharply curved like Wulfric's.

Yet she did not think she had guessed wrong, and said, "You have his eyes, not as dark, but still his."

He nodded thoughtfully. "True enough. We share the same father, though I was born in the village."

A bastard then, which was common enough. Some even inherited—if there was no legitimate heir. Still, a brother, which had Milisant wondering why she did not feel the same rancor for this one as she did the other. Mayhap because this one actually seemed nice, with his crinkling eyes and quick laugh. Certainly he seemed non-threatening, so mayhap they were nothing alike after all.

"What do you out in these woods?" she asked curiously.

"Looking for those who are stupid enough to make war on a lady."

Jhone was the lady he spoke of, obviously, those assailants on the path the ones he sought. Had Sir Milo enlisted his aid? She could not fathom why he would, when Dunburh had plenty of household knights and over fifty men-at-arms.

"Should you not come down from there, ere that limb breaks?" he suggested.

"I am not big enough to break it."

"Aye, you are small," he agreed, then added cryptically, "but older than you appear, methinks."

"Why say you that?"

"You are too discerning, for a villein, least for one as young as you seem."

She realized then that he did not know who she was any more than his brother had known—until he'd been told.

But he was not finished, said also, "And too audacious for one. What are you then, lad? A freeholder?"

"A freeholder wouldst be preferable to what I am, sirrah. Nay, I am Nigel Crispin's daughter."

He winced and she heard him mumble, "Poor Wulf," which she was likely not meant to hear, as insulting as it sounded. So he pitied his brother, did he, for being contracted to wed her? No pity for her, of course, for being forced to marry a callous brute. But then when was a woman's lot ever taken into consideration by men?

In two carefully placed steps along the tree trunk, she dropped onto the ground in front of his horse, making it shy back a ways. She spared a moment of concern for the animal, putting her hand out to it and saying a few comforting words in Old Saxon. He came forward to nuzzle against her.

The knight blinked. She didn't notice before

she glared up at him to say in parting, "Aye, your brother deserves to be pitied, for he'll have no peace if I am forced to join with him."

She was turning to disappear again in the woods when she heard, "Do you wear that dirt for concealment, or are you a believer that bathing is unhealthy?"

She whirled back around. As if it was any of his business what she wore . . .

"What dirt?" she demanded.

He smiled then, his eyes crinkling again with it. "The dirt on your face and hands, demoiselle, that covers what might be perceived as a woman's skin. Very deceiving in keeping one from noticing to begin with that you are indeed a woman. You do it apurpose then? Or mayhap it has been a while since you have seen your own reflection?"

Milisant gritted her teeth. "Gazing in mirrors is an utter waste of one's time, and not that 'tis *any* concern of yours, but I bathe more often than most, nigh once a week!"

He chuckled outright. "Then you must be due for a bath."

She refused to drag a sleeve across her face to see if it would come away dirty. She did not doubt that it would, though. Jhone was forever dabbing at dirt smudges on her face—when Milisant would stand still long enough. She just was not used to having someone mention it. But as if she cared, she snorted to herself. How silly and—and womanish, to be concerned with vanity.

And even if she was due for her weekly bath, she'd avoid one now just on general principles—

at least until Wulfric was gone from Dunburh, which could not be soon enough to suit her. If his brother had noticed she was dirty, then he likely did as well, and all the better to send him away pleased with a broken contract.

So she smiled in parting and said, "Worry about your own bathing habits, sirrah, for you are not like to have time enough to find a hot tub here."

With that she slipped back into the woods and was quickly gone from his sight.

Eight

Milisant was feeling the effects of missing both supper and dinner that day, but she was too anxious to visit the kitchen before she sought out her father. He was a creature of habit, and 'twas his habit to retire at precisely the same time each evening, whether he had guests or not. And she wanted to catch him at just the right time, when he was alone in his chamber but not yet asleep.

So she slipped into the small chamber in front of his where his squires slept, and waited for them to leave the inner chamber after preparing him for bed. She did not have to wait long. Soon both squires appeared, and recognizing her, gave her no more than a curious look as she passed them and closed the inner door behind her.

The thick curtains on her father's bed had been closed to keep out the drafts, so she cleared her throat to let him know he was not alone. She had no worry that he might not have been alone before she entered.

He had never taken a mistress, at least none that she ever heard of. Instead he slept with the memories he had of the one he still missed. Milisant sorely regretted not knowing her mother, a woman who could inspire such devotion even after her death. She had been only three when she'd died, and could recall no memory of her other than sweet smells and a gentle voice that could banish all fear.

"I have been expecting you," he said as he moved the curtain aside and patted the bed next to him.

She approached slowly, unable to tell by his tone just how angry he was. She knew he had sent others than just Jhone to look for her, for she had dodged them repeatedly throughout the day.

"You are not too tired to talk?" she asked carefully, sitting beside him.

"Talks with you are always interesting, Mili, because you do not think as one might expect you to. So nay, I am never too tired to talk to you."

She frowned. "You find me interesting, do you? But I'll warrant you do not think others find me so."

"If you seek a denial of that from me, you will not get it. Others do indeed find you— strange, rather than interesting. 'Tis well that you do not delude yourself of this and so cannot be offended by it. When you make a concerted effort to be other than what you are, daughter, you must accept the consequences. 'Tis human nature to cling to what is normal and traditional, and to question, even fear, what is not."

"I am not feared," she scoffed.

"By those who know you well, nay, you are not. You *are* normal to them, because they have long known you to be the way you are. And you have been deluded by this acceptance to think that you can continue to do as you would like indefinitely. 'Tis just not so, Mili."

She noted the sadness in his tone. She did not take his words to heart, though. She would *not* change her ways just because some folks would find her behavior strange—for a woman. She had fought against such limited restrictions all her life. Why would she stop that fight now? But she knew why her father would want her to change—at this time. Because of de Thorpe.

In the same vein he continued, "You are old enough now, and certainly intelligent enough, to realize that benefits can be reaped from compromising."

She stiffened. "Meaning?"

"Meaning that it would have cost you little to don the appropriate clothes to make a favorable first impression on your future husband. To have him pleased with you would greatly be to your benefit and yours alone. Instead, you do not even make an appearance. Was it necessary to embarrass me in front of my friend's son this way?"

"Nay, Papa, you know that was not my intent!" Milisant protested.

"Yet was that the case," he replied. "Would it really have inconvenienced you so much to treat our guest with the respect due him?"

"He is due no respect from me," she mumbled.

Nigel was now frowning. "He is due every respect from you. He is your betrothed, soon to be your husband."

"But I would have it otherwise."

"Otherwise?"

This was what she had come for, and she rushed to get it all said before he stopped her. "I do not want to marry him, Papa. The thought of it terrifies me. I would mar—"

"This is normal—"

"Nay, it is not, for 'tis *just* him. On the path this morn, he meant to strike me down, would have if Jhone had not prevented it, and only because I questioned why he did not go after the attackers ere they escaped."

She knew she was misleading her father. She should have mentioned that Wulfric had not known who she was. Unfortunately, her father guessed so much.

"He thought you a lad, Mili, and a villein at that. You know yourself that villeins can be dealt with severely for questioning their betters. Some have been hung for less. 'Twould seem he would have been most lenient, merely to think of striking you."

She flushed furiously. "You find that acceptable, that he will beat me?"

Nigel snorted. "I doubt me he will ever do that. And be honest, daughter. You choose to provoke him, so the choice is in fact yours, whether you live with him in harmony or not."

"I do not want to live with him at all! I want to marry Roland Fitz Hugh of Clydon instead. I know him well. We are friends."

"Is that not Lord Ranulf's son?"

"Aye."

"And is he not one of Guy de Thorpe's liege men?"

"Aye, but—"

"You would have me wed you to the son of one of his vassals, when you could be wed to his own son instead? Do not be a fool, Mili."

"If you were not friends with the earl, if you had not saved his life, I would *never* have been considered for his precious heir! You know that."

"All the more reason to be honored that you were considered. He made the offer himself. 'Twould have been the gravest insult to refuse such an offer. You should be pleased with it. You will be an earl's wife."

"What would I care for titles when I know I will be miserable? This is what you want for me? To condemn me to a life I will hate?"

"Nay, I want you to be happy, Mili. The difference is, I know you will be, once you get over this silliness of thinking you cannot love Wulfric. There is no reason for you *not* to love him."

It was on the tip of her tongue to give him one very good reason, that in the space of mere seconds, Wulfric had not only killed one of her pets, but nigh crippled her for life. But since her father had never known about her broken foot, with Jhone going about pretending to be her during those three months she had stayed to her chamber to recover, so she would not be missed, he was not like to believe her. And even if he did believe her, he would still discount it, because Wulfric had only been a boy at the time,

and boys could be forgiven for their childhood
misdeeds.

So she gave him another reason, albeit one
that was not true as yet, but she had every confidence that it would be. "I cannot love Wulfric
de Thorpe when I already love Roland and
know I can be very happy with him. I would
not fear him, because I know that he would
make me a good, tolerant husband, as you have
been a good, tolerant father."

Nigel shook his head slowly. "You speak of
feelings you developed as a child. That is not
love—"

"It is!"

"Nay, you have not even seen him for nigh
two years—aye, I remember his visit here. A fine
lad. I was much impressed by his manner. No
doubt he would make a tolerant husband. But I
have done you no good favor, being tolerant of
your preferences all these years. More tolerance
is *not* what you need now. 'Tis time for you to
accept what you are, a woman, soon to be a
wife, soon after that to be a mother, and to con-
duct yourself accordingly. Or do you intend to
shame me for the rest of my days, as you have
shamed me thus far?"

She blanched. She had never heard him speak
so before—nay, that was not exactly true. He
had mentioned many times the embarrassment
she brought him with her unnatural tendencies,
but he had not seemed to really mean it. She
had not taken him seriously. But now . . .

"You are ashamed of me?" she asked in a
small voice.

"Nay, child, not ashamed, just very disappointed that you cannot accept your lot, what the good Lord decided you should be. And very tired of not being heeded. You do not realize how disrespectful it is when you disobey me, or how others perceive it and lose respect for me also—"

"Nay, that is not so!"

"Unfortunately it is, Mili. If a man cannot control his own daughter, how can he expect to command men or have their respect? Not once have you ever done as you were told. Well, I am asking something of you this one last time, ere you leave my house for good. Honor this contract that was made for you in good faith, and that does you such honor. Do this for me if not for yourself."

How could she refuse? Yet how could she willingly condemn herself to marriage with a man she truly did not like?

Her dilemma must have been obvious, because Nigel added, "You need not wed him on the morrow. Will a time to know him help? A month, mayhap, when you can come to see that he will indeed make you a good husband?"

"And if that is not my conclusion after a month's time?" she asked.

Nigel sighed. "I know you, daughter. You have an uncommon stubbornness. Can you set that aside and try this afresh? Can you be fair and truly give him a chance to change your mind about him?"

Could she? Feelings were hard to ignore, especially when they were so powerful. She could not honestly answer him, and said so. "I do not know."

He smiled, if only slightly. "That is at least better than a nay."

"And if I can never like him?"

"If I know you have tried, really tried . . . well, we will see."

That was small hope to offer her, but she was afraid it was the only offer she would be getting from him, as set as he was on this joining.

Nine

Milisant went down to the kitchen after leaving her father, not because she was still hungry but only because that was what she had intended to do. She had utterly lost her appetite, not surprising when she now had so much bile churning around in her belly.

In fact, she found herself standing in the center of the kitchen with no idea why she was there. She did not even recall walking there, so full was her mind with what she had more or less promised to do.

Give him a chance? Had she really agreed to do that? When she already knew what he was like? Boys did not outgrow their natural tendencies when they were men. She'd seen the proof of that this very morn, for Wulfric's tendency was still to lash out with his superior strength, and woe betide the one he should wield it against.

"So this is where you didst hide all day?"

Milisant whirled around, incredulous. He was standing there in the doorway, filling it with his great size. The room was warm with the many ovens banked for the night, but dimly lit, making his large figure all the more ominous, his shoulder-length hair blackest black, his blue eyes shadowed so that they appeared black as well. It was the broad shoulders, though, and the thick arms, that made him so menacing.

Roland was taller, maybe half a foot taller than Wulfric, a true giant like his father, yet he did not inspire fear in her. She hated that this man could make her afraid when she was usually so bold. It was the pain he had put her through in her youth—it had to be only that and the vivid memory of it, yet that was enough to make her tense and near tremble in his presence.

She was to give him a chance to prove he was worthy of her regard? Sweet Mary, how could she do that? He paralyzed her. The only time she hadn't feared him today was when she'd shouted at him this morn, and only because she had been so furious with him for not chasing after those men. Anger had been the buffer that had let her deal with him. But she could not use that as a defense, not if she was to do as her father had asked.

"Are we adding selective hearing to the list?" he said into the silence that had greeted his first question.

Milisant stiffened. "A list of my faults? Aye, add it, for it does sound like a good one. And nay, I was not hiding here. But what do you here? Were you not fed today?"

"I had no stomach for food earlier. Now I do. Ask me instead why I had no stomach for it."

Milisant frowned, clearly sensing his anger

now, and aware that he was blaming her. Mayhap she was at fault. He had certainly been to blame for her own lack of appetite today.

She said as much. "If you are as upset as I over our joining, I understand."

He nodded. "I see."

Instead of feeling insulted, Milisant took hope. If he was as displeased with their upcoming marriage as she was, he might speak to his father about it. Speaking to hers had not helped, but he might have better luck. Mayhap they could even work together to get out of this dilemma. If that was possible, then honesty might be the best way to deal with him just now.

Carefully she tried it. "You may have gathered that I do not want to wed with you." To lighten the blow, she added a little lie. " 'Tis not you in particular—but that I love another."

That did not lighten the blow enough, apparently. His expression grew darker. "As do I, but what difference does that make? So we will have a typical marriage."

"My parents' marriage was not like that," she informed him curtly. "I expect better."

He snorted. "Your parents were a rare exception, not the rule. You know as well as I that the marriages of nobles are political alliances and naught else. Love is never once taken into consideration."

"It should not be that way!"

"But it is, and you are childish to think it would be otherwise."

"Childish! You like this no better than I," she pointed out. "So why do you just accept it? Why do you not speak to your father about undoing it?''

"Think you I have not already?"

She felt her hope dwindle. He had already spoken out as she had, and by the sound of it, he'd had no better luck.

"Do you ask me, you gave up too easily," she mumbled bitterly, aware that she had as well.

"I did not ask you, wench, nor would I, when your behavior shows you to still be a child. The opinions of children carry little weight with me."

This was the man she was supposed to give a chance to? A chance to insult and belittle her? Aye, he'd make a worthy husband—about as worthy as the slop pigs that were penned near the kitchen.

Her face suffused with angry heat, she asked him, "You wouldst recognize an opinion if you heard one? Strange. Men like you tend to only hear their own thoughts."

As a rebounding insult, it hit its mark. His face was now as red as hers felt. But he also took several steps forward, bringing him too close for comfort. She had forgotten how *he* dealt with what he did not like hearing—with his fists.

She did not cower back from him, though, was still too angry for that, even when his hand rose and gripped her chin, not hurting, but a strong grip. She found she could not escape the warning look he gave her.

"You will learn, wench, to talk sweetly or not at all," he told her.

"Will I?"

He smiled at the quaver in her voice. 'Twas

not a pleasant smile, though; it spoke of wicked and dastardly things that put a queasiness in her belly.

This close, his size overwhelmed her. Why did she never feel this small when she stood next to Roland, who was actually taller? Mayhap because she had never been so aware of Roland as she was so intensely aware of Wulfric.

He leaned even closer to answer her bravado. "Aye, you will, since what you will learn quickest is that I am not your father. So do not presume that you can have your way, as you have had with him."

"You know naught of what I have been allowed."

"I can *see* what you have been allowed, and I like it not. I will expect you to be dressed properly when next I see you. I cannot tell what I am getting when you look like the veriest beggar."

She gasped and shoved her way past him, rushing out of the room. Behind her she heard a chuckle and the question, "What? You are not going to fetch your future husband something to eat?"

She waited until she had reached the stairs leading back up to the hall before she shouted back, "Only if 'tis your own tongue you would like served!"

Ten

"'*Tis time, m'lady.*"

"Is it?" Milisant mumbled into her pillow.

"Aye, look yonder out the window," the maid said. "The sun rises."

"You look yonder, Ena, while I sleep a bit more."

"But you never sleep late."

The cover was being tugged on. Milisant grabbed it back with a low growl. "I never miss sleep either, but such was the case last eventide, and since I got none then, I'll have some now. Be gone, Ena. Come back in an hour . . . or two . . . or three. Aye, three sounds about right."

There was a *tsk*ing sound, but then the door closed behind the servant. Milisant sighed and went promptly back to sleep. But it was not long before her cover was being insistently tugged on again.

"If you do not rise now, you will miss dinner," she was warned.

Milisant sat up with a gasp. "Dinner? You let me sleep *this* late?"

Dinner, the larger of the two main meals of the day, was served a bit before noontime. She had never in her life slept passed Terce, let alone nearly to Sext.

The servant was giving her a long-suffering look, as if to say, *I tried, but you did not.* Young Ena made an excellent maid, had been serving both sisters for many years now, but she did often have a condescending air, due to her long years of service.

Milisant ignored her and pushed her way out of the big bed she shared with her sister. Jhone, of course, would have risen at a normal hour and had no doubt been entertaining their guests all morning, one of the many tasks that fell to the lady of a keep. And Jhone was considered the lady of Dunburh, since Milisant had never aspired to that distinction, and there was no other to take it since their mother had died.

She dropped the bed robe she slept in during the winter months on her way to the garderobe, where she snatched up a clean tunic and braies. She was half dressed when she recalled that she should be dressing in something other than her normal attire today. In fact, she had promised her father. But she quickly shrugged off that thought and continued wrapping the silver cord to cross-garter her leggings. Dress differently just because Wulfric had ordered her to? After the way he had insulted her with that remark about looking like a beggar?

She snorted to herself before she looked around the chamber for her footwear. Not spotting them, she asked Ena, "Where are my boots?"

"Under the bed where you left them."

"I never leave them there. I leave them at the washbowl. You know I cannot sleep with dirty feet. You heat the water for me yourself."

That had been a quirk of hers ever since she had removed the boot from her mended foot those many years ago and had been treated to the stench of it after wearing the boot for three months. Ever since then, she had been unable to get to sleep at night unless she washed both her feet just before getting into bed.

Ena bent down by the bed and rose with the missing boots in hand and a told-you-so smirk on her lips. "Mayhap that is why you did not sleep last eventide?"

Milisant blushed. She had been so upset last night that she had forgotten something like that. She recalled wanting, nay, needing to talk to Jhone, but her sister had been fast asleep and she had been loath to wake her. So she had gone to bed without sharing her worries, and thus they had preyed more heavily on her mind.

Her belly reminded her, loudly, that she had not been kind to it yesterday, so she hurriedly finished dressing, eager to rectify that. When she reached for her thick woolen cloak, though, the maid held out another.

"If you are not going to dress as your dear papa would like, at least wear this in honor of the guests below," Ena suggested.

She was holding out a long mantle better suited to be worn over a bliaut. But it was a fine piece of rich blue velvet trimmed in black fur. Milisant supposed she could concede that much and nodded, letting the maid drape it over her

narrow shoulders and fasten the golden clasps
and chains that would keep it from falling off.

It did not do what the maid had hoped,
though, which was let her lady realize that it
would look much better with the light blue bliaut it had been designed for. So Ena was left
sighing as Milisant rushed out of the chamber.

The Great Hall was noisy, the castle folk already gathered for the midday meal. Milisant
nearly ran down those last few steps in the
north tower, her rumbling belly prodding her to
haste. But she came to an abrupt halt as she
entered the hall and found Wulfric right there
at the bottom of the stairs, as if he had been
waiting for her. And so he had been, she realized, when his eyes moved over her slowly, then
his head shook just as slowly.

"Only half done, wench. You will take yourself back upstairs and finish the other half."

Her back went stiff. Her jaw set stubbornly,
her eyes flashed. She was about to retort when
he continued.

"Unless you would like my assistance. So go
now and dress yourself properly, or I *will* dress
you myself."

"You would not dare," she hissed at him.

To that he chuckled. "Would I not? Ask your
priest about marriage contracts, and you will
learn that we are all but wed, verily, missing
only the bedding ceremony. Which means I
have rights where you are concerned, wench,
that supersede your father's rights. When you
were contracted to me, that gave my family the
control of you if they so wanted it. My father
could have dictated your education, where you

would live, and aught else to do with your up-
bringing, could even have put you into a nun-
nery until the wedding. That he left you in your
family's care was obviously a mistake, but one
I am in a position to rectify. So you will honor
me today by looking like the lady you are supposed to be. If I must help you to do so, so be
it. *Do* you need my help?"

Milisant stood there in shock. Furious beyond
common sense, she opened her mouth to heap
invectives on him, but noticed her father across
the hall frowning at her and closed her mouth
again. To Wulfric she gave the most baleful look
she could manage, but she did indeed turn on
her heel to remount the stairs.

This was intolerable. The man had no sensitiv-
ity, no tact, no understanding. Everything he
said to her was intended to provoke her to argument. Was he hoping she would fly into a rage
so he would have an excuse to use his great
strength on her again? She did not doubt it.
Nothing too despicable was beneath his doing,
the churlish lout.

Eleven

Wulfric smiled to himself, well pleased. Lord Nigel had been correct after all. The girl would obey him, simply because she did not know him, and so did not know how much he would tolerate from her. She also did not know what means he would use to force any issue between them; thus she would not be eager to find out.

He still was not happy with her, doubted he ever would be. She would never give him the tender care he could expect from a wife. *Jesu*, she actually admitted she loved someone else. So she would never be happy in their marriage either, and she was not like to let him forget it. Her ways were abrasive. He could expect a never-ending battle with her. But he *would* make a lady out of her. She would not embarrass him.

The lady Jhone rushed past him and up the stairs, her expression concerned, so she had likely witnessed her sister's upset. He sighed, regretful that she had not been the eldest daughter, for she was lovely in every way, would have made him a fine wife indeed. Compassionate, soft-spoken, eager to please—everything her sister was not.

Nigel tried to summon him to table, but Wulfric declined for the moment. He was not leaving his position by the stairs so that the wench could sneak past him again and be gone for another entire day. However, he was reminded that she had gone up these stairs yesterday, yet had disappeared from the keep without coming down them. He asked a nearby servant if there was another exit and he moved to the stairs next to the chapel instead.

Sure enough, he soon heard the light steps of a woman coming down the other stairs. She was a crafty one, he had to admit, one with a sharp wit. He had actually gone to bed last night somewhat amused over her parting remark. Serve him his tongue indeed.

But he was wrong about who was coming down the stairs. He was surprised to see that it was Jhone instead—and then not so surprised as another thought occurred to him.

" 'Twould seem I moved to this location too late," he said to her when she reached the bottom step. "She was not up there, was she?"

"She?"

"There is no need to stall for her, Jhone, by playing dense. So she thinks to hide from me for yet another day? She will not—"

"You are mistaken."

"Am I?" He frowned and indicated she should precede him up the stairs. "Then you will show me—"

"I already have," she said cryptically, and slipped past him to hurry into the hall.

His frown got much darker. He did *not* like riddles, which was what he had just been served. He debated whether to climb the stairs himself to search out his betrothed, when he was already sure she would not be up there, or to follow her sister to find out what she had meant.

With a low sound of aggravation, he entered the hall to follow the lady, only to find that there were . . . two of them. He stopped short and simply stared at the two women sitting on either side of their father, both wearing gowns of light blue velvet with a darker blue chemise, both wearing blue wimples, both—identical.

'Twas the lighting, of course, it had to be— yet daylight streamed in the windows, casting no shadows. He took a few steps closer and could still see no difference. They were shaped the same, dressed the same, both incredibly lovely, both—identical. A few more steps and he noted one gown was embroidered about the neck and sleeves with gold thread, the other with silver, but that was the only difference. Their faces were the same—identical.

Why had he not seen it sooner? But then he knew why. Each time he had looked at Milisant Crispin he had seen the outrageous clothes she was wearing and looked not much further. He'd seen her legs, clearly defined by tight leggings, and had been annoyed that every other man could see them as well. He'd seen her dirt-stained skin and had not seen what was beneath the dirt. And he'd been clouded by anger each time, that she was just as he had feared she would be.

He continued now to the high dais where the lord's table sat, uncomfortably aware that he did not know which woman to sit next to. Neither of them was watching him, which might have given him a clue.

Wulfric rarely felt such uncertainty, and liked it not at all. Nor did he like feeling like an idiot, which was exactly how he felt for not having known that Nigel Crispin had twin daughters. His father had no doubt mentioned it to him at some point in his life, but he had either not been paying attention or he had just never been interested enough to remember. Either way, he could fault himself for not knowing.

The odds were even that he could make the right choice without looking like a fool, so he moved to the first seat that he came to, which would put him next to the twin nearest the stairs.

She was kind enough to correct him, though, before he sat down, turning to whisper to him, "Are you sure you wish to sit here?"

Obviously not, and so he continued on to the empty seat next to the other twin. However, this one, too, turned to whisper to him before he sat down, "I am Jhone, Lord Wulfric. Do you not wish to sit with your betrothed?"

He flushed then, and flushed worse as he heard the other twin giggle. Lord Nigel even coughed, likely aware of what Milisant had done, or used to such antics from his identical daughters.

Wulfric was not amused, not in the least, especially since he was forced to turn about to return to the other end of the table. He could only be grateful that he had not compounded his embarrassment by thanking the first twin for her misleading warning.

Reaching her again, he lifted the bench Milisant sat on, literally off the floor, to move it back so he had room to sit down. He heard her gasp, and grab the table for support, and felt much better as he took his seat next to her.

She was now glaring at him, which helped even more to soothe his disgruntlement. But she was also quick to hiss, "Next time give warning ere you move the furniture."

He raised a brow at her. "Next time do not pretend to be who you are not."

"I pretended naught," she insisted. "I merely asked you a logical question. Considering all the frowns I have received from you since your arrival, I assumed you would not want to share this meal with me."

"When you dress like a villein, wench, one must worry about catching lice. Little wonder you elicit frowns."

She was blushing now, profusely. "Think you I would lose my lice just from changing clothes?"

He chuckled. "Nay, I suppose not. *Am* I like to catch them from you?"

She smiled tightly. "One can surely hope."

He did not get to reply to that as the food was being ushered into the hall by a long line of kitchen folk, and a servant leaned between them to set down the large crust of bread that they would share as a trencher. Another came to pour wine, then another . . .

Wulfric gave up the idea of conversation for

the moment and sat back to wait until their trencher was filled. He was almost smiling, and amazed, actually, that he felt like it, after the red cheeks he had just worn to the table.

Who would have thought that he would find Milisant Crispin amusing. Her attitude was not. Her habits were not. Yet what came out of her mouth either infuriated him or amused him. And he could not say why it amused him, when that was certainly not her intent. Nay, her intent was clearly to insult, last eventide and again now.

Mayhap that was all it was. As insults went, hers were paltry at best. But then, he had never been insulted by a woman before, and that might be why as well. 'Twas not exactly a talent most women aspired to perfect, when a typical insult could lead to drawn swords.

By courtly custom, he was supposed to feed his lady, finding the choicest meats and offering them to her. Wulfric simply could not resist saying, once the servants stopped hovering, "Since you prefer to take the manly role, mayhap you would like to do the honors and feed me?"

She glanced at him with what might be construed as an innocently curious look before she said in a neutral tone, "I had not realized how brave you are, to trust my knife near your face."

She then stabbed a chunk of meat with her eating dagger and stared at it for a moment before moving it toward his mouth. He quickly grasped her arm to push it back, but caught the challenge in her green-gold eyes and let go. Incredibly, she was daring him to trust her, after implying that he should not. Actually, she was making him regret that he had provoked her.

But he continued to meet her gaze rather than watch her dagger, though he did warn, "Keep in mind that most actions cause reactions, and do you get clumsy with that dagger, you will not like mine."

"Clumsy?" She snorted. "Who said aught about being clumsy? I mentioned trust only because this hand would likely prefer to take a few chunks from your hide rather than feed you, and I had assumed you were smart enough to realize that—after forcing me into these blasted clothes."

Blasted clothes? So that was the cause of her present rancor? He should have known she would not give in on that point gracefully.

"When you look so fetching in those clothes, how can you abhor them?"

Having said it, he realized just how true that statement was. She really did now look like the one he had been so pleased with yesterday, when he had thought Jhone was his betrothed. To look at them now, there was no difference; Milisant was as pleasing to the eye as her sister was. 'Twas only when she opened her mouth to speak . . . And in that, there was a mighty big difference in the two women.

" 'Tis a matter of comfort and ease of movement," she told him. "Why do you not try wearing a bliaut and chemise and see if you like all that material dragging at your legs with every step."

"You exaggerate. Priests do not find difficulty with their robes."

"Priests do not hunt on foot."

He chuckled, conceding that point with a nod. She stared at him curiously for a moment, as if he had surprised her.

That worried him, making him add what was so very obvious. "Nor do women need to hunt."

"There is need . . . and then there is need. If I need explain the difference to you, then you are not like to grasp it."

"If you are trying to say that hunting is the only thing you can find happiness in, you are correct. I would not be able to grasp that notion—nor would I believe it to be true."

She appeared thoughtful. "Most men retain their opinions no matter if proof to the contrary is served them on a golden platter. Black will still be white and white will still be black because *they* say so—at least if that differing of opinion involves a woman. Do you disagree? Or have you not just proven that very thing?"

He almost laughed. If she were not being so serious about this, he would have. Did she really believe that, that men would adhere to their opinions despite proof to the contrary, regardless of who offered the proof?

"Methinks you exaggerate. I merely note that there are many things that can make one happy. To base all of one's happiness on a single thing is—silly."

"And if I say it is not silly, you will, of course, disagree, because your opinion is the only correct opinion, is that not so?"

" 'Twould seem you are determined to argue with me, no matter what I say."

"Nay, 'twould seem you are determined to disagree with me, no matter what I say."

"Not so. I agreed priests would find difficulty with their robes if they hunted."

She snorted. "For all of five seconds you agreed, only to point out that women would not find the same difficulty because they do *not* hunt."

He was near to growling now. "Why do you not concede that 'tis not the woman's place to be the provider?"

"Mayhap because not every woman has someone providing for her."

"An untruth! If not the men of her family, then the men of her husband's family. If neither of those, she has her king to provide her a guardian."

Milisant rolled her eyes. "You speak of ladies of property, who are no more than tools of bargaining—for a man. What of the women of the village or towns who lose their kin? Why do so many of them turn to begging or whoring to put food on their table? When they could as easily learn to hunt their own food?"

He was now red faced. "Are we correcting the ills of the world now at this sitting? I had not realized a mere compliment on how fetching you look would turn to a deep discussion on the inequities of—"

"Faugh, you do not want to have a discussion, you want merely an echo of your own opinions," she said in disgust. "Very well, shall we discuss the food instead? Or mayhap the weather? Are those safe enough subjects for you? On *those* subjects you might get an agreement from me, but do not count on any others—"

"Enough!" he snapped. "Mayhap we can agree to a little silence, ere my appetite grows as cold as the food is like to be now."

She smiled at him. "Certainly, Wulfric. Far be it from me, a mere woman, to disagree with you."

As he glowered at her last response, he had to wonder, after all of that, if her intention had not been, from the very start, to turn his mood sour. If so, she surely had a unique and quite skilled knack for doing so.

Twelve

Nigel suggested a hunt to amuse the visiting knights for the afternoon. This would not be the kind of hunt that Milisant enjoyed, though, since her father only hunted with his falcon these days, and the falcon, therefore, did all of the work, and thus got all the enjoyment out of it.

Jhone agreed to go along. She did have a sweet, well-behaved tiercel that she used for such occasions. He was a smaller hawk, and so not really classed as a hunting falcon, which were the much larger and more aggressive females of the species.

Milisant declined to join the hunt. She had had more than enough dealings with her betrothed for one day, plus she had never taught her own bird to hunt, kept her only as a pet. It was named after the first Rhiska that Wulfric had killed, and thus she perhaps pampered the second Rhiska more than she should. She also doubted her father would appreciate if she brought her bow along instead, so being unable to contribute to this hunt, she saw no purpose to her accompanying them.

Wulfric thought otherwise; in fact, detained her when she tried to leave the hall after the meal was finished. "You *will* join us."

Two orders from him in the same day! Did he think to control her every movement? Or did he think she was incapable of making logical decisions on her own?

But she did not owe him an explanation. "I prefer not to," she said, which should have sufficed, but nay, not with him.

"Your father has informed me that you require a month to become accustomed to me ere we marry. If that is so, then you will needs make the effort to be with me to accomplish this—or I will think you do not need this time, after all, and we can proceed with the wedding."

She wanted to reply that growing acquainted did not require all of her waking hours each day, but it was too dangerous. Keep him company or get married immediately was what he was actually saying, and in that case, she would, of course, opt for the lesser of those two despicable choices.

So they all adjourned to the bailey where the falcons and horses were being fetched. Milisant had to fetch her own horse, since none of the stable lads would do other than toss Stomper his feed from a distance. She would have taken a smaller mount, except Stomper did need the exercise.

It was well known to all who lived in Dunburh how she'd come to own the destrier, just not a pleasant memory, at least for her. He had been a horse much abused, belonging to a visiting knight who'd used brute force to control him, but had done so one time too many.

'Twas ironic that the horse should go mad and try to kill the knight in her presence. The animal had no longer been of any use to the knight. He had known that and ordered it killed. She had intervened, claiming she could tame him. The knight had, of course, scoffed, and told her if she could tame him, she could have him.

Mayhap she should not have done it so quickly. The knight had been enraged at how easily she had mastered his animal. Much as she'd hated the idea of any animal belonging to such a vicious man, she had offered to give him back to soothe the man, whom her father had hoped to hire as a household knight. His pride had refused to accept her offering. Nor had he stayed in Dunburh, but left immediately.

Her father had, of course, been very wroth with her for causing his abrupt departure. He'd later apologized when they'd learned that that particular knight had found employment elsewhere, and had betrayed his employer, opening the lord's keep to an attacking army.

Since then, Milisant had equated vicious tendencies with deceit, and considered anyone who showed such qualities to be untrustworthy. And as far as she was concerned, her betrothed fell into that category.

As usual, it took her a while to get the horse saddled, something else she had to do on her own, other than having the saddle fetched for her. Then it took a while longer to acquaint him with her skirts, which he was unaccustomed to her wearing.

She did have her leggings and boots on underneath the womanly garb, however, and so sat him as she usually did, her bliaut split up the sides anyway, and wide enough that most of her legs remained covered beneath it, so *he* would have naught to complain about.

She had to use the mounting blocks kept near Stomper's stall to get on his back, he was so huge, and so she rode him out of the stable, talking soothingly to him all the while, to keep him calm amongst the crowd in the bailey. Yet she no sooner cleared the opening than she was being dragged off his back and shouted at in the process.

"Are you utterly beyond common sense, or just lacking any sense at all!?"

Her feet did not release from either stirrup immediately, the action happening so quickly, so both of her arches were caught and bruised by the metal despite her boots. The arm about her waist was like a vise, keeping her from breathing for the moment, and hurting as well as she was roughly carted away from Stomper. It took her a few dazed seconds to even figure out what had happened, that she'd been "rescued." She rolled her eyes mentally.

"Methinks your father should have locked you up for your own safety long ago," she heard now in a furious tone. "Never in my life have I seen aught so stupid." And then Wulfric called to one of the servants, "You there, take that animal back into the stable."

She knew, without having to look, that he

would not be obeyed. He realized that himself after giving that order to several others and getting a lot of wide-eyed head shaking in return.

He set her down on her feet then and lifted her chin so she could not miss his furious expression. "How the devil did you manage to get near a warhorse, let alone get on him without having him kill you?"

As calmly and as drolly as she could manage, she said, "Mayhap because he is mine?"

He snorted, not believing. And he turned to see to putting the destrier back in the stable himself, only to find the horse had come up right next to him, having followed Milisant. That surprised him, but not enough to give him pause. He still reached for the reins.

Milisant only managed to get out, "Do not—!" before Stomper made a concerted effort to bite the hand he did not recognize.

Wulfric swore, and immediately raised a fist to clout the horse. Milisant lost her own temper at that point, shoving him aside, stepping between them. Stomper's large head came to rest over her shoulder and she soothed him by petting his nose.

To her betrothed, she snarled in the loudest of tones, uncaring who else heard her, "Never again will you hurt one of my pets! When I say something is mine, I do not lie. If anyone is lacking in common sense here, 'tis you. If I can mount the animal, which I so obviously did, 'tis logical to assume he is tame for me."

Since the proof of her claim was there before his eyes, he could hardly doubt her further. Yet he was not appeased. And he turned to Nigel, who had come forward to help her remount the animal. "Why have you let her keep such dangerous *pets?*" Wulfric demanded.

Nigel led him away before answering, "Because they are no danger to her. I did warn you she has a way with animals, large or small, wild or merely frightened. It matters not, she can tame them. So be easy, Wulfric, that horse will never hurt her. For yourself, though, treat it as you would any other destrier, with extreme caution. Her pets are tame for her, not necessarily for others."

Milisant was still slightly trembling with anger. He had done it again, shown her that he had no care whatsoever for animals, that they were nothing to him if they did not serve his personal needs, and even *then* were likely nothing to him. Kill them, beat them—what did it matter? They were just animals. Marry a man like that? Never!

Thirteen

"*You should not* have shouted at him in front of his men, Mili."

Milisant turned to see that Jhone had moved her small palfrey near, though not too close to the much larger Stomper. They had both fallen behind the others, though, so there was no need to worry that they would be overheard even with the distance between them.

"Think you I care if he gets embarrassed?" she told her sister.

"You should. Some men react very badly to that, even seek revenge for it of one kind or another. We do not know yet whether he is such a one."

Milisant frowned. Several of Wulfric's knights had been present in the bailey during their altercation, including his brother Raimund. So Wulfric had likely been embarrassed—if he had stopped being angry long enough to notice.

"Was I supposed to thank him for nearly hitting Stomper?" Milisant mumbled.

"Nay, of course not. 'Twould merely behoove

you to make sure no one else hears what you say to him—if what you have to say is less than pleasant."

Milisant grinned and replied, "Less than pleasant, eh? Verily, I will needs speak to him always in whispers then."

Jhone smiled back. "You jest, but just keep it in mind and your temper in hand. 'Tis easier for a woman to swallow her pride than for a man."

"Is it? Now, I would think 'twould be the opposite, since we have the smaller throats."

"Faugh, you will not take advice today, will you? I am merely—"

"Advice today will fall on deaf ears," Milisant cut in. "For I expend all my effort on not bursting into tears after seeing how horrid that man can be."

Jhone's eyes widened. "Are you truly that miserable?"

"In the space of a few hours, he threatens me with mayhem if I do not dress to his liking, then threatens me with an immediate wedding if I do not join him on this hunt. He means to put me on strings, able to move only at his command. I am supposed to be happy with him?"

Her sister wisely noted there was more anger in that response than misery. "You are used to doing as you will because Papa has allowed it. A husband will be different—any husband."

"Roland would not."

"Friends do not think to command friends, but once a friend becomes a husband—Mili, do not deceive yourself that Roland would never try to direct your doings. He would be more lenient, surely, but there would still be times when he would deem it necessary to command you—and expect to be obeyed. Marriage does not make us equal with them. We merely go from one authority to another."

"And you can accept that?" Milisant asked with stinging bitterness.

"How can we not when that is the way it is, the way it has always been, and the way it will always be?"

And that was the reason Milisant despised the body she had been born into. It should *not* be that way. She was a grown woman, capable of rational, logical thoughts. She should have a say in directing her own life, the same as men did. Just because they were bigger and stronger did not mean they had any more intelligence or common sense than she did. They only *thought* they did.

"Did William treat you thusly during the short time of your marriage to him, ordering you to do this and that just because he could?" Milisant asked curiously.

Jhone smiled. "Will loved me, and so he did all he could to please me. And there is your key to happiness, to have your husband love you."

Milisant snorted. "As if I'd want *his* love."

"That is just it, you do want him to love you, for then he will want to please you, and you will have more freedom that way. Do you not see how easy that would be? And I did not say you have to return that love, merely that you would find it useful if you could have his."

"Mayhap if I was forced to wed him, but I still mean to stop that. Papa has allowed me a month ere I must wed. He seems to think my opinion will change about Wulfric during that time, but it will not happen."

Jhone sighed. "Nay, it will not, not when you will not even try."

Milisant stiffened perceptibly. "You *want* me to marry him?"

"Nay, 'tis just that—unlike you, I do not think aught will prevent it from happening, and since it will happen, I want you to find happiness with it. Did Papa actually say he would set the contract aside if you are not satisfied with Wulfric after the month?"

"Not exactly, but he did say we could then discuss it further."

"Do you ask me, Papa is certain you *will* change your mind, and that is the only reason he said what he did. Keep that in mind, Mili, during this month. It would behoove you to make an effort to see Wulfric in a better light."

"The brightest summer day would not supply a light bright enough for that."

Jhone *tsk*ed. "Surely there is something you could like about him? He is very easy on the eyes, with such a handsome face. His teeth are not rotted, his breath not foul. He is young, his physique not gone to slouch or fat. Verily, there is naught wrong with him in any way—"

"Until he speaks or raises his fist," Milisant cut in. "Then I find him as foul as any gutter rat."

Jhone shook her head, giving up, though she had one last comment. "You tame the most savage beast to eat out of your hand. What makes you think you could not do the same with yonder knight?"

Milisant blinked, having never considered such a thing. "Tame *him?*"

"Aye, to your liking."

"But—he is not an animal."

Jhone rolled her eyes. "To hear you describe him, one would think he was."

"I would not even know how to go about it— if I cared to, which I do not."

"You give the animals what they most need, yes?" Jhone pointed out. "Trust, your compassion, a gentle hand, so they do not fear you."

"That man does not need compassion, nor does he need to trust me. What harm could I do him, after all? And 'tis doubtful he would feel a gentle hand if I clouted him on the head with one."

Jhone chuckled. "You call that gentle?"

"Nay, just that he would not *feel* it. So what does he need that I could tame him with?"

Jhone shrugged, but then grinned. "William was fond of saying that all a man needs is a good lusty romp in bed to keep him happy."

"Jhone!"

"Well, he did."

"And that was all it took to make him happy?" Milisant asked incredulously.

"Nay, he was happy just being with me, but then he was very much in love. If you do not want Wulfric's love, then just catering to what will keep him content might suffice to make living with him agreeable."

Milisant smiled at her sister. "I appreciate what you are doing, Jhone, truly, and your advice might be beneficial if I was forced to live with him. But I would prefer that not happen.

To live with a man I could not trust to never raise a fist to me? He has been reared to react with violence. He did it as a boy, he still does it."

"But that, too, can be curbed, if you would but gentle him with taming," Jhone pointed out.

"Mayhap, yet that is not his only fault. He means to do exactly what you are suggesting I do, tame *me* to his liking. Think you I can bear such constraints and not soon wither away?"

"There *has* to be a middle ground here, Mili."

Milisant snorted. "That would entail a measure of equality, yet were you not the one who just pointed out that very lack in any marriage? He does not *have* to give any ground here. He is the man, his opinions all that matter, his might able to enforce his whims. While I am less than naught, a woman who must concede all. Sweet *Jesu*, I hate this!"

Jhone's expression turned bleak. It was not the first time she had heard how much her sister hated the woman's body she had been born into. And all those times before, just as now, there was not much she could say to make it easier for Milisant to accept.

It could not be disputed that a man could direct his own actions—at least most of them. But a woman could direct none of hers. Most women never questioned the rightness of this, that they were considered property by the church, by their king, by their families—by their husbands. Those who did question it, like Milisant, would never be happy with their lot.

Fourteen

They stopped in a small clearing to release the falcons. There would not be many birds for prey at this time of the year, not that many small animals either, for that matter, but whatever there was, the falcons would spot them from their soaring height and swoop down for the kill.

For a hunter, it was a compelling sight, to witness a regal falcon in action. Though Milisant preferred to hunt using her own skill rather than that of a bird, she could still appreciate the sight of a born predator trained to perfection.

The Dunburh knights all had their own birds; the visiting knights did not, however. Though many people did travel with their own falcons, Wulfric and his men had not traveled with hunting in mind.

Most of the nobility, though, men and women both, owned such creatures, and some were so prized and beloved that they were never left at home. In fact, such birds would be regularly brought to table, no matter whose table, and

were hand-fed the choicest meats. A prized falcon could usually be found on its owner's wrist
or the back of his chair.

But like Milisant, Wulfric was there merely to
watch. Ironically, she found herself watching
him instead of the falcons in flight.

She wished Jhone had not pointed out how
handsome he actually was, for she found that
she could not disagree with that fact. The lines
of his face were clearly defined and clearly mas-
culine, even though he adhered to the old Norman fashion of keeping his cheeks and jaw
smooth of hair. King John sported a beard, and
most nobles followed the fashion of their king,
but not Wulfric.

His hair was a bit longer than usual as well;
actually, was as long as her own. This made her
feel somewhat—strange. Though she did not begrudge him such a thick mane of lustrous, raven
dark locks, she found herself wishing her own
hair were a bit longer—actually a lot longer,
which was absurd really.

He looked quite regal, sitting on that fine
black stallion, his voluminous gray cloak spread
back over the animal, halfway down its tail.
Even when he was relaxed, Wulfric's posture
was straight, emphasizing the broadness of his
shoulders, the trimness of his waist.

Jhone had spoken true; there was no excess
flesh on his body. She had not mentioned the
muscles, though. Verily, he had those aplenty.
They rippled beneath his black tunic. They were
prominent on his long legs. Even his knee-high
boots seemed too tight because of them.

There really was naught about him that was

not pleasing to look upon. It was too bad that he was a typical brutish knight, and that she expected much better than that for a husband. She knew she was being unrealistic in wanting a man who was violent *only* on the battlefield, but there it was, that *was* what she wanted— and what she could have if she could have Roland instead of Wulfric de Thorpe.

She had stared at Wulfric too long. He must have sensed it, for his dark blue eyes fixed on her suddenly and stayed there, as if he were now taking stock of her as she had done to him. It gave her a funny feeling to think so, and an even stranger feeling when he did not approach, just continued to gaze at her intently.

She tried to look away but could not. His gaze was too magnetic. She barely felt the cold, felt warm actually . . . That very fact chilled her and had her wrapping her cloak tighter about her body, an action that caused him to smile, as if he *knew* he was responsible for her discomfort.

And then he was riding toward her. She was only surprised that he had waited this long to approach her, after he had *ordered* her presence in the hunting party—then proceeded to ignore her as soon as they left the castle.

It took him a few moments to reach her side, since she had kept the greatest distance between them that she could manage while still being considered present. But reaching her, he meant to keep *his* distance from Stomper. His stallion had other ideas, however, and headed straight for Milisant's hand for a gentle nose scratch, despite Wulfric's attempt to jerk him away from her.

She heard him swear when he could not control his animal, then, *"Jesu,* what have you done to my horse?"

"Naught but make friends with him," she said, smiling at the stallion as she scratched him. Stomper merely tossed his head to the side for a look, to make sure naught was threatening her.

" 'Tis witchly, your way with animals."

Milisant snorted, then wished she had not. Perhaps it could benefit her if Wulfric thought her a witch. He might not be overly harsh with her if he thought she might get even with him in some unnatural way. The thought was a pleasant one.

"The animals I befriend simply know I will never hurt them. Does your stallion think the same of you?"

"Why would I hurt him?"

"You just did," she said pointedly, "in trying to get him away from me."

He flushed red, then scowled. "Lady, you do try my patience."

She nodded thoughtfully, then smiled. His scowl grew darker. Her smile got brighter. Mayhap it was not wise, to provoke him, even subtly, but she simply could not resist the opportunity.

He tried again to get his stallion to move back, less harshly, but still without success. Finally he ordered her, "Release your hold on him."

"I am not holding him," she replied calmly. "Mayhap if you apologized for hurting him, and showed him that you care about him, he might obey you."

To that Wulfric growled, dismounted, and led

the stallion some distance away on foot. Milisant managed to keep from chuckling as she watched his difficulty, but she did call out, "Do not forget the apology."

He ignored her—at least, he did not glance back at her to reply. He did say a few words to his horse, though, which she was unable to hear. Likely threats and dire warnings about not embarrassing him again.

After a few more minutes, he remounted and tried once again to approach her. He just made sure he kept his distance this time, and kept his stallion turned partially away, so the animal would have trouble noticing her.

This worked, and the knight was able to relax somewhat. Which was why Milisant knew, to the second, when he realized that she was looking down on him, even at the extra distance between them.

Due to the huge size of the destrier, Wulfric's greater height still did not put them at eye level. It was close, but not quite enough. And it was so very obvious that he did not like having to look up at her, even if only a few inches.

Perversely, Milisant straightened up in her saddle, adding a few more inches. Wulfric, seeing this, made a sound of disgust and turned his stallion about to leave her.

Then she gasped in pain.

It was completely involuntary. She certainly would never have drawn him back to her intentionally. It was merely her surprise at hearing the arrow as it neared her, then feeling the sting of it on her upper arm. It only nicked her, continued on to embed in a nearby tree, yet she was still staring incredulously at the blood appearing on her cloak as Wulfric turned back to her.

His reaction to seeing the blood was a bit faster than her own. He had her off of Stomper and buried in the cocoon of his chest, arms, and cloak within seconds. His shout of "To arms!" swiftly followed, to bring his knights to him.

She was trying, in vain, to find an opening in the voluminous cloak wrapped about her, so she could at least get her head out of it. No luck. And then the stallion was galloping away, so she gave up trying.

She was feeling a bit dizzy as well, and her efforts had made that worse. And she was also noticing that the sting on her arm was getting increasingly more painful with each jarring bounce of that wild ride back to the castle.

By the time the drawbridge was reached, Milisant had lost all feeling. For the first time in her life, she fainted, not because of the pain, which she could withstand better than most, but from blood loss. Since she was hidden under Wulfric's cloak, neither of them could see just how much blood she had continued to lose.

Fifteen

"*What is taking* the castle leech so long?" Wulfric asked.

"Mayhap the fact that I did not send for him," Jhone said quietly in answer.

"That should have been the first thing you did when you arrived. See to it now."

Milisant tried to open her eyes to see them, knew they were standing nearby, but simply could not muster the strength. Her senses were still spinning dizzily. There was a ringing in her ears that made hearing difficult. She needed to sleep, she knew, to regain her strength, but the burning sting on her arm kept her from succumbing.

"Do you bring him, I will bar the door," Jhone told the knight. "He can do naught for Mili that I cannot do. Faugh, look at her! She has lost so much blood already, she cannot afford to lose any more."

"Nonsense—"

"Think what you like, but it has been our experience, my sister's and mine, that leeching may do fine for certain illnesses and infections to draw out the poisons, but for simple injuries and clean wounds, we have never seen them improve the condition. More like, the blood-sucking they do worsens it. Besides, my sister hates leeches and would not thank you for being responsible for bringing them, when she is too weak to tear them off of her."

"I do not seek her thanks, merely her recovery," Wulfric said stiffly.

"Then leave me be to tend to her. Do you wish to be helpful, tell my father that it is a simple wound and Mili should be fine after a few days of rest."

A moment of silent indecision, then, "You will inform me if aught changes with her condition?"

"Certainly."

"I wish to see her when she awakens."

"As soon as she agrees to see you."

There was a snort, then the order, "I do not ask for *her* permission. Summon me."

The door closed behind him rather loudly, proof of how annoyed Jhone had just made him. Milisant still could not manage to get her eyes open, to make sure he was gone. But she did manage to part her lips.

"Do not . . . summon him," she whispered.

Jhone's gentle hand came immediately to her brow, and her voice was soothing by her ear. "Shhh, you intend to sleep for nigh a week. He would not be so churlish as to disturb your sleep."

"Would . . . he . . . not?"

Jhone *tsk*ed. "I will see that he does not. Now,

brace yourself. 'Tis lucky you did not wake for the stitching, but I still need bandage you."

"How many?"

"It took six stitches," Jhone said, understanding the question. "I was careful to leave no puckers."

Milisant would have smiled if it would not have cost so much effort. Jhone would hover over her until she was well, she did not doubt.

She was almost asleep when it occurred to her to ask, "Did they find him?"

Again Jhone did not need to ask who. "Nay, not yet. Papa was directing the search when I left the clearing. He is furious, Mili, and rightly so, that one of our hunters could be so careless."

" 'Twas no hunter . . . or accident," Milisant said as the last of her strength gave out. She slurred the rest. "Someone wants to see me dead."

"Wulfric has placed guards outside the door—nay, do not look alarmed. 'Tis not to keep you in, but to keep everyone else out." Jhone was whispering, as if those guards could hear her and would be reporting every word. "He took to heart what you said."

Milisant sat up in bed, where she had spent the last three days. They were beneficial. If not for the pain on her arm, she was feeling almost normal.

"What I said? What did I say?"

"What you told me the day it happened," Jhone explained. "That it was no accident, that arrow hitting you. I repeated this to Papa— while Wulfric was present. They both agree with you. 'Twas too soon after that first attack for the second to be unrelated.''

'' 'Twas not just that—I had not even thought of that yet. 'Twas that I know our own hunters, as well as those from our neighbors. None of these men are careless. And none of them would dare to hunt anywhere nearby when Papa was hunting in the area. And Papa's party was impossible to miss hearing or seeing that day.''

Jhone wrung her hands before she exclaimed, "I hate this! Verily, I have never despised aught so much as this threat to you. *Why* would anyone want to do you harm, Mili? You have no enemies.''

"Nay, but *he* likely does. And how better to hurt him than to keep him from collecting the fortune that comes with me to the marriage?''

"I cannot credit that. 'Tis too complicated,'' Jhone said, shaking her head. "Much easier to just kill the enemy directly, yet no attempts have been made against Wulfric—well, at least none that we know of.''

"These attacks happened with his arrival, Jhone. If I do not believe that they come from an enemy of his, then that leaves me only one other thing to believe, that Wulfric has arranged for them himself.''

Jhone gasped. "You *cannot* think that!''

Milisant lifted a brow. "Can I not? After he admitted to me that he loves another? After he admitted that he spoke with his father to get released from this joining, yet he had no more luck than I did? To eliminate me would get him what he wants, would it not?''

"Lord Guy is an honorable man. I have to

believe that his son was raised to be just as honorable. 'Tis absurd to think he would resort to murder.''

Milisant shrugged. ''Stranger things have been done for love. But I am inclined to agree with you, which is why I think that it is the doing of an enemy of his. We need just find out who.''

Jhone nodded, then gave her a pensive look. ''There is more.''

''More?''

''*He* is convinced that he cannot protect you here. Dunburh is large, with too many mercenaries, he said. Men for hire are not known for the greatest of loyalties, are actually known to take the highest offer.''

''You speak of betrayals?''

''Not me, him. I am merely repeating what he told Papa. Shefford, on the other hand, is manned by knights whose allegiance is owed to the earl. There are no mercenaries there, and those household knights who make their living there have been loyal to Shefford for many years.''

''In other words, he trusts all the men-at-arms there, but here they come and go frequently. Thus here we have men aplenty who might take a bribe or payment—to do murder.'' Milisant snorted. ''And did Papa believe that reasoning?''

''He did not discount it totally. But he did agree that we get a lot of strangers here, since it is well known that Dunburh is a good place to find work. The gist of it is—we leave for Shefford on the morrow.''

''What?! I was given extra time. Papa cannot

change his mind about that now, just because—"

"You will still have the time, you will just have it there rather than here."

Milisant frowned, not very appeased, and still not liking it that 'twas his idea. "You said 'we'?"

Jhone grinned. "I told Papa you were not well enough yet to travel without me. So he agreed you would not go unless I accompany you."

Milisant gripped Jhone's hand as she said, "Thank you," then added in a conspiratorial whisper, "But pretend to be ill as well. Then we can both stay home."

Jhone *tsk*ed at the suggestion. "What difference, here or there? You will still have the allotted time."

"Shefford is his domain. I will not be comfortable in his domain."

"Methinks you will not be comfortable wherever he is, so again, what difference?"

"True," Milisant conceded, then sighed. "On the morrow—should you not be packing?"

Sixteen

"*What the devil* are those?"

Milisant followed Wulfric's gaze to the servants coming forth with four cages in different sizes. They were all gathered in the bailey, where it had ended up taking two baggage wains to accommodate all that the twins deemed necessary for the journey. Milisant's pets were the last thing to be loaded.

She was very proud of the wooden cages she had made when she was a child. She had made them for her fostering at Fulbray Castle, as she had refused to leave her pets behind then. She was not about to leave them behind now.

To answer his question, Milisant said, "My pets travel more comfortably in their cages, at least some of them do."

His dark blue eyes swung back to her where she sat on the end of the baggage wain that she would be riding in. "You keep *four* pets?"

"Well, nay, there are more than that, but only those four do I cage."

He looked back at the cages that had gotten

close enough now for him to see inside them. "An owl? *Why* would you make a pet of an owl?"

"I did not, actually. 'Twas more that Hoots made me his owner. He followed me home and raised havoc in the bailey until I agreed to keep him."

"Until you agreed—" He broke off repeating that, deciding it was not worth pursuing, and still staring at the cages, said next, "Think you I will not feed you, that you must bring along your own dinner?"

She followed his gaze again and this time gasped. "Do *not* even think it. Aggie has been with me since she was a chick. She is *not* for eating."

"Chickens are not pets!" he insisted in exasperation.

"That one is!" Milisant insisted right back.

"And what is that ball of fur, or dare I ask?"

She chuckled at that point, starting to enjoy his amazement, or rather, aggravation. "Actually, that is not fur, but spikes—'tis my hedgehog. I call him Sleeper since he spends most of the year doing just that."

He rolled his eyes, then frowned when he saw Stomper tied to the other side of the baggage wain. But that was naught compared to his expression when he finally noticed Growls, who had just pushed his nose between Milisant's arm and side so he could see who she was talking to.

"A wolf? You keep a wild wolf?"

"Growls is completely tame. He is pathetically friendly toward anyone."

"Then why do you call him Growls?"

Her pet, unfortunately, chose that moment to growl at Wulfric's tone. Milisant grinned before she answered, "He was not always so friendly—and still does not like it when people yell at me."

"I was not yelling! I damned well should be, but I was not!"

"Verily, I can hear that you were—not," she replied mildly.

He scowled at her. "These pets stay here."

She stiffened. "Then I stay here."

"This is not open for argument."

"I agree—it is not."

Jhone *tsk*ed as she came up beside them. "My sister's pets will be no trouble on the journey, Wulfric. Verily, you will not even know they are with us, once they get settled in. But do not ask her to leave them behind, when she is so attached to them. Truly, they are like her children, the way she protects and cares for them."

He started to argue further, had his mouth open to do so, but obviously changed his mind as he ended up smiling at Jhone instead. It was not the first time Milisant had seen him smile at her sister. She had just never noted it quite so clearly before.

It was apparent, to anyone with half an eye for observation, that Wulfric would have greatly preferred Jhone for a bride. She wondered if Jhone would mind trading places with her. They need not tell anyone. They had switched places too often, with no one the wiser. It would be easy.

As the thought took form and started to excite her with its possibilities, a vision of Jhone and

Wulfric embracing sneaked up on her and seemed to affect her with a physical jolt. She actually blinked, several times, to banish it, then shoved the thought of trading places away completely with a mental sigh. As ideas went, that was not one of her brightest, simply because she would not wish a brute like Wulfric, who was also proving to be quite the tyrant, on anyone, least of all her sister—at least, that was what she assured herself.

They lost Wulfric's attention for a few moments as he answered questions from one of his men. When he glanced back at them, the cages were being set into the baggage wain behind Milisant. He gave a disgusted sigh, acquiescing to their presence without further comment.

But he parted from them with a question for Milisant that surprised her, coming from him, especially after he had insisted they leave this morn. "Are you sure you are well enough to travel?"

She assured him she was, and he was quick to leave them after that. For a short while she thought that question had come from concern, and that confused her. Then common sense quickly prevailed. It was more like he was concerned that she would slow down their progress on the road.

She didn't slow them down, but the two baggage wains certainly did. The day-and-a-half journey was now going to take two full days instead—at least that was what they thought until it started snowing late that afternoon. It was not a heavy snowfall, just enough to drop the temperature and make traveling in it quite unpleasant.

Bundled in their cloaks, even with two extra blankets covering them, the sisters were still unable to keep the wet cold at bay. Those riding fared no better, which was why Wulfric ended the journey earlier than planned, when they reached Norewich Abbey. The monks did not have accommodations for everyone, of course, but their stable was warm, and there were enough rooms for the women and knights to share.

Jhone and Milisant took their meal in the room they had been assigned, well aware that the kindly monks would prefer not to associate with women if it could be avoided. They retired right after eating, since Wulfric had warned he wanted to be on the road in the morning much earlier than the start they had gotten today.

Milisant would have retired early anyway. She was more exhausted than she cared to admit, still affected by her accident. She really should have delayed this journey a few more days, at the very least, until her arm stopped hurting. As it was, she went to sleep with it throbbing something fierce after that jarring ride all day, but thankfully, she was too tired for it to keep her from sleeping.

Seventeen

Milisant could not say what woke her in the middle of the night. Whatever it was, she felt a clear unease, as if whatever it had been was not normal. Because of it, even with nothing else occurring to cause alarm, she could not get back to sleep.

She needed to see for herself that the quiet and windowless room was as it should be, empty except for her and her sister. It was too dark to see even a few shadows. The fire had burned down to mere embers, giving off no useful light, and the candle she had left on the table next to the narrow bed had been extinguished before they slept.

She knew, though, as alert as she was, that she would never get back to sleep until she'd checked every corner of the room. So she grabbed the candle, rolled carefully over her sister with a whispered, "Shhh," in case it woke her, and stumbled toward the fire on that side of the bed to stick the candle in the embers to light it.

She really was not expecting to find anything there. She expected to scoff at herself for her silly unease and get right back to sleep. So it was quite a shock to see the burly fellow standing a few feet from the end of the bed with a dagger clutched in one hand.

He was no one she had ever seen before, nor was he a man easy to forget, with a scar on his face so wide it cut a deep groove through his scraggly beard. Clearly he had come from outside. There was still snow melting on the top of his woolen cap and his brawny shoulders.

Jhone had indeed been awakened when Milisant climbed over her, and had waited silently, still half asleep, to find out what that "shhh" had been about. She gasped and sat up in bed as soon as the light revealed their intruder.

He stared back and forth between the two of them. There was not much intelligence in his dark eyes, but whether that would help or hinder remained to be seen. At the moment he seemed somewhat panicked.

"Which of you is the elder?" he asked.

Considering he held a dagger in his hand, Milisant was quick to protect her sister with the truth, claiming, "I am." Only Jhone had gathered for herself what the man was doing there and said exactly the same thing, at nearly the same instant, causing him to growl in frustration.

"The truth, or you'll both have to die. Better just one than both, eh?"

Better neither, but pointless to tell him that. Yet Milisant was at a loss on how to deal with him. She should not *have* to be dealing with him.

Faugh, Wulfric's method of protecting her left much to be desired, and she would be sure to tell him so. At least at home she would have been safe in her own bedroom, where Growls and Rhiska would tear anyone apart who entered to threaten her. But here, both pets were in the stable, doing her no good whatsoever.

They certainly could not fight him off, not without risking serious hurt. He was just too brawny. And while he held a dagger, they had no weapons of their own. Her bow had been left in the baggage wain as well, assumed to be unneeded in an abbey.

That left only persuading him to seeing reason. So in a commanding tone she told him, "I wouldst hire you, sirrah, and I will pay you much, much more than you could ever imagine earning."

He blinked. "Hire me?"

"Aye, to protect my sister and me. You seem like a capable fellow, and smart enough to know where the greater benefit would lie. Or are you no more than a lowly serf, bound to some lord for life?"

He flushed at the derision she intentionally added to her tone, and nearly growled, "I am a free man."

"Then it would behoove you to guard your own interests, would it not?" she pressed her point. "To look to the greater gain?"

She had sparked his interest; it was evident in his avid expression. He was tempted. But he must have imagined what would happen if he gave in to the temptation, some sort of retribution only he could envision, because he as quickly looked very frightened. Then that emotion, too, was gone, and he was back to appearing exceedingly menacing and resolved to doing what he had come to do.

"Honor and loyalty count for more'n coin, lady," he told her to appease his momentary fear.

"Those traits do not feed you, nor do they make you rich," she pointed out.

"What counts for rich if you will not live to enjoy it?" he replied.

"Ah, the truth then. You are merely afraid of your employer," she sneered.

That had him flushing again, but this time with anger. "Methinks it will be a pleasure to finish my task here," he said, looking straight at her.

But before he could take a step toward her, he obviously recalled that there were two of them. Glancing at Jhone again, he knew he still faced a dilemma. And Milisant could just imagine his thoughts. One of them could escape while he made the effort to kill the other. And the one who escaped could be the one he was supposed to eliminate.

She took advantage of his hesitation to say, "Who sent you on this task? Give us a name."

"Think you I am a fool?" He snorted. "There is no need for you to know."

"You could have just said you do not know," she said in scoffing derision.

That merely angered him the more, but at least his anger gave her warning that she was out of time.

As soon as he took that step toward her, she

sent the candle flying at him. The flame extinguished on the way, yet he was too slow to dodge the candle itself. His yelp was telling, that the hot wax had at least hit him on bare skin, likely his face. But while he was distracted by that, she grabbed the cover on the bed, lifted it high, and threw it in the direction where he had been standing. His muffled curse said her aim had been accurate in that as well.

She had shouted at Jhone to leave to get help, even as she'd thrown the candle. Thankfully, Jhone had been quick to react. The door was thrown open only seconds after the cover landed on the man.

With that small bit of light that came in from outside, Milisant was able to at least see the outline of the bed to dive over it and try to get out of there before the man untangled himself. He must have done some diving himself, though, for she didn't quite reach the open door before she felt his hand on her lower calf and she went down hard, right in the doorway—landing partially on her wound.

Tears of pain filled her eyes, completely blinding her for the moment. But she heard her sister screaming for help. She heard other doors opening. She just couldn't see if any help was coming yet. And the man still had his dagger. It was that knowledge that struck a desperate fear in her and had her kicking against his hand with her other foot, her breath coming so hard now in her exertion that she almost didn't hear his cry of pain.

She did feel his hand go slack, though, and release her. She didn't wonder what part of him she had hit to make him let go. She merely jumped to her feet to escape, and slammed into Wulfric before she knew he was there.

His arm clamped immediately around her waist as he half dragged, half walked her away. "Be at ease," was the only reassurance she got that it was he and not some other assailant.

The guest rooms in this part of the abbey faced an outdoor courtyard that was barren this time of year and, with the absence of a moon, not much lighter than her room had been. But he took her no further than the room next to hers, where his brother had lit a candle.

Jhone was there, huddled beneath a blanket that had been given her, trying not to stare at the nearly naked knight wearing no more than his braies. She rushed to Milisant to take her from Wulfric's side and enclose her in the blanket. This room had no fire going either, and none of them were dressed for the cold coming in the open door.

"Are you hurt?"

"My stitches may have opened, but otherwise I am fine," Milisant assured her sister.

She turned to see that Wulfric was still there, when he should have returned immediately to capture the assailant. She was distracted for a moment, because he, too, was wearing no more than braies, and that was just too much male skin, *his* male skin, for her senses to handle all at once.

It took some very strong willpower to tear her eyes away from that broad expanse of chest to find out why he was still there. Yet she hesitated to point out his duty, recalling his reaction the

last time she had insisted he apprehend someone, that day on the path.

She compromised by merely mentioning, "He
is going to escape."

"He goes nowhere—ever again," Wulfric
replied.

Only then did she notice the blood smeared
across the end of his sword. "*Jesu*, you killed
him? You do not think questioning him would
have been preferable?"

"Mayhap, yet was there little time to decide,
when the weapon in his hand was descending
on you."

It was jolting, to realize she had been that
close to death. She had known it, had felt the
fear at the time, but to hear it had really been
so . . .

She conceded the point with a nod, though
she would not thank him for saving her life,
when he was responsible for protecting her. He
had taken her away from her home to do so,
yet was thus far doing a dismal job of it. *That*
she could complain about, and did.

"You take me away from the safety of my
home—"

"Your home was *not* safe."

"Neither was this abbey. There should at least
have been a guard at my door."

"There was." She blinked, but he did not notice, had already looked toward his brother to
say, "Find out what happened to him."

Raimund nodded and abruptly left the room.
While he was gone, Jhone pulled Milisant closer
to the candle and, under the cover of the blan-

ket, pulled the sleeve of her tunic down to examine her wound.

"There are only a few drops of blood," Jhone whispered, still shaken from the whole ordeal. "The wound only opened slightly, though the stitches still hold."

Milisant smiled tiredly, grateful. To have had to undergo more stitching tonight would have been more than she could endure.

Raimund was quick to return and impart what was already half expected. "He is dead, Wulf. A dagger to the heart—thrown, 'twould seem. He was then dragged and set behind that tree in the courtyard."

Wulfric frowned thoughtfully, then looked at Milisant again. "Who wants to see you dead?"

"A question you should have asked ere now, do you not think?"

He ignored that. "Who?"

She shrugged. "Obviously someone who would like to prevent our joining."

"I see no *obvious* to it, yet might it be possible. If so, then we should be wed immediately. And if not, then we should still be wed immediately, so I need not worry about the competence of whomever I set to guard you, since I wouldst be doing the guarding myself."

"There is *no* need to be that drastic," she hastily assured him. "I will merely keep my pets with me henceforth. They can protect me well enough."

He snorted at that idea. "They can die as easily as you."

"They can kill as easily as you," she countered, her chin lifting stubbornly.

His frown darkened for a moment, but then he sighed. "Very well, I will stand duty at your door for the remainder of this night, and we do not stop on the morrow, no matter how harsh the weather or how late into the night it takes, until we reach Shefford."

She readily agreed to that. Obviously he did not like his suggestion that they marry posthaste any more than she did. Thank God for alternatives.

Eighteen

The last two hours had been traveled in the
dark. Wulfric had been true to his word; they
had not stopped once this day, not even to eat,
merely chewing on crusty bread and cheese
bought from the monks as they rode. The snow
had not continued, and what little had stuck to
the ground had melted by midmorn. So at least
the ride had not been as uncomfortable as it had
been the previous day.

Still, considering their near dawn start,
many of them were fully exhausted by the
time they rode over the drawbridge into Shefford Castle that night. Milisant was one, having been unable to return to sleep the night
before. She could blame Wulfric for that. She
had simply been unable to relax, knowing he
stood guard outside her door. What should
have made her feel safe made her feel—anxious instead.

She was not at all sure why she had felt so.
She certainly had not thought he would come
in and harm her. Even if he was behind these

attempts on her life, he would not risk seeing to the deed himself.

Besides, if he wanted her dead, it would be to his benefit to wed her first and collect her dower, then see to eliminating her. So she was inclined to feel foolish now for even suspecting him, especially now that one of his men had been killed, and he had himself killed the intruder.

Although she and Wulfric had managed to avoid each other over the many years of their betrothal, their parents had visited each other often, either at Shefford or Dunburh, and for weeks at a time. So she knew Shefford well, might have actually felt at home there, if not for the unwanted marriage. She also knew Wulfric's parents well, so she was not really surprised to wake up finding Anne de Thorpe in her chamber.

Both Anne and Guy had most likely been present last eventide to greet their arrival, but Milisant had been too exhausted to recall much of it, other than her eagerness to find a bed. And she *would* have slept longer if given the choice, but Wulfric's mother was of a different mind.

Anne was speaking of preparations for the wedding, of guests who were being invited, including the king. She was fair bubbling with excitement, and seemed to be so very glad to be arranging this joining. Jhone, already up and dressed, though still in the chamber the sisters would be sharing, was graciously being a rapt audience for the lady. Milisant seriously thought about hiding her head under the pillows.

She did *not* want to hear about these grand

preparations that would bind her to Wulfric de Thorpe. But she didn't want to insult his mother either, by telling her that she abhorred her precious only son. That might be a guaranteed way to get out of the marriage contract, but she couldn't do that to her father. She needed some other reason that wouldn't reflect on his parents and wouldn't shame her father.

Roland still seemed the most likely option—citing her love for him. It would help, it really would, if it were true. But she would worry about that later. The time was not right to mention Roland yet. She still had to abide by her father's month of giving Wulfric his chance to prove himself worthy, to get Nigel's support. It was going to be a very long month.

She was not able to get back to sleep even after Anne left the chamber. Jhone mentioning that 'twas Growls howling down in the bailey that had awakened her reminded Milisant that she hadn't properly seen to her pets upon their arrival. Her exhaustion was no excuse to not at least have found Stomper a warm stall, when she knew very well no one else would risk getting near him to do so.

She found all of her pets in the stable; to her amazement, even the destrier was happily munching away on feed in a stall of his own. When she asked one of the stable lads who had managed to get the horse into the stable, she wasn't truly surprised to hear it was Wulfric who had done so. But that answer had her quickly examining Stomper for whip marks or wounds. Finding none was what *did* surprise her.

Nor could she leave it go at that and just be glad that her pet had been well cared for. She did something she never thought she'd do, she actually sought out Wulfric.

After much questioning of the castle folk, she found him in his own chamber. She didn't think about the fact that it wasn't appropriate yet for her to go there. She had questions, and in her typical fashion, the direct approach was more important than what might be considered unseemly.

He appeared only momentarily surprised at her entrance. He was in the process of scraping the hair from his face. The sharp blade he was using suspended briefly.

Milisant's thoughts suspended a bit longer. But then she hadn't expected to find him half naked. Verily, this second time she saw him so was as bad as the first had been. It was nigh impossible for her to concentrate when all that bare skin on his chest and arms was there for her to look upon.

His voice finally recalled her to her purpose when he questioned, "I hesitate to ask if you mean to be here, or are you lost?"

She ignored his dry tone to answer seriously, "Lost in Shefford when I have been here so frequently over the years?" But then she couldn't resist adding, "Of course, you wouldn't know that, never having been here when I was."

He smiled. "You imply that was deliberate. Let me assure you it was *most* deliberate. Mayhap someday you will ask why and we can discuss it without rancor. Truly, I doubt me that time is now."

She almost snorted. For herself, she doubted that time would be ever, but refrained from saying so. But now her questions were suddenly much less important than a quick retreat. For a reasonably large chamber, as his was, it seemed *much* too intimate with only the two of them present, and she liked it not at all, how nervous he made her when she didn't have anger as a buffer to shield her from it.

So she meant to ask only the one question that she was most curious about, and then exit posthaste. "I was told you stabled my horse. Why did you?"

He shrugged nonchalantly. "It annoyed me to see him left in the bailey, when your servants saw to all of your other pets."

She had been hoping his reason *wouldn't* show him to have even that small measure of decency, not after the conclusions she had drawn pertaining to his treatment of animals. Of course, he had mentioned annoyance. Had there not been other pets involved that had been seen to, he might not have given Stomper a second thought. She needed to be wary of giving him kind qualities that he did not truly possess.

However, he had attended to her horse when he hadn't had to, and her face lit with color from unwanted gratitude for his having done so. She nigh choked on the words that needed saying. "Thank you."

He grinned, sensing her feelings. "That was difficult, wasn't it?"

"Aye, likely as difficult as your handling Stomper was," she retorted.

"Actually, the horse was no trouble once he scented the sugar I offered."

So that was why there had been no whip marks. He was smart enough to tempt, rather than coerce. Too bad he hadn't tried the same approach with her. Not that she was so gullible, but anything other than his typical "do it or else" would be an improvement. Of course, that was from her viewpoint. From his viewpoint, his "do it or else" was working just fine . . .

Which brought her aggrievement with him to the fore and prompted her to say curtly, "I'll disturb you no longer, Lord Wulfric."

She'd already turned toward the door when his voice stopped her with, "Do you not agree 'tis time you called me Wulfric? Even Wulf would do."

She didn't agree at all. Using his given name implied a friendship, or at the least, a solid acquaintance, which they did not have.

But instead of insulting him so early in the morn by pointing that out, she turned back to him with a new question. " 'Tis an old English name you have, unusual for a Norman. How came you by it?"

"To hear my father tell it, a pack of wolves came to the edge of the woods near Shefford the night I was born, and set up a howling for hours—till I was born, and howled louder than they. He felt it was prophetic, that the pack should quiet upon hearing me, and thus I became Wulfric, despite my mother's preference to name me after my grandsire. Actually, he did compromise. He would have named me just Wolf."

Loving animals as she did, Milisant found that amusing. His grouching tone indicated that he didn't. So she merely said, "An unusual tale to match an unusual name," then turned again to leave.

But again he stopped her, this time more directly when he asked, "What is your hurry, Milisant? You seem always to be in a rush. I wonder, do you ever take time to admire the flowers in bloom?"

What an odd question from him, yet did she reply truthfully, "Were there such to smell this time of year, aye, I would stop to smell them. I am, in fact, more at home among nature's bounties than inside a cold stone building."

She was immediately annoyed with herself for telling him something that personal. It was certainly nothing that he needed to know.

"I wonder why I am so little surprised by that," he said in a soft tone as he took a step toward her.

Alarms went off in Milisant's head. He had no *reason* to get close to her that she could think of, other than to intimidate her with his large size. That he did easily enough, whether he was across the room from her or standing right next to her. He was apparently determined to stand right next to her, though . . .

She should have bolted. She realized that later. He would have called her coward and she wouldn't have minded at all—if it had kept her from finding out what his kiss was like. But she didn't bolt. She stood a bit transfixed by the sensual expression he suddenly wore, which so greatly changed his demeanor. He was handsome normally, but there was an added attraction now that disturbed her, causing her to feel strange things, causing her to feel trapped, as if she'd been snagged by a lucky fishing hook and was being yanked to an unknown fate.

The touch of his lips upon hers broke the spell he'd put her under. She jerked away, ending the contact. His hands on her shoulders drew her right back to him, much closer now, and ended her formal protest for the moment as his mouth captured hers more fully.

Devouring came to mind. The trapped rabbit came to mind. The falcon swooping down on his prey came to mind. Not one image offered escape, but held her immobile in fear—and something else. It was the something else that she hoped to forget, but doubted she would, that small, tiny urge to relax against him and let him have his way.

The taste of him was—pleasant. The heat of his lips was—pleasant. The feel of his body pressed to her was—more than pleasant. However, considering how she felt about him, none of that should have been so and was rightfully confusing. But she only thought of that afterward. During the kiss, she thought of nothing, and that was the most frightening, that she could be rendered witless.

She had to wonder what might have happened if that kiss had continued. Thankfully it was interrupted by a servant's sharp rap on the door, causing him to release her and step back to his previous position. She vaguely noted that he seemed somewhat embarrassed now.

Still in a daze herself, Milisant didn't think before asking baldly, "Why did you do that?"

"Because I can."

Had she expected some romantic answer from him? More fool her. The answer she got had her own cheeks flushing with angry heat. So typical of the male of the species. I can, therefore I will. Bah, would that a woman could ever say the same and not have someone tell her why it would never be so.

She gave him back his own answer, as derisively as she could, as she left him to deal with the servant who entered as she opened the door. "I wonder why I am so little surprised by that."

Nineteen

Because I can?

Wulfric amazed himself sometimes, and this was certainly one of those times. He could not think of a more stupid answer to have given Milisant, and hardly the truth. But the truth had caught him by surprise, that he could desire her so suddenly, and so strongly, when verily, there was so little about her that he liked—nay, that wasn't entirely true.

She was an exceptionally comely wench when she wasn't wearing more dirt than clothes. And she had a sharp wit that he found more and more often amusing. Of course, she used it to try and insult him at every opportunity, but her daring in that also amused him.

She was unusual to be sure. She had too much pride. She was too opinionated. Her pursuits were unseemly in the extreme. Yet he had no doubt now that he would have little trouble bedding her; nay, he was sure now he would find much pleasure in that. So although he was still not thrilled with their approaching marriage, he couldn't say he still found it utterly abhorrent either.

Which was likely why he refrained from mentioning his reservations to his mother when he joined her at the Great Hearth before the midday meal, though previously he had considered enlisting her aid.

Also, she couldn't have helped noticing his sour mood when he had left here last week to collect Milisant. But in her typical fashion, she would have ignored it. Unless and until she was actually confronted with a dire situation directly, she found it quite easy to explain away any portentous signs of approaching disaster.

So she would have had warning, if he cared to discuss with her the many reasons, and there were still many, why Milisant would not make him a suitable wife. But he chose to bide his time and keep silent on the matter, well aware that the taste of Milisant, still fresh in his mind, was likely the only thing to decide him.

Cynically, he had to wonder how many decisions of great import were based on a man's sexual needs, without his even being aware of it. Too many, no doubt. Even kings were not immune to self-interest in the sexual arena. King John was a prime example in that.

Unfortunately, he should have realized that his mother would want to talk of nothing but the wedding—and the bride. He didn't even get a proper greeting from her before she launched into those very subjects, when he joined her on her favorite bench.

"Ah, I am glad you have come ere the hall begins to fill for dinner, so I can tell you how pleased I am that you have finally fetched your betrothed. You are truly lucky, Wulf. She is such a lovely girl. Verily, betrothing you to her at her birth as was done, we could not know how she would turn out, could we? Yet did it work out exceptionally well for you."

He managed to keep from laughing. Did she really have no idea how unusual Milisant was? But then he realized she really might *not* know. The girl could, after all, turn herself out decently and behave when she cared to, and mayhap she had cared to do just that whenever his mother had been present over the years.

Then, too, had he not been fooled himself into thinking only good thoughts about Milisant when he thought she was Jhone? How often were others so fooled as well?

He could have just let it go without comment. But he was too curious to know whether his mother was just deluding herself, as she so often did, or whether she really didn't know the Milisant he did.

So offhandedly he asked, "What think you of the way she dresses?"

Anne frowned at first, as if not understanding why he would ask, but then smiled with the memory. "You mean her fondness as a child to wear the garb of her playmates? But of course, she outgrew that."

"Actually, Mother—"

She was quick to cut him off. But then he should have known better than to use a word like "actually," which would be too negative for her peace of mind.

"And she enjoys hunting," Anne said. "Which

should please you, much as you like to hunt yourself."

"She doesn't hawk."

"She doesn't? But I know her father mentioned more than once—"

"That she excels with a bow?" he cut in, quite dryly.

Anne chuckled. "How silly, Wulf. Of course she doesn't use a bow. And I've seen her hawk. A splendid bird. Rhiska, I believe she calls it, named after a bird she had in her youth that some brute of a boy killed for spite. But then I am sure she will tell you the story if she hasn't already. 'Twas a most unpleasant experience for her, so the telling of it should draw her closer to you."

He stopped in shock. If, as he suspected, he was the boy his mother had just mentioned, who had killed Milisant's first Rhiska, no wonder she was at his throat.

"Brute" would have been the girl's word, not his mother's. Anne never resorted to name calling or passing such character judgments as that. So Milisant had obviously related the story to Anne, just kept silent on who the brute had been, since Anne very likely wouldn't have believed her if she'd tried to convince her that her son was the culprit.

Jesu, he wished he'd known before now that that had been the result of getting the attacking hawk off of him that day. He certainly hadn't meant to kill it, if this was indeed the hawk in question. But how else was he to have gotten the thing off of him, when it had been making every effort to rip off his fingers?

Still, if he'd known the bird hadn't survived hitting that wall when he'd shaken it off of him, he might have stayed to make some attempt to comfort the enraged girl for her loss. And they might both have ended the day without such horrid memories.

"Speaking of birds," he said now, "have you seen all of her pets?"

"All?"

She was frowning again, then just as quickly smiling as she obviously figured she knew what he referred to. As usual, she guessed wrong.

"The wolf, you mean? A strange pet, aye, but so friendly. Believe me, I would trust it ere I would one of your father's dogs. It slept at my feet once, did you know? I wasn't even aware that it was there until I kicked it by accident, and it didn't even growl—oh my," she added with a giggle. "She calls it that, doesn't she? Growls? But that is *so* inappropriate, when it's as tame as a kitten."

He got the impression that his mother thought he was worried about the wolf. He could have clarified that he was referring to Milisant's great number of pets, rather than one in particular. His main worry was that she would turn the marital chamber into a stable, but he decided there would be no point in pursuing the issue. His mother would turn any concern he might have into a minor consequence of no import. He loved her greatly, he truly did, but sometimes her attitude left him distinctly frustrated.

It was just as well. He didn't really want to complain to her about his bride-to-be, at least not at this time. That kiss was still too fresh in his mind, and if anything, his thoughts were more centered on when might be an opportune time to have another taste of her—just to assure himself that he hadn't imagined how nice was the first taste.

He did need to warn his mother, however, about the attacks against Milisant. Since she was like to be much in the girl's company, 'twas not something he could keep her ignorant of to shield her from worry.

So he said without preamble, "I mean not to cause you great alarm, Mother, but you need be aware that someone is trying to kill Milisant."

She gasped. Not surprisingly, she didn't believe him. "Wulf! 'Tis not a subject to jest about!"

"Would that it were only a jest. But there have been two, possibly three attempts made against her in a mere matter of days. I tell you only because you will be often around the girl, and should take note of anyone who comes near her whom you do not recognize."

Her sudden pallor said she took him seriously this time. "Who? Sweet *Jesu, why?*"

He shrugged. "I cannot guess who, but as to the why—unless she has an enemy she is not owning up to, I would suppose someone either hopes to hurt me through harming her, or mayhap prevent the wedding."

"Then you must marry immediately."

He chuckled. "She is not like to agree to that. 'Twas already suggested."

"I'll speak with her—"

"It won't do any good, Mother."

"Of course it will," she said confidently. "She

is a reasonable girl. If it will stop these attacks, then she must agree."

Reasonable? He was afraid now that his mother really did think Jhone was her sister. But there was no point in beating her over the head with the truth, that Milisant wanted no part of their joining. She would find that out for herself if she attempted to rush the wedding.

So he merely said, "Do as you will."

Knowing his mother, she would anyway. And as long as she had been warned to be wary of anyone she might find suspicious, he was satisfied.

Twenty

"Idiots, the whole lot of you! I give you a simple task to do, and it was a *very* simple task, and you botch it repeatedly. What, I ask you, am I paying you for? To be told how incompetent you are?"

Ellery's first thought was that he should stop sleeping in hostelries where Walter de Roghton could so easily find him. His second thought was that he would as soon kill Walter as the girl Walter had hired him to kill. Course, that wouldn't be good for his reputation, so it was merely a thought, albeit a nice one.

He didn't hang his head in shame either, though he knew that was the reaction the lord was seeking. His two accomplices, Alger and Cuthred, accommodated Walter well enough, both looking suitably chastised, but Ellery looked him in the eye and merely shrugged his indifference.

"Circumstances, m'lord," was all he said by way of excuse. "We will do better next time."

"Next time?" Walter all but screeched, red-faced in his rage. "What next time? You had access to Dunburh, you will have no such access to Shefford, which is kept like a stronghold under siege. No one enters who has no legitimate business there. Even merchants must be known to the guards, or they are turned away."

"They will hire—"

"You are not *listening!* Shefford is an earldom. An earl does not hire, he draws from his vassals and villages service owed to him."

"There is always a way, m'lord, to gain what is needful—if not through hiring or bribery, then by trickery or stealth. There will be villagers who come and go. There always are. There will be wagons that enter—and whores. I know a wench I can use if needs be. She has worked for me before and knows a thing or two about poisons. What is not needful is you telling me how to do my job."

Ellery couldn't care less that it was a lord he was slighting, when he could claim no such title himself. He was a free man, and that gave him all the rights he needed, far as he was concerned, to speak his mind to noble and serf alike. He'd been born to a London whore, had no idea who his father was, and had been cast off onto the streets to fend for himself 'fore he was barely weaned. He had survived starvation, beatings, and sleeping in the gutter in the dead of winter. A blustering lord was naught to him.

That Walter looked like he was about to froth at the mouth, said clearly he was not accustomed to being addressed so by someone he would consider far beneath him. Too bad. If Ellery had learned anything about life, it was to take what he could, by arms if needs be. What worth was life, after all, if one must grovel and eat dirt, just because some noble, born in his gold-lined bed, said so?

Ellery didn't mind this job. He had killed others for hire. But he didn't like being told how to do the deed. He didn't like being yelled at either. He was a big man, bigger than most. If his size did not make other men hesitant to rail at him, his demeanor did. He had been told that although he was a somewhat handsome brute, he looked meaner than sin. So he was used to being treated with a degree of wariness, if not actual respect.

As for the job in question, that it was a woman he was to kill made only one difference. He had seen her in all her beauty, or rather, seen her sister, who was reputed to look exactly the same, and he had a real fondness for pretty women. He'd kill her well enough, but he wanted her first. But Walter didn't need to know that, was like to insist that she not be touched other than with a blade.

Cuthred and John weren't of the same mind and had simply tried to kill her as Walter wanted. But Cuthred had a lousy aim with a bow, and John, well, he hadn't come back from that monastery.

Truth was, she would have been dead now if Ellery didn't want a taste of her first, because it would have been easiest to kill her that day on the path near Dunburh, rather than try to take her as he'd done. He was beginning to wonder, though—and not because Walter was railing at them, but because of John's death—if having her

first was worth the risk he was putting himself
and his friends to.

Mayhap he should just hire the whore he was
acquainted with to get into Shefford Castle and
poison the wench. Then again, he hadn't tried
yet to get into Shefford himself. He would have
to see if that was as difficult as Walter was
claiming first, 'fore he decided.

He did have one complaint, though. He didn't
mind not being told why a job needed doing.
That was no concern of his. But he did object to
not being told all the particulars of a job that
might be pertinent to his success or failure.

He said so now, "You should have warned
us, m'lord, that the lady is betrothed to an
earl's son."

"That wouldst have made not a *bit* of difference if you had done the deed when you should
have, ere de Thorpe went to collect her. She was
the veriest fool, behaving no better than a peasant, even going off into the Dunburh woods
alone. She was easy to get at, at any time prior
to de Thorpe's arrival. But since you have thrice
bungled the job, she is now like to be guarded
more greatly than a queen, especially now she
is ensconced inside Shefford."

Ellery wondered, if she'd been so "easy to get
at," why the arrogant lordling hadn't done the
deed himself. Likely because he was as competent with a blade as he was with the drivel that
came out of his mouth.

Of course, he'd yet to meet a "lord" who
wasn't all bluster that hid the veriest coward
underneath. He knew there were exceptions out
there, true knights who trained diligently and

were quite competent at war and killing. Ellery had just never met one, but then he wasn't like to, since such men as that wouldn't need the sort of services that Ellery provided, were quite capable of taking care of such things themselves if needs be.

He didn't say this to Walter, he said instead, "If she behaved like a peasant before, what makes you think she won't continue to do so? Methinks she is her own worst enemy. We need not get to her, she will come to us."

"Would that you could depend on that, but you cannot," Walter said, though he did seem to be somewhat reassured. "Do not forget there is a time constraint. She needs to die ere the two families are joined in marriage, *not* afterwards. Is that understood?"

"Aye, but we will still be prepared to take advantage of her own foolishness."

"Suit yourself, but do not fail me in this, or you will know a king's wrath, as well as my own."

Ellery burst out laughing, causing Walter to flush a mottled shade of red. Why did petty lords think that invoking the king's name was like threatening the wrath of God? That might have been the case with the last king, known to be as lionhearted as he was called, but with his weak-kneed baby brother?

Walter, incensed, finally found his voice enough to say, "You dare!"

Ellery waved a dismissive hand, not the least impressed with the lord's fury. "Threaten me with de Thorpe and I might worry. Even I have heard rumors that he is a knight of worthy note.

But your petty king deals only in intrigue and lies. He is a threat to no one but his own faithful nobles. Now be gone, m'lord, and leave me to plan this murder in peace. I will finish the job I started because I choose to, not because I worry over your displeasure."

Again Walter was too incensed for words. Stiffly, with all the hauteur of his class, he marched from the room. Ellery couldn't care less that he had gravely insulted his employer. He'd been paid half the promised fee, and would collect the other half when the time came, from the lord's hide if need be.

Outside the room, Walter was thinking along the same lines. He had already intended to have the mercenaries killed once they finished the task he'd set them, just as a precaution to assure the job was never spoken of. Now he was thinking he would do the killing of them himself, and enjoy it immensely.

Twenty-one

"*You seem much* subdued today, and that worries me," Jhone said.

Milisant had paused on the circular stairs on their way down to the Great Hall. That she paused to gaze longingly out one of the arrow slits at the countryside beyond Shefford's outer walls, Jhone tried to ignore for the most part, sure that there was something else bothering her sister, other than her near confinement here.

Trying to ferret out what it was, she continued, "Are you still tired from the trip?"

"Nay."

The brevity of that answer had Jhone even more worried. "Very well, what maggot are you chewing on?"

Milisant glanced back at her with a slight smile. "If I liked maggots—"

"You know what I meant," Jhone cut in impatiently. "You also know you cannot hide your distress from me, no matter how much you try."

Milisant sighed and said simply, albeit in a whisper, "He kissed me."

Jhone blinked. "When?"

"This morn."

"But that is a good thing—"

"The devil it is," Milisant snapped back.

"Nay, truly," Jhone persisted. "Do you not recall our conversation, about the benefits you can have if he desires you? Verily, that he would kiss you when there was no other reason for it but that he wanted to, then—"

"Oh, he had a very good reason for doing so," Milisant said with remembered anger. "Because he could."

Jhone stared for a moment, then chuckled. "How silly. Of course that is no reason."

" 'Tis the reason *he* gave."

"Mayhap, but still not *the* reason."

"And I suppose you know *the* reason," Milisant asked in exasperation.

"Do you think about it, the answer will come to you easily enough," Jhone replied. "Would a man kiss you if he did not *want* to kiss you?"

"I can think of other reasons besides wanting," Milisant scoffed. "There is the kiss to establish peace, the kiss to establish domination, the kiss to punish, the kiss to frighten, the kiss to—"

"Enough," Jhone cut in, all but rolling her eyes. "Why do you fight to deny that he could desire you? We decided that would be to your benefit."

"Nay, you decided that," Milisant reminded her. "I decided I want no part of his desires."

Jhone frowned. "You didn't like his kiss?" Milisant's blush was answer enough and had

Jhone smiling in relief. "Well, we can at least be grateful you didn't find it completely horrible."

"I mind it not when Growls licks my cheek either. Does that mean I *want* him to lick me?"

"The wolf and the, er, Wulf"—Jhone paused to giggle over the similarity of names—"cannot be compared."

Milisant snorted her disagreement. "Speak for yourself. I find it quite easy to compare Wulfric to a wolf—not *my* wolf, but wolves in general."

Jhone sighed at that point. "I've said it before, but I did not think you would *really* be stubborn about this to the bitter end. Yet you are determined to prove me wrong, aren't you?"

"Stubborn about what?" Milisant asked defensively. "About not liking him? About not wanting him to kiss me? Jhone, you did not experience the pain he put me through when he broke my foot, the dread and fear of being lame. 'Tis a miracle I walk not with a limp today."

"I did experience your dread and fear—not the pain, but the horror of your possible lameness. But, Mili, that was so *long* ago. He has become a man since then. Do you honestly think he wouldst cause you that kind of pain today? He is Lord Guy's son. You know how kind Lord Guy is. How can his son be so different?"

"Easily. I am a prime example of a child who grows to be in no way like either parent."

"Untrue! I have heard Papa say many a time how much you remind him of our mother."

Milisant rolled her eyes now. "Because she had a bit of a temper. Think you she behaved otherwise like me?"

"Verily, you are not the best example to use,"

Jhone conceded with a chuckle. "Yet have I spoken with Wulfric when he thought I was you, and he was all things gallant, courteous, knightly—"

"And I spoke with him when he thought I was a lad, and he was all things brutish, arrogant, and surly."

Jhone threw up her arms in exasperation. "Faugh, I give up."

"Good," Milisant just managed to get in before Jhone continued.

"You give new meaning to the word *stubborn*. He is not going to treat his wife like a disrespectful servant, which is what he *thought* you were that day he arrived."

"Nay, he'll as like treat his wife worse," Milisant countered. "Because he *can*."

"*Jesu*, that really enraged you, that remark of his. I sense that now."

Milisant snorted. "I couldn't care less—"

"Mili, do not try to fool me—you know you cannot. Would you rather have heard him say that he looks forward to bedding you? That you tempt him to not wait for the actual joining? Would that not have embarrassed you terribly? And why did he even make such a remark? If you tell me you actually asked him why he kissed you, I will clout you myself."

"Of course I asked him," Milisant mumbled. "I was nigh daft from that kiss of his. I asked the first thing that came to mind."

"Daft?" Jhone asked with interest.

"You know what I mean."

"Actually, I am not sure," Jhone replied thoughtfully. "Do you mean daft as in greatly disturbed? Or do you mean daft as in you felt so many things that you could not sort them out enough to think straight? Nay, never mind, either daft is good, do you ask me."

Milisant made a low sound very close to a growl. "I do *not* like being unable to put two thoughts together, which is what that kiss did to me."

"Did I ever tell you about the time Papa's squire kissed me?"

Milisant blinked. "Sir Richard? And Papa didn't have him flayed alive?"

Jhone chuckled. "I didn't tell Papa, of course. No harm was done, after all, and the lad apologized profusely afterwards. I was flattered, truth to tell. But I was already in love with William."

Milisant leaned back against the wall. "You have a point to make, I suppose?"

"Of course." Jhone grinned. "When do I not? Being kissed by Richard was of so little moment that it was no different than if Papa kissed me. Like a flea bite, it was nigh forgotten the next day. It stirred no feelings in me. But when William did first kiss me, I nearly swooned, so many emotions did I feel. It was so exciting, Mili. There is just no comparison, what desire can make you feel."

Milisant was blushing before Jhone had quite finished, but that last remark had her denying hotly, "I do not desire him! How could I want him when I hate him?"

"Mayhap because you do not truly hate him. You want to hate him, there is no denying that. You are giving it every effort. But you are finding it difficult to do so."

"That sounds good, Jhone, even logical," Milisant said with dripping sarcasm. "But you forgot to take into account the anger he causes me. He makes me so furious I could spit. Signs that I want him?"

Jhone gave her a hurt look. "I am trying to help you, to make this easier for you, but you wouldst rather adhere to your misery."

"Nay, I wouldst rather find a way to avoid this altogether—which I have said repeatedly now, but *you* fail to listen. Help me out of this joining, Jhone, not into it."

Jhone put a commiserating hand on her arm. "But I fear there *is* no way out. And I wouldst rather you be prepared and accepting of that fact than face it unprepared and be so very unhappy when the time comes."

Milisant hugged her. "I mean not to take out my upset on you—"

"Nay, better me than him," Jhone said, then, "Very well, I will speak of it no more—for today. And we had best go down, ere they send someone looking for us. You look lovely in that rose color, by the way."

Milisant looked down at the rose bliaut that Jhone had lent to her and snarled, "Just the thing to say to ruin my appetite."

Jhone chuckled and pulled her sister along down the circular tower stairs, teasing, "I am beginning to think your problem is you have too much vigor and not enough activities to use it up, thus you vent it all into being as surly as you can be."

"I'm not surly," Milisant grumbled.

"You are. But Dame Elga confessed to me

once, the easiest way to expend all vigor and have none left for moping—or aught else for that matter."

"I suppose this is some great secret you are about to impart?"

"Nay, and a simple enough solution it is, too." But she moved a bit ahead on the stairs before she ended, "Just have lots of babies," then raced down the remaining stairs before her sister could clout her.

Twenty-two

He saw them enter the hall. They were not dressed identically today, yet were they still identical. One was laughing, the other scowling. For once, it was so easy to tell which was which.

Wulfric railed silently once more at the fates that had gifted him with the unnatural sister, rather than the normal one. And yet, oddly, looking at Jhone now, so lovely, glowing in her amusement, he felt not the least attraction to her, not like he'd felt when he'd thought she would be his. But looking at her sister . . .

Blast and bedamned, he could feel his blood stirring. He just couldn't understand why. He had never liked women who threw tantrums, who were caustic and disagreeable. When a man wanted some bed sport, he did not want to deal with tempers. Yet when had his betrothed not been in a temper of one sort or another? And even now, when she was obviously annoyed, judging by her expression . . . how could she stir him?

"Must you frown so when you look at her?" Guy asked in a tired voice.

Wulfric glanced at his father. He hadn't heard him approach. Nor had they spoken of Milisant again since his return, other than of the attacks on her. He had reported those last eventide before he'd found his bed, and in much greater detail than what he had told his mother.

He relaxed his expression now and replied simply, "I had not realized I was frowning."

Guy made a *tsk*ing sound. "Your feelings for her need not be made so public. Nor will it benefit you to have *her* know how displeased you are with her."

Wulfric almost laughed aloud. He did smile wryly before admitting, "She already knows. And furthermore, she feels the same way. She loves another, Father. She admitted as much to me."

Guy frowned for a moment, but then scoffed, "Faugh, a defensive reaction, no doubt because she could not help but sense your dislike."

Wulfric could hardly discount that possibility when he had himself done exactly that, lied to her about loving someone else when she'd told him that she loved another. However, that did not account for her very real animosity. Because he had killed her bird? He could hardly credit someone carrying a grudge for that long over an animal. Because he hadn't gone after those curs who'd attacked her that day on the path? More likely. Yet even that was not enough for her wanting out of their contract, which she surely did.

But he wasn't going to stress that to his father.

In fact, he said lightly, "No matter. She and I
are—adjusting. Her father has allowed her a few
weeks to do so."

Guy raised a brow. "So you are no longer so
averse to this joining yourself?"

Wulfric shrugged. "Let us say I am not *as*
averse. I still think she will give me naught but
difficulties, but mayhap those difficulties will
be—interesting, or at least not as unpleasant as
I thought. Her father thinks that once she settles
into marriage, she will change—you *did* know
that she wishes she had been born male? And
that she prefers manly sport to that of her
own sex?"

Guy flushed. "I know that she is sometimes
lacking in the female graces—"

"Sometimes?" Wulfric cut in with a snort.
"You could have warned me that she goes about
dressed like a man. I nearly clouted her when I
thought she was a serving lad with a surly
tongue."

"*Jesu*, how could you mistake that soft
skin . . . ?"

"Mayhap because she also dresses in dirt."

Guy winced. "I know she used to dress so.
Nigel could not help but lament her boyish
ways to me when he was deep in his cups. Yet
did I think she would have outgrown that pecu-
liarity. And look at her. 'Tis not as if she does
not know how to behave properly."

"Merely that she would rather not."

Guy cleared his throat uncomfortably before
he said, "Well, I am of the same opinion as my
friend. Wed, bed, and get her with child, and
you are sure to find her more agreeable, and

certainly more womanly, though I have never seen her otherwise myself."

Again Wulfric wondered if his parents had ever really met the true Milisant, or if they'd thought her sister was she, but to the subject he merely said, "Actually, he thinks love is the answer."

"Love *can* change people," Guy agreed. "I have seen it happen time and again. But then I have also seen a brutal knight treat his child with extremely tender care, and a shrewish woman turn into a saint after she has had a few babies, so do not discount the wonders of siring offspring as a means to turn the lass around."

Wulfric chuckled. "Now, I wonder why you wouldst stress the latter. Mayhap because of the pleasures involved in that direction?"

"There is much to be said for—pleasures. Just as a foul-tasting medicine can be made palatable with a dose of honey, so, too, can—" Guy paused when Wulfric rolled his eyes. "You are determined to disagree with me as usual," his father ended up mumbling.

"Not so," Wulfric protested with a conciliatory grin. "I just would not compare a wife to foul medicine, when the one is taken and as quickly forgotten, but the other is like to linger for the rest of your days."

"Never mind the comparisons, as long as you see the point. You *did* see the point, aye?"

"Assuredly, I always grasp your meanings, Father. Rest easy on the matter of the girl."

Guy stared at him for a moment, then conceded, "Very well, on this subject I will. On that other matter, though . . . have you given it more thought, on what I asked? We must know who is behind these attacks."

When Wulfric had spoken to his father about them last night, Guy had asked him to come up with some names. He'd been hard-pressed to do so.

"I have had no serious altercations with anyone that I can recall," Wulfric said, "other than with one of John's mercenary captains."

"King John?"

"Aye."

Guy frowned. "What sort of altercation?"

"Naught that I had thought to worry about. I had just lost one of my men to a Welsh arrow and was in no mood to listen to his belittling of our efforts. I clouted the fellow. When he recovered some hours later, he was heard to say that he would see me rotting at the end of a spike."

"You should have dispatched him permanently."

Wulfric shrugged. "The king does not take lightly losing his captains to petty squabbles. Besides, I did not take the threat seriously. He was an idiot, thus do I think him incapable of plotting this sort of revenge. He would go straight for me, not try to hurt me through another."

"Who else then?"

Wulfric chuckled at his father. "Think you that I have enemies aplenty? Verily, I can think of no one else. But what of yourself? You wouldst be hurt as well, does this marriage not take place."

Guy seemed somewhat taken aback. "I had not even considered that, but you are correct, we should. I will give it some thought. Unlike you, I have made numerous enemies over the years."

Wulfric gave him a doubtful look. "Numerous? You? When your honor is so sterling it would take a complete fool to question it?"

Guy grinned. "I did not say I had honorable enemies. Far from it. 'Tis those lacking all scruples who have reason to fear and revile an honest man, and want revenge when they are exposed—if they manage to escape a hanging. But I want more than just precautions taken where Milisant is concerned. Who have you assigned to watch her?"

"Aside from Mother?"

"You jest, though your mother *is* diligent in her duties, and she will consider the girl one of her duties."

"All passages out of the castle are being watched, Father. Milisant will not step foot from the tower that I do not know it."

Guy nodded. "I will also tighten the restriction on who may enter Shefford. But when the wedding guests begin arriving with their own servants, I think we may needs confine her to the women's solar."

"She will balk at that," Wulfric predicted.

"Mayhap, but 'tis necessary."

"Then I will leave it for you to tell her when the time comes." Wulfric grinned.

Twenty-three

The castle folk were beginning to fill the lower trestle tables for the meal. The long table on the raised dais where the lord and his retainers would eat was still empty. Typically those welcome to eat there waited until the lord took his seat at the center. However, Lord Guy was still deep in conversation with his son.

Milisant had noticed Lady Anne approaching her, but thrice she was detained by servants needing her attention. She hoped the lady did not want to talk of the wedding again. She wasn't to find out, though, since Anne, at last free to continue on her way, changed direction now to gather her husband instead, to start the meal—which left Wulfric alone for the moment, and turning his attention to her.

Before he could fetch her, if he thought to do so, she grabbed her sister's hand and dragged her to the table, which was quickly filling now, so they could find two seats together that would leave no room for him to join them. She cared not that it would appear to Wulfric as if she were trying to avoid him. She was. And she did find one narrow bench left, with room for only two.

"What *are* you doing?" Jhone hissed as Milisant pushed her down on the bench.

Milisant whispered back, "Making sure he cannot speak to me in private."

Jhone sighed. "A useless endeavor, Mili. Does he want words with you, he will have them, will you nil you. And you *should* be sitting with him."

Her jaw tightened stubbornly. "Why? So he can spoil my appetite?"

"You give me too much credit, wench," Wulfric said as he sat down beside her.

Milisant stiffened and glanced his way, to see that the old knight who had been sitting next to her on that side had moved down the row of benches to accommodate her betrothed. She made a sour expression that she turned on Wulfric.

"So good of you to join me, m'lord."

"Sarcasm does not become you," he replied tonelessly and without expression.

"I wish you would leave. Is that better?"

"Much. The truth is always preferable—even when it avails you naught."

She snorted and turned back to her sister, to begin a conversation that was so mundane that even did he overhear it, there would be little for him to comment on. It worked. He did not try to intrude.

Would that his silence was all that was needed to ignore him. But alas, even though she crowded Jhone to keep from touching Wulfric at thigh, shoulder, or anywhere else, not for a moment could she forget that he was there, next to her, just inches away.

It caused a tension in her that did indeed affect her appetite. She ate, but she knew not what she ate. She drank, but the wine could have been vinegar, for all she noticed. It was almost a relief when she heard his voice again.

"Give me your attention, wench. We are supposed to at least look like a betrothed couple."

Wulfric's tone was distinctly surly. She was beginning to realize that he called her "wench" when he was not pleased with her.

She turned to raise a curious brow at him. "And how wouldst such a couple appear?"

"Happy?"

She almost laughed. She did smile wryly. "When most marriages, like ours, are arranged? What, pray tell, would cause happiness in such a case?"

He appeared thoughtful for a moment. "Well, there is the fact that neither of us is impaired, overly short, or cross-eyed, things to cause great joy."

An image of him crossing his eyes was too much to keep her from laughing, which was too bad. Their supposed happiness was a subject she could have sunk her teeth into in all seriousness. Now she would feel silly doing so.

She crossed her own eyes instead, and heard him burst out laughing as well. So much for letting the castle folk know they were unhappy with each other. Actually, the amusement had her relaxing, which *was* preferable to the tension he had been causing her.

"Now I must recant my own words. You are a vision, lass, even with crossed eyes."

She blushed. Actually, she blushed profusely. Compliments from him were extremely difficult to take, and she couldn't even say why that was so. Had someone else said what he just did, she would barely have noticed. Yet his words went right to her gut and stirred things there.

She reached for her wine, and nearly spilled it. *Jesu*, were her hands trembling as well? But gulping down what was left in the chalice did seem to help somewhat. She was at least able to look at him without blushing again.

It was still a mistake, to glance his way again. The humor he still wore in his expression added a sparkle to his deep blue eyes and softened the hard edges of his mouth. It made him seem so different, hardly brutish. It also pointed out once again just how very handsome he was.

It must have been the surprised wonder in her own expression that caused his to alter, but suddenly he looked as he had earlier that morn, just before he kissed her. Her breath caught and held. Her belly churned. Her pulse seemed to thunder in her ears.

He looked away first, thankfully, for she'd been unable to do so herself. And he seemed a trifle disconcerted, mayhap even embarrassed. She saw him rake a hand through his hair, just before her eyes flew elsewhere.

She thought to get up and leave the hall. That was her first instinct and would be the wisest action. Simply get far away from him until her senses returned to normal. She could give him any excuse, or none; she did not think he would try to detain her after what had just passed between them—whatever it was.

But when she heard, "I wouldst speak with you, after the meal," she abruptly changed her mind, afraid that he would follow instead.

"Speak now if you must," Milisant said without looking back at him, and in a voice that she barely recognized as her own, it was so breathless.

"In private," he stressed.

"Nay."

"Mili—"

Alarmed now, and in absolutely no doubt about what he wanted in private, she cut in, "Nay, there will be no more kissing."

"Why not?" he asked simply.

The question so surprised her that she turned to stare at him again. And he did seem genuinely confused, though no more than she was, since she had not thought she would have to give a reason. Nor did she have one that would not embarrass them both.

So she avoided an answer by countering, "Think you a woman needs a reason to say nay?"

"When 'tis her betrothed she is telling nay, aye, she does."

"We are not joined yet."

"I do not mean to bed you—yet—so what can you object to in a simple kiss?"

Jesu, she had known the subject would scald her cheeks again. And what could she say, that his kiss disturbed her so much, she could not take it in the light way he seemed to be thinking of it? Simple? There was naught simple about his kiss, nor what it made her feel.

She took a defensive tack. "You love another. Why do you even *want* to kiss me?"

His lips tightened. He obviously did not like the reminder that she was not his choice for a mate, any more than he was hers.

"Is that why you think to deny me? Because *you* love another? You will forget him, wench. The *only* one who will be kissing you henceforth is me, so best you resign yourself to that soonest, ere you cause us both grief."

Having ground out those words, he abruptly left the table. Dislike the reminder? Nay, nothing so mild as that. It had made him furious.

Twenty-four

"*How many men* will you shatter today, ere you figure out what is bothering you?"

Wulfric glanced at his brother, who had come up beside him, then at the row of knights and squires Raimund was staring at, who were sitting nearby, nursing various bruises and contusions after the vigorous workout Wulfric had just put them through.

"There is naught bothering me," Wulfric denied, though he did sheathe his sword and shake his head at the squire who was next in line to test his skills against him. He then scowled at his brother. "I should have looked for you instead."

Raimund gave a hoot of laughter. "Thank you for sparing me. And you barely worked up a sweat. Or are those ice crystals I see on your frowning brow?"

"Mayhap you *are* due for a workout," Wulfric rejoined menacingly.

Raimund grinned. "And mayhap you are due for a large tankard of mead and a shoulder to—bite on."

"You should apply at John's court for the position of buffoon, brother. Methinks you would be hired right quickly—and what has *you* in such silly humor?"

"I spent a very pleasant eventide with my wife, so why would I not be in good spirits? You, on the other hand, are obviously in an even worse mood than you were on the way to collect your betrothed, and I had thought naught could possibly get worse than that. What has occurred since I parted from you yestereve?"

" 'Twould be better to ask, what has not occurred."

Wulfric said it in a mumble as he walked away, not really for Raimund's ears, yet did Raimund follow him quick enough to hear each word, and replied with a grin, "Very well, what has *not* occurred?"

Wulfric glanced back to give him a glare. His only answer was a snort. He continued on his way, entering the nearest stable, stopping by two occupied stalls. His stallion was in one. Milisant's destrier was in the other. Surprisingly, it was the destrier, rather than his own horse, that Wulfric offered the sugar crystals to, which he pulled from the pouch on his belt. More surprising was that he did it at all.

"I wouldst fear for my hand," Raimund remarked quite seriously.

"Nay, he has the veriest sweet tooth. There is not a mean bone in him when it comes to sugar."

" 'Twas brave of you to find that out." Raimund chuckled, then, curiously, asked, "You offer her horse, but not yours?"

Wulfric shrugged. "Mine is spoiled enough."

"Think you she does not spoil hers?"

Another shrug. "If she does, she will not be able to much longer. Once the guests begin to arrive, she will be restricted to the keep."

"A wise precaution," Raimund agreed. "But what is the immediate problem, that has you decimating the lower ranks?"

Wulfric sighed and raked a hand through his hair, so rankled that he forgot it was coated with sugar crystals, nor did he notice. "I find that I want to kill a man I do not even know."

"Understandable. I wouldst be livid with rage did someone try to harm my—"

"Nay, I do not mean the one trying to harm Milisant," Wulfric cut in. "That one will wish for a score of deaths ere I am done with him, once I have him. I mean the one she has given her heart to. I did not give him a thought at first. Now I can think of little else."

Raimund was amazed. "When did you switch from hating her to liking her?"

"Who said aught about liking her?" Wulfric countered. "She is my betrothed, Raimund. I find it intolerable that I will be competing with someone I have never even met."

"You have a name then, to know that you have never met him?"

Wulfric frowned. "Nay, 'tis a name I am wanting."

"What keeps you from simply asking her for it?" Raimund ventured.

"And have her think I mean to do him harm?"

Raimund chuckled. "Is that not what you

were just saying you wouldst like to do? Kill him, I believe were your exact words."

Wulfric waved a dismissive hand. "An exaggeration, and give me none of your doubtful looks, brother. I cannot figure out how to end her attachment to him until I know why she did form one, and I cannot know that until I know who he is." His look then turned thoughtful. "But methinks you can aid me in this."

Raimund raised a brow, guessing. "You want *me* to ask Lady Milisant?"

"Nay, not her. She wouldst tell you no more'n she would me. But her sister, Jhone, she is a much different lass, sweet, biddable, hardly the suspicious sort. She would know who this man is, and is more like to tell you than me."

"And if she does not, I suppose I could beat it out of her," Raimund said, tongue in cheek.

"You jest when this is a matter of serious concern to me?"

"*Jesu*, I hope the priest was eloquent in the burial of your humor, brother. Nay, what I *think* is you make too much of this. Even if your lady is fond of another, 'tis you she will marry, you she will keep faith with. Or do you have reason to believe otherwise? Think you she wouldst betray you?"

"Nay, I think she would honor what vows she makes. That is not my concern. Let me ask you this, then. How wouldst you feel if, when making love to your wife, you know, *know*, mind you, without any doubt, that she is imagining you to be some other man?"

Raimund's cheeks lit with heated color. "I'll speak to her sister today."

Twenty-five

It amazed Milisant, the things women did gossip about. It had been years since she had been forced to sit and listen to such idle chatter. Nor would she have done so today if Lady Anne hadn't fetched both her and Jhone right after the midday meal, putting them to work on the huge tapestry she wanted finished before the wedding.

It was set up near the Great Hearth on a large rack. Nigh a dozen needles plied it at once, and without crowding, so big was this tapestry. Milisant stayed, but only because Anne stayed to supervise, and she didn't want to argue with that determined lady.

Yet she only pretended to use the needle she had been given, because it really was a beautiful tapestry, or would be when it was finished. It depicted a lordly knight and his entourage on horseback on a lovely hill in summer bloom, surveying an approaching army. Yet so little concerned by the impending threat was the knight that a hawk perched on his wrist, and he was nigh laughing. Was he supposed to be Sir Guy? Or Wulfric? No matter, it would be petty of her to ruin the tapestry with her unskilled stitching.

As for the gossip flying about her, the subjects ranged from the gory details of childbirth, to the intimacies that caused such conditions, to the exaggerated size of a certain man-at-arm's sword—it had taken Jhone to whisper to her what sword they referred to before the ladies got the expected blush out of Milisant that they had been trying for.

They soon gave up, though, when they realized that she was not a bride-to-be easy to tease, which had been their harmless intention. Standard fare that all new brides must endure, yet Milisant was not a standard new bride, thus her reactions were not what they did expect—quite a few glares and only one blush.

It was during this time, while she was sitting among so many, that Milisant felt eyes on her that did not belong. Just an odd little feeling that she shook off, since the ladies were making a great deal of noise in their laughter, and so would be drawing eyes their way.

That she felt the eyes on her in particular was a moot point. She just happened to be among the many—at least, she tried to convince herself of this, rather than accept her first thought, which was that she was being guarded so closely that men had even been set to *watch* her, which she would find intolerable. But in either case, she was quick to take herself from prying eyes just as soon as Lady Anne left the hall.

She was able to do so because Jhone wasn't

there either. She had gone up to the chamber they shared to fetch an unusually bright blue thread she'd been hoarding from the treasures their father had brought back from the Holy Land, which she wanted to apply to the lead knight's eyes on the tapestry. A kind gift on her part, since the tapestry wouldn't grace Dunburh. But at least she wasn't there at the moment to try and prevent Milisant from sneaking off.

But her escape was not as quick as she would have liked. She was halfway down the stairs that led out to the bailey when her way was blocked by Wulfric's half brother, who was coming up them. Having already been told that morning when she went to check on Stomper that she would not be leaving the keep henceforth without an escort, even to go just to the stable, she had already determined to be Jhone the next time she tried to leave the keep.

So whereas she herself would only have given Raimund a nod lacking in expression, she gave him instead a demure smile. She did, after all, have much practice in copying her sister's ladylike mannerisms.

She had hoped, with him thinking she was Jhone, that he would not try to detain her. She had not figured 'twould be just the opposite.

"Lady Jhone, might I have a word with you? You *are* Lady Jhone, correct?"

It was on the tip of Milisant's tongue to tell him the truth now, in hopes *that* would send him on his way. Yet his expression aroused her curiosity.

But rather than lying, she said simply, "Can I help you?" which avoided answering his question and left him to his own conclusions. Sop for a guilty conscience, that it wasn't entirely her fault if he drew the wrong conclusion—just mostly. And he did.

Raimund nodded. "Aye, m'lady, 'tis my hope that you can. It has come to my attention that the lady Milisant bears a certain fondness for a man other than her betrothed. Yet is my brother not one to share his possessions, even if the fondness is of a harmless nature."

Milisant immediately recalled Wulfric's fury at the meal they had shared, and what she had thought was the cause of it, that he didn't like being reminded that he loved another yet was forced to marry her instead. That had been her first thought, yet she had wondered briefly, after his warning her to forget "him," if there was not a bit of jealousy involved—though she couldn't imagine why, when his feelings, *other* than his wanting to kiss her, quite clearly demonstrated his dislike of her.

Yet as Jhone, she wouldn't know any of that, and so was forced to question, "What do you mean?"

"It would annoy him, did he think another man was pining for his wife."

Or that his wife was pining for another? And what about the wife who knew that her husband would rather have married another?

She wasn't in love with Roland. She knew she could be, given time, but at the moment he was merely a dear friend. Yet Wulfric could not say the same, did in fact admit to loving another.

She sighed inwardly, frustrated that she could not mention any of those thoughts to Raimund.

Each would lead to an argument from him in an effort to defend his brother. Yet Jhone did not argue.

So she said, "I wouldst think a man would gloat instead, for being the possessor of said wife."

He grinned, allowing, "Some might."

She raised a brow at him. "But not your brother? Then are you saying he has a jealous nature?"

"Nay, just that it would annoy him."

Milisant really wanted to say, "So?" but Jhone would be much kinder in her response.

"Feelings are a strange malady that one has very little control of," she said with a slight smile. "A man can hardly be blamed for falling in love with a woman he has no hope of winning for his own. Such things are random. Neither can a woman be blamed for the feelings of another, as long as she does not intentionally solicit those feelings."

Her smile got brighter. *Jesu*, but that was likely exactly what Jhone would have said. It had been quite a while since she had pretended to be her sister, but she hadn't lost the knack for it.

"Wulf is not placing blame, m'lady," Raimund assured her. "It would have been much better if he did not know of this other man, but your sister saw fit to mention him, and her own feelings for him."

"So that annoys him as well?"

"Nay, I doubt me that annoys him at all. He wouldst be confident that given time, his wife's affection would be his and his alone."

Milisant had to bite back a snort. Confident indeed, the conceited oaf. And she was fast losing patience with the pretense she was fostering. Her curiosity had been satisfied—except for one thing.

"Is there a reason for this discussion, Sir Raimund?" she asked pointedly.

She realized her mistake when she saw his blush. The question had been too direct for Jhone. Jhone strived never to cause anyone any discomfort, including embarrassment, whereas Milisant was known for her bluntness, which could, and often did, cause many red cheeks.

"I had hoped to be able to assure my brother that he has allowed himself to become annoyed over naught. Actually, I was hoping you would give me the name of this other man, so that I could speak with him and learn whether he returns Lady Milisant's affections. It wouldst be a fine gift for my brother's wedding, to be able to tell him that he need have no further concern in the matter."

"It would indeed," Milisant said tightly, "yet can I not aid in delivering this gift. You will have to speak to my sister, Sir Raimund. The name you seek has never been divulged to me."

So much for not lying directly. But she was not about to have Roland badgered about this matter when she had yet to even let him know she wanted to marry him.

Not surprisingly, Raimund appeared doubtful. "Never? You and your sister are twins, which implies a closeness more solid than most siblings. I had not realized you refrained from sharing confidences."

Milisant chuckled; she couldn't help it. "Nor do we. Yet some things my sister holds too personal to discuss, even with me. I do know of her . . . fondness for this man, but she has never actually called him by name, or rather, by his real name. She calls him her gentle giant."

Raimund sighed. "I will have to speak with your sister then."

Milisant smiled. "Good luck, sirrah. If she would not mention the name to me, she is hardly like to give it to you. But by all means, do try."

Twenty-six

Milisant didn't go outside after all. Because she was a twin, and because it was extremely difficult for most people to tell her and her sister apart by sight alone, the guards posted at the door had been ordered to keep both sisters inside the keep.

Blasted precautions. Wulfric thought of *everything*, much to her own frustration. And yet what was she doing here in Shefford Castle if she was still in such danger? If she had to have an armed escort wherever she went, she could have stayed home in Dunburh. His point in bringing her here was that he could trust his own people, that there wasn't a mercenary among them.

She was so annoyed, she almost sought him out—until she recalled how they'd parted earlier, with him so angry. It would be soon enough to make her scathing remarks when she saw him for the evening meal. So she spent the rest of the afternoon taking out her frustration on the poor tapestry, plying a needle for real this time.

Fortunately for the tapestry, her sister worked right beside her and calmly undid the horridly uneven stitches without comment. Milisant barely noticed, so preoccupied was she with her aggrieved thoughts.

She would like to know, along with everyone else, who it was who was trying to harm her. But she knew that she would never find out with the type of protection she was presently being afforded, because whoever it was wouldn't be stupid enough to make another attempt against her when he would have so little hope of succeeding. Far better to leave her to her own devices, let the attempt be made, and let *her* thwart it.

Not that she thought she was invulnerable, or capable of dealing with every situation—just most of them. But her pets could protect her, and be much less intimidating than four burly guards, which was how many had lined up ready to follow her out of the keep.

She determined to start keeping her pets with her at all times from now on—at least Growls and Rhiska. Growls in particular seemed utterly tame at first glance, despite his being a wolf. Yet could he rip through three adults in a matter of seconds, while Rhiska could panic several more. They could easily keep her safe outside the keep, yet still within Shefford's high walls.

However, out in the countryside, which she wasn't familiar with here, she would agree with the need for an armed escort. She wasn't stupid, after all. But no one was going to shoot arrows at her within the walls of Shefford, when they would have no escape. Nor would anyone be able to get her out of Shefford with its closely guarded gates.

She was fully prepared to present this reasoning to Wulfric when he joined her for the evening meal. She had collected her pets, had Growls resting beneath the table at her feet, and Rhiska perched quietly on her shoulder. She was armed with logic. And then he didn't show up.

The meal progressed and he still didn't show up. The meal was nigh finished and he still didn't show up. She wasn't just annoyed now, she was furious. *He* was the one who had insisted they spend so much time with each other each day, yet she had seen him hardly at all that day.

It wasn't until she was actually leaving the dais that she saw him enter the hall. He paused there at the entrance to survey the large room. His dark blue eyes passed over her, then came back. His expression, or lack of one, didn't change, nor did he move, other than to lift the large grouse leg that he clutched in his fist to his mouth, to rip off a chunk of the fowl. There had been grouse served with the meal, along with the standard fish and deer.

So he had gone to the kitchens for sustenance, rather than sit beside her for the lavish meal? Unlike Dunburh, where the kitchens had been moved inside the lower regions of the keep many years ago, Shefford's kitchens were out in the bailey. This kept the smoke well away from the hall, yet the food wasn't quite as hot when it arrived at the tables, especially during the winter months.

Yet being outside, the kitchens here were easy

enough for anyone to access without making an appearance in the hall—at least they were easy enough for Wulfric to access, since he was not restricted to the keep. So if he wanted to avoid her, he need not starve to do so.

Would that she were allowed the same choice, at least of avoiding him. But had he not proved at the earlier meal that such was not to be her choice? More fuel for the fire of her anger.

She didn't wait for him to come to her—actually, it appeared that he would not be doing so, since, after several moments of staring at each other, he was still standing where he had entered the hall, and still without expression of note. Not that she cared what mood he might be in, when her own was so foul.

She went to him. "I wouldst like a word with you—in private."

Wulfric's black brow shot upwards sharply, and not surprisingly. She had forgotten that he had made the same request earlier—and been denied.

Yet she guessed his thoughts, and fairly growled, "Nay, not for kissing."

"Then best you say what you mean to say right here. Do I find myself alone with you again, wench, there *will* likely be some kissing."

Why those words caused her cheeks to heat and her belly to flutter, she couldn't say. They were not exactly uttered in sensual tones, far from it. The tone had been surly at best, nor was his expression neutral anymore, was quite a perfect scowl.

Oddly, 'twas not his testiness that put a dent in her own, but that strange fluttering—at least, her own tone was not nearly so sharp as she'd intended when she replied, "I wish to discuss my imprisonment here."

He snorted. "You are not imprisoned."

"Yet does it seem so when I cannot even go to attend my horse without four behemoths surrounding me."

"Behemoths?"

"The guards you ordered to follow me."

He stared blankly for a moment, then he actually smiled at her. "Nay, not my order. I have taken precautions of my own, yet for the guards, you may thank my father. Or did you not realize you wouldst be under his protection now, as well as under mine?"

Milisant bit back a scathing retort, said merely, "This is intolerable."

" 'Tis like to get much worse ere the matter is ended," he replied.

"I can think of naught that is worse, and not even necessary. Look at them."

She nodded to Growls, who had followed her and sat staring at Wulfric curiously. She then took Rhiska from her shoulder with her gloved hand, and gripping the bird's taloned feet so it would know not to leave her, she lifted her hand sharply. The bird didn't try to fly, but it did reflexively spread its wings wide. She had to lean her head to the side to avoid the long reach of them.

"These two are all the protection I need within Shefford. Speak with your father and tell him so."

Perhaps she shouldn't have said it in the form of an order. His brow rose again, though not as sharply. But the tightening of his mouth was a better indication that he didn't like her tone.

He nodded toward the Great Hearth. "There he sits. And you have a tongue that you use most—eloquently."

He started to walk away. She quickly put a hand to his arm. "He is more like to listen to you."

"And I am more like to listen to *you*, wench, when you learn how to make requests in a more . . . womanly fashion."

"You expect me to plead with you?" she said, aghast.

"That would be interesting, but—"

"I'd sooner cut off my tongue."

"—*but* unnecessary," he finished, then chuckled. "I was merely suggesting a pleasant tone. Ironic, that that is so foreign to you, you did not even consider that it was what I meant."

She snapped her mouth shut, glared at him for the insult he'd just dealt her in his roundabout way, and walked off. Talk pleasantly to him? When she could not manage a conversation with him without having her temper pricked? He provoked her at every turn, and she was beginning to suspect he did so deliberately. And what did that say for their having a peaceful marriage? That it wouldst never happen.

Twenty-seven

A week passed without incident, other than the fact that the wedding was approaching much too quickly for Milisant's peace of mind. She managed to go through the week without arguing with Wulfric again, but only because they barely spoke. Even when they shared meals now, he didn't insist that she make a pretense of enjoying his company, just for the benefit of those watching.

She found his silence, for the most part, unnerving, mayhap because she detected a frequent tenseness about him that was undefinable. It did not bespeak anger, at least not that she could detect, yet did it cause her to be constantly on guard, awaiting she knew not what.

Lady Anne came up with a number of entertainments for her ladies during the week, including a small gathering in the solar to celebrate the finished tapestry with wine and sweet cakes. The tapestry now hung above the Great Hearth. With the bright blue thread Jhone had contributed, the lead knight now looked more like Sir Guy than his son, for which Milisant was grateful. The resemblance was still there, though, and she caught herself staring at the tapestry often.

Passing minstrels had also been allowed entrance on two nights. And there had been a night of dancing, an amusement that even Milisant enjoyed immensely, causing her to forget for a short time that she wished she were anywhere else, rather than inside Shefford Castle.

Wulfric's mother had decided that Milisant should remain close to her side for most of each day, so that she could get used to the daily running of such a large castle. Milisant didn't have the heart to tell the lady that the tasks she performed were foreign to her. She instead managed to say the right things, to keep the lady blissfully unaware of her ignorance.

She did marvel at the woman's boundless energy. Lady Anne rarely got a moment's rest, with the castle folk and her ladies coming to her with their many questions, to receive new tasks, or to report problems of one sort or another, yet did she never seem tired. Nay, 'twas as if she thrived on being in such constant demand.

The only drawback to being in Anne's company for most of each day was the fact that the lady rarely left the keep. She'd conferred with her cooks in the kitchen only once, since they usually came to her in the Great Hall to discuss the day's menus. And any other task that might have taken her out to the bailey, she assigned to others.

Lady Anne confessed she didn't like the cold of winter, and thus avoided being out in it as much as possible. Milisant was just the opposite, since she thrived on being in the midst of nature.

In fact, she missed the sunshine, even from a weak wintery sun; thus she gave in and accepted her escort to get out of the keep at least once a day. The storm that arrived later that week put an end to that pleasant excursion. She didn't mind the cold, but snow depressed her if she couldn't get out in the countryside to view it in its untouched beauty. And out in the bailey, it took no more than an hour after dawn for any new snow to be thoroughly turned to an ugly gray-brown slush.

Nay, actually, Milisant enjoyed Lady Anne's company and did not really mind following her about. There had been one uncomfortable moment, though, when Anne had suggested that the wedding be changed to a sooner date.

They had been alone in the lord's chamber, where Anne had been taking stock of her foreign spices, so precious she kept them locked in her husband's coffers. Yet when they had been in the kitchen she had mentioned wanting to use some of them for the wedding feast, which was when the subject had first been introduced.

Milisant had been hard-pressed to come up with a reason other than the truth for why she would not agree to that, and she'd had plenty of time to think of one, since Anne had gotten distracted in the kitchen and didn't mention it again until they were in the lord's chamber. The month that Milisant's father had given her to "get to know" Wulfric wasn't enough of an excuse in the face of the attacks that had been

made against her. At least, that was what Anne
had stressed earlier, and she did so again later
when she recalled the subject.

"A week sooner will make no difference
really, you must agree," Anne said. "Once the
joining has been made, you will be in no further danger."

"We have only assumed that to be so," Milisant was quick to point out. "The attacks could
be for a completely unrelated reason."

"Very doubtful—"

"But possible. It could just be some crazed
person who has imagined some grievous wrong
against me, and have naught to do with enemies
of Shefford."

Anne frowned, considering that. "But were
you not set upon by a group of men? That does
not indicate that it is just some madman with
an imagined grudge."

" 'Tis well you note the difference in the attacks, Lady Anne. 'Tis my opinion that first encounter was by different men altogether."

"Why think you so?"

"Because they seemed more to want to steal
me away, mayhap for ransom. While the other
two attacks were definitely an attempt to kill
me. And consider, the man who tried it the second time is now dead. Thus there could be no
further danger at all—except from that other
group who had hoped to profit by my father's
tender regard of me. And they, too, could have
given up the idea, having been so thoroughly
thwarted in their first attempt."

Milisant wished she could believe that; however, she knew that man who had died had been

working for someone else. However, Anne didn't need to know that, and did seem to be giving the matter new thought.

Milisant was able to add to the doubt by reminding Anne, "Besides, if it can make no difference a week sooner, then it can make no difference a week later. And have the invitations not gone out long since? What if the king has decided to attend the ceremony? Would he not be furious to arrive and find the wedding over?"

That brought a frown to the lady. One did not intentionally enrage the king, after all—at least, not their current temperamental king. And although no one *really* expected John to show up for the wedding, when he was in the process of planning another campaign across the channel, it was not an absolute certainty that he wouldn't. He'd been invited only because it would have been an insult not to invite him. There were many other guests coming, though, who would be inconvenienced by a change of dates.

This was likely why Anne finally agreed, "Very well, we will just have to assure that you are kept safe, and that can be done easily enough, I suppose, as long as you are never left alone."

Milisant had the feeling that that solution had already been in effect, since the lady did indeed try to keep Milisant at her side constantly. Amazingly, she found that she liked Anne's company. When she'd mentioned that to her sister, Jhone's explanation had been simple.

"She is a mother, after all, who has raised many daughters. And you and I have both lacked a motherly influence, and mayhap missed it without realizing it. This is why you do not mind her treating you like a daughter. I for one bask in her tender regard when she thinks I am you. I do not doubt she has the same effect on you."

Milisant didn't argue with that reasoning. She in fact admitted how nice it would be if she could keep Anne for a mother-in-law, if only she didn't have to accept her brutish son in the bargain.

Twenty-eight

The winter storm howling outside brought with it a marked chill inside the keep. Icy drafts gusted through the Great Hall and the stairwells, entering with each opening of the doors and through the arrow slits in each tower, which were difficult to cover completely. Heavy winter cloaks were worn indoors. More mead was drunk than usual to fight off the chill. And the crowd gathered before the Great Hearth was thrice the normal size.

That evening Lady Anne sent Milisant to her chamber to fetch an extra mantle, since it was too early for her to retire yet and seek the warmth of her bed. And those still in the hall were being entertained by an old Dane with stories from his homeland, so Anne was enjoying herself—except for the cold.

Milisant nearly suggested to the lady that she ought to wear leggings beneath her skirts as she did, but in the end she decided Anne would be shocked. But even more thickly dressed than most, Milisant still raced up the icy stairwell.

She had left Rhiska with Jhone near the fire in the hall, since the bird had been noticeably shivering a lot herself that evening. But Growls padded up the stairs right behind her, unaffected by the cold with his gray coat grown thick for the winter months.

She supposed she could blame the lighting, or lack of it—the torch at the top of the circular stairs had burned out, likely because of the draft—and her haste for her hard collision with the man who was just entering the stairwell from above.

She heard him grunt as they impacted. She heard Growls growl. She turned to quiet the wolf before she apologized, then thought better of it, at least until she knew who she had slammed into.

But the wolf quieted on his own, no doubt because he could smell the man now, and knew him not to be a threat. Would that Milisant felt the same.

But that was not the case at all when she felt those strong hands on her shoulders, steadying her, and heard Wulfric say, "Dare I hope that you followed me up here for a reason I might find to my liking?"

There was light farther down the corridor behind him, so he had had no trouble seeing who she was. The question that came to her mind, though, was *how* he had known it was she, rather than Jhone, to make a remark like that, when she and her sister had worn matching bliauts today.

However, she addressed his question first. "I

am on an errand for your mother. But be assured that if I *had* seen you come up here—"

"If you say you would have run in the opposite direction, I may thrash you," he interjected.

Milisant stiffened slightly. She *had* been about to say something of that sort. Now, instead, she remarked, "Now, why does that not surprise me overmuch?"

Wulfric sighed, very loudly, before he said, "That was a jest, wench."

She refrained from snorting, just barely, said merely, "Was it?"

But she didn't want an answer. She wanted to be on her way, which she tried to do. But his hands didn't release her shoulders, though he did allow her to come up the last step, tugged her up it, actually, so she didn't feel quite so . . . dwarfed in his presence.

"Your tone implies you doubt me. When have I ever given you reason to think that I might beat you? And do *not* mention that time when I thought you were an insolent peasant. Even then did I stay my hand against you, because I thought you must be mad to be that foolish."

She did not need to mention that time. She had other memories of much worse pain and terror.

So she said in answer, "If you can beat an animal, Wulfric, you can beat a woman." She was also quick to remind him, "And you did in fact raise your fist to Stomper, would have hit him if I had not got in your way."

He actually smiled at her. "You compare yourself to an animal?"

His humor was not appreciated. "Nay, but I compare your impulses to one."

That did indeed end his humor. His hands tightened on her noticeably. He hadn't liked that answer at all. And she wished now she hadn't given it, that she could practice at least a little restraint where he was concerned. But no, instead she had given him an excuse to keep her here arguing with him, when she would prefer to be on her way.

To correct her blunder, she tried to distract him with a simple question that could be answered briefly. Hopefully that would be the end of their discourse.

"How did you know 'twas I and not my sister? I could have sent Growls with her. In fact, she has Rhiska with her now. So with my pets divided atween us, how could you know? Or did you only guess?"

"Aside from the smell of you, which is quite unique, there is your habit of holding your lips tightly compressed, as if you are in constant annoyance—which, given my experiences, does seem to be the case."

"And given my experiences with you, do you wonder why?" she shot back.

"Think you I enjoy arguing with you, wench? I assure you, I do not, yet can you say the same?"

So much for this being a brief, dismissable subject to get her on her way. Actually, his last remark did give her an excuse to end it.

She gave him a tight little smile and said, "There is an easy way to avoid arguing, and I will do that right now and bid you a good eventide."

She again moved to pass him, but still he did not release her shoulders. "Not so fast. You have accused me of having the impulses of an animal. And lest I disappoint you, mayhap I should demonstrate some of those impulses."

It dawned on her in shocking clarity in the moment following those words that they were utterly alone there at the top of the stairs. And no sooner did her heart skip a beat with that knowledge than he pulled her up against his hardness and his mouth took possession of hers.

It was a kiss fraught with passion, frustration, and . . . tenderness—a unique combination that didn't so much frighten as intrigue. It was the molding he was doing to their bodies that was frightening, because that was what was setting her senses to rioting this time. And it was a continuous molding and positioning with his hands, so that it seemed he almost rubbed her against him.

Sweet *Jesu*, the things this made her feel were nigh impossible to contain, even more impossible to resist. The sensations were wonderful, deep within her, spiraling, churning, clamoring to culminate. Without even realizing she did it, her arms went around his back.

He took note of it, though, and must have assumed a complete surrender, for immediately she was lifted, then carried. This brought her to her senses right quickly, reality jolting her and setting off a panic.

"Why do you carry me?" she gasped out.

" 'Tis quicker."

"Quicker for what?"

"To get where we are going."

"Which is where? Nay, never mind where. Just put me down."

"Aye, I intend to."

He did, but not on her feet. The bed he laid her on was soft and she sank deep into it when his body came to rest on top of hers. Her panic soared when she realized she could not budge the huge weight that kept her pinned there. Yet in no more than five minutes, mayhap less time than that, it slowly receded and then was gone, due to a combination of the sensual kissing that Wulfric began almost immediately, and the strategic adjustment of his weight.

Actually, it was his weight that won the skirmish for him, not because it kept her there beneath him, which it did easily enough, but because of what it caused her to feel. It was that incredible new sensation she had felt when he had held her close, yet amplified tenfold. It made her want to put her arms around him and pull him even closer to her. It made her want to return his kisses. It made her want . . .

As before when he had kissed her, her thoughts deserted her altogether, leaving only the feelings as each new sensation made itself known. And he provoked so many! First with his body, as he moved it subtly against her until she was gasping and moaning under his kisses, then with his hands as he began to caress her.

There was no chilling air against her skin to give her warning when he lifted her skirts, because of the leggings she wore under them. So she was unaware that he had even done so until she felt the heat of his hand on the bare skin of her belly. It was there only briefly, though, for quickly did it move lower until . . .

It was the most incredible feeling as his fingers slid between her legs. She had a vague notion that he shouldn't be doing so, but like her other thoughts, the notion didn't stay long. His hand did, though. It was so intensely pleasant as his fingers moved slowly against her there, so relaxing, yet not relaxing, so nice. But then suddenly a tension was added, came unexpectedly, a coiling, a gathering, and in the end, an exquisite bursting . . .

There was a cough. When that produced no response, some throat clearing was added, then another cough, much louder, which was finally heard.

Wulfric swore most foully. The weight left Milisant. It still took several more moments for her to realize there was someone else in the room with them. When she opened her eyes, she found Guy de Thorpe standing near the door to his own chamber—that was where Wulfric had carried her—nonchalantly examining his fingernails.

She probably could have cooked something on her face, it exploded with such heat. She had never been so mortified as she was in that moment. And rather than stay and endure such shame for even another second, she shot off the bed and straight out the door, without a word or another glance toward Wulfric's father.

Nor did her embarrassment lessen after she returned to the hall and was forced to tell Lady Anne that her son had distracted her from her errand. The embarrassment just grew worse the more she thought of what she had been doing, and what Guy de Thorpe must think of her now. And there was no excuse she could offer, even for her own benefit. She had not protested over-much, what Wulfric had been doing to her. Far from it. In the end, she *had* returned his kisses and let him have his way with her—and enjoyed every moment of it.

Twenty-nine

"*Your timing, Father,* leaves much to be— lamented," Wulfric grouched as soon as Milisant's racing footsteps could no longer be heard.

"Verily, I thought the timing was rather fortuitous myself, considering you have another week ere you have the church's blessing to dally as you just were."

Wulfric snorted. "Spare me any lectures you would not care to hear yourself."

Guy chuckled at that reply. "No lectures. Nay, 'tis just lucky for you that I was the one to open that door, rather than your mother, or neither of us, I am sure, would have heard the end of it. What the devil could you have been thinking, to bed the lass in *here?*"

Which was when Wulfric finally blushed. He hadn't exactly cared where he bedded her, as long as it was in a bed near to hand. It was disconcerting, though, to realize that he *hadn't* cared. When had he ever been so thoroughly thoughtless in such a matter? Never, that he could recall.

She made him forget himself, whether in anger or passion. She made him overlook place, and time, and consequence. What was it about her that could so rattle good common sense? Even if he could figure that out, it would not change the fact that he behaved most erratically when he was around her. It wouldn't change the fact, either, that he only had to see her now, even if across a crowded room, to want her. And *that* fact was the hardest to deal with.

Another week until the joining? At the moment it seemed like an eternity.

To his father, standing there awaiting an answer, he said, " 'Twas thoughtless, aye, but there was not much thought involved—if you know what I mean. I was looking for you. She was on an errand for Mother. 'Twas not intentional, that we should meet up here."

Guy nodded in understanding. After all, what man had not been carried away by passion at one time or another in his life, particularly when it was unexpected, rather than a planned seduction?

So Guy let the subject pass. "Was it of import, the reason you sought me?"

"Nay, not really," Wulfric replied with a careless shrug to belie just how important it actually was—to him anyway. "Merely a curiosity."

Guy raised a brow when he didn't continue with an explanation. "Well?"

"Who do you know who could be described as 'a gentle giant'?"

After a moment of thought, Guy replied, "King Richard, of course, was considered a giant at well over six feet, but gentle?" He gave a short laugh.

Wulfric shook his head. "Nay, not Richard, and not someone no longer among us."

"Ahh, well, my vassal Ranulf Fitz Hugh could also be termed a giant, and many do call him so. Verily, aside from Lionheart, I have never known anyone as tall as Ranulf is. But again, gentle? Ranulf made his living by the blade ere he became my vassal through marriage to Reina of Clydon. And what man of war can be called 'gentle'?"

"Gentle would be a matter of opinion, I wouldst suppose. But Fitz Hugh is too old."

Guy snorted at that, insulted on Ranulf's behalf. "He is in his prime—"

Wulfric waved a dismissive hand. "Nay, I do not mean old as in old, just too old for who I am looking for. Someone more my age?"

Guy frowned at that point and asked, "What need you of a giant?"

Wulfric hedged with the reply, "I have no need of one, I merely heard of one mentioned, and found myself curious as to who he might be."

"Why do you not ask the one you heard mention him?" Guy advised.

An excellent suggestion, but the last place that Wulfric was like to get an answer, which was why he grumbled, "If that were an option, I would have done so. Bah, never mind. As I said, 'twas merely curiosity. It is a contradictory description, after all, as you just pointed out—gentle and giant make an odd combination."

Guy chuckled. "Now you have me just as curious, so if you do discover who this gentle giant is, I wouldst like to know myself."

Later, after finding out if the ice would break on his old swimming hole in the east woods—it did—Wulfric took his time returning to the castle. There was nothing like a dip in frigid water to clear one's thoughts—and passions.

The storm had yet to abate, though the wind had settled down for the time being, leaving only a soft flaking of snow that was little more than a nuisance. The white blanket on the ground kept the path from being totally dark, despite the absence of a moon. And the torch-fire off in the distance was an easy beacon to follow, though he did so absently, his thoughts occupied still with discontent, Milisant Crispin and her "gentle giant" at the center of it.

After Raimund had repeated the conversation he'd had with Milisant's sister, Wulfric didn't doubt that Jhone had lied about knowing who her sister had given her heart to—and that the twins obviously felt the need to protect this man. However, that made it more imperative that Wulfric discover who he was. If there was no chance of his ever meeting him, then there would be no need to hide his identity. So obviously it *was* possible that he might someday have dealings with the man, not knowing who he was, and *that* Wulfric found intolerable.

He had not realized he had ambled so far afield until the torch-fire became a campfire instead, and he was almost upon it. There were three men huddled there for the warmth. He did not hesitate to approach them, sure that he had not wandered so far that he had left Shefford lands.

"What do you here when there is a castle near where you could have sought hospitality for the night?" Wulfric asked when he drew up his stallion in front of them.

They had stood up, all three, as soon as he had been noticed. They had waited for him to speak, though, warily watching him, hands near the hilts of their blades. That was not unusual. They knew him not, after all, and though he seemed alone, many an ambush had been laid by sending in one man as a distraction.

One of the three was quick to volunteer, "We are not poachers, m'lord."

They had the look of mercenaries, which was why Wulfric said, "Be at ease, man. I had not thought so. A poacher tends to go home when the sun sets."

"We are merely passing through these lands," another thought to mention. "We left the road to make camp, as a caution against road thieves."

Wulfric nodded. That was plausible enough and practiced by many. Also, strangers to the area wouldn't know that thieves feared to operate on Shefford land. Of course, there were King John's enemies who might want to bedevil Shefford simply because Shefford was still loyal to the king. Yet his father had mentioned no such problems.

So he took them at their word. "If you are looking for work, Shefford would have none to offer you, yet on a night like this, spreading your pallet near a fire under a roof wouldst be preferable, would it not?"

It was a test. That he did not get an immediate answer led Wulfric to his first suspicion, that the three men were not what they seemed after all. His instincts alerted, he was forced to give them a closer look.

The two who had spoken appeared to be of peasant stock, but the third was a large, handsome brute with a look of keen intelligence. There was also a condescending air about him that said clearly he *thought* he was in no danger, that he was sure he could take Wulfric if necessary. Usually when a man felt that way, he was either stupid—or so expertly skilled that he was right. Wulfric wondered if he would ever find out in this one's case.

Possibly, though apparently not tonight, for the man made an effort to correct the blunder their silence had caused, saying now, "A roof and fire wouldst be appreciated. We had heard Shefford was closed to travelers, which is why we did not expend the effort to try their hospitality. Are you sure they make exceptions due to the weather? We would not care to break camp here only to be turned away at their gate."

"I can assure you entrance."

"And who would you be?"

"Wulfric de Thorpe."

"Ah, son of the great earl himself," the man said with a smile. " 'Tis a pleasure, my lord. Your reputation precedes you."

"Does it?" Wulfric replied skeptically. "If you are coming, be quick about it. I have been out here long enough to be feeling the cold myself now, so I am sure you are as well."

They did make haste now and returned to

Shefford with him. But whereas he would have merely told the guard he turned them over to to see to their comfort and their departure in the morn, he now told the fellow to have them followed at a discreet distance. He wanted to be assured now that they did indeed leave Shefford lands on the morrow.

He could have wished his suspicions had been groundless, though. Yet were they proven correct when the man who was sent to follow them the next day did not return, and after an extensive search, was found half buried in the nearby woods, his throat cut. The three men were not seen again, though the patrols were given their description and were ordered to apprehend them on sight.

Wulfric even added a bonus for their capture, chagrined as he was that he had not seen to the matter himself. But if their leader was as intelligent as he had seemed, Wulfric doubted they would be found. Unfortunately, he also doubted they had left the area.

Thirty

The guests began arriving. King John had been invited, but no one actually expected him to come. Thus it was a surprise when his huge entourage was seen approaching Shefford five days before the wedding.

Having the king of England as a guest could be viewed as an honor or a disaster. If he only stayed a day or two, it was usually an honor. If he stayed longer, though, it was nearly always a disaster, since stores would be utterly depleted, leaving a castle hard-pressed to feed its own people until the next growing season.

That John was going to be at Shefford at least five days due to his early arrival, mayhap longer, might have put a crimp even in a demesne the size of Shefford, if the earl hadn't planned well in advance, and had many holdings to draw from. Extra stores had been shipped in from townships as far away as London, and his many vassals had contributed from their own stores as well.

The castle huntsmen and falconers had also

been kept busy in the prior weeks, so there was an abundance of smoked and salted meats available. There would be food aplenty. The only problem being that each meal needed to be lavish to impress someone of John's stature.

To that end, Lady Anne would be using more of her precious store of spices than she'd counted on, yet she did not begrudge the need. Her husband might bemoan the fact that the king would be in residence, but Anne was delighted that it was so, for with John came the highest-ranked ladies in the lands, including the queen, and naturally, entertaining gossip.

Milisant might have been excited to be meeting the king for the first time if she were not in a constant state of panic as her wedding got closer and closer to becoming a fact. And that her father had yet to arrive, or even send word of when he would, only increased it.

She was afraid he had no intention of showing up, which would be the easiest way for him to avoid sticking to their bargain. He had given her a month's grace, yet he hadn't wanted to, and he had been confident that she would change her opinion about Wulfric during that time. However, he wouldn't really want to take any chances about this. If he didn't come, his reasoning could be that she was there, the groom was there, and the groom's parents would see the wedding accomplished, which was what everyone wanted—except her . . . well, and except for the groom.

Actually, she wasn't so sure about the groom anymore, not after he had nearly made love to her that night in his parents' chamber. *That* would have put an end to any hope of avoiding their joining. She knew it. He had to know it as well. And even before that, he had been behaving as if he were now completely resigned to having her for wife.

He might still wish it were otherwise, yet was it obvious that he was no longer expecting something to prevent it. But then he could afford to give up. A marriage, after all, would not prevent a husband from seeking love, as well as happiness, elsewhere, whereas a wife could not do the same—if she did not want to find herself killed in a jealous rage or locked away in some tower for the rest of her life, which in some cases just might be preferable.

The wife had no choices. The husband had as many as he cared to pursue. Yet another reason for Milisant to rail against the despised female body that she had been born into.

John's arrival brought all this to mind again. And worse, as they watched John ride through the portcullis that day, Jhone pointed out that the king's presence nearly made the wedding mandatory. After all, he was there to witness a joining. To not have one now . . . How could that be explained, without making one of their two families appear utter fools whom the whole country would soon hear about?

Could Milisant do that to her father, or to Lady Anne, for that matter, whom she had become so fond of? Yet what was the alternative? To accept the brute. To accept her every enjoyment henceforth being curtailed by a husband who took pleasure in gainsaying her. Nay, she could not. There still had to be a way to escape the shackle awaiting her.

Milisant was officially presented to the royal couple that evening before the meal. Jhone saw to it personally that she was dressed befitting the occasion. The cumbersome bliaut and chemise of rich royal blue velvet were as heavy as the dread weighting her shoulders. Yet the queen remarked on their beauty—the sisters were presented together—which at least pleased Jhone.

The queen herself was an amazing sight. It had been rumored that she was a woman whose beauty was beyond compare. To find that the rumor was indeed fact was disconcerting, and led most people to simply stare, utterly bemused by such radiance. Even Milisant, who put little store in such things as appearances, was impressed. But then she was also impressed by King John.

For a man in his middle years, John was still a very handsome man, and charismatic, with an engaging smile that could put one quite at ease. It was hard to believe that half the country could be his enemies. But then, that half likely did not include women, for John was known to be at his most charming where women were concerned. What could be wondered was if he was still the womanizer he had been in his youth, now that he had a wife so exquisitely lovely.

Milisant was to find out for herself, unfortunately, when later that night one of John's servants sought her out, to bring her to the royal presence. The pretext, not that one was needed since one did not refuse a summons by the king,

was that the royal couple wished to congratulate
her in private on her brilliant match. And since
Milisant considered her match anything but brilliant, she was understandably not in a pleased
state of mind as she followed the servant to the
king's chamber.

Jhone, aware of her feelings without being
told, had cautioned her to at least be civil, and
to keep in mind that John's presence meant he
must approve of her marriage. Not that his approval was needed, since Nigel had mentioned
once that King Richard himself had given his
blessings on the joining of the two families. But
Milisant knew better than to pour out her grievances to someone of John's reputation. He was
a sovereign who could not be trusted to give
aid unless he himself might benefit from it. This
was such common knowledge that one didn't
have to attend court or be involved in royal intrigue to hear of it.

The queen, on the other hand . . . Milisant did
in fact consider confiding in. Isabelle was young,
had seemed very approachable. If anyone was
likely to understand her aversion to marrying a
man of violence, Isabelle would.

But Milisant was undecided whether to en-
treat the queen for help. She wanted to speak
with her in private first, to determine if she
would even be sympathetic. Some women, she
knew, wouldn't be.

She hoped she would have the opportunity
during this meeting, but when she was led into
the chamber, she saw that Isabelle was not
there—at least not yet. She thought nothing of
that, however, even when the door closed

soundly behind her. The queen was merely
tardy to arrive—or the servant had fetched Milisant prematurely.

John was there, though, and completely alone.
Unusual to imagine a king without his servants
and lords of state hovering over him, even in
his bedchamber. He was dressed in a simple,
long tunic, loosely belted about his hips. He had
been bathed as well as cologned—at least there
was a pleasant smell in the chamber.

Brazers in every corner made the room nigh
too warm. But no expense would be spared for
the king's comfort, she was sure, even to wast-
ing precious fuel.

He sat in a high-backed chair, nearly throne-
like with carvings and inlaid silver, that was set
out in the center of the room. It no doubt traveled with him. He sipped from a gem-encrusted
chalice, staring at Milisant over the bejeweled
rim, another item that no doubt came from his
own treasure rooms. A king would not want to
leave all his luxuries at home, after all, just because he must journey about his kingdom.

Milisant noticed all this in utter silence. The
silence, and his staring, continued overlong,
though, causing a slight unease. Mayhap it was
his habit, but one she was not accustomed to—
found rude, in fact.

She was close to breaking the strange quiet
herself when he said, "Come here, child. We
wouldst have a closer look at you in the light."

The room was well lit. His eyesight must not
be as keen as it used to be. She was not about to
remark on it, though, since he might be overly

sensitive about his age. She approached his chair instead.

As she stood in front of him, he stared at her some more, thoroughly looked her over, actually, from head to toe. This habit, he might find very useful in dealing with his barons, to cause them nervousness, thus putting them at a disadvantage. Milisant found it quite annoying. The only thing she feared was that she would say so. So it was an immense relief when he ended the silence again, though she could have wished for a different subject, never comfortable with compliments.

"He should have mentioned how pretty you are," John said in a chiding tone.

"Who should have?" she asked.

Instead of answering that, he added cryptically, "But there are other ways to accomplish the same goal, are there not? Some ways even having the added benefit of being pleasant."

"I am afraid I do not know of what you speak, Your Highness."

"Come, sit here, and I will explain," he replied, and patted his lap.

Milisant said merely, "I am beyond the age of knee sitting."

He chuckled, his green eyes crinkling with the laughter. "A woman is never too old for that."

Perhaps she wasn't sophisticated enough to figure out what he found amusing. She just knew she did *not* want to sit on his lap.

He might be old enough to be her father, and want to act in a fatherly manner toward her, but he in no way reminded her of a father. Far from it. His smiles were too sensual. And he was looking at her, well . . . the way Wulfric did, which was highly disconcerting, considering who he was.

Not that it meant anything, of course. He was wed to an incredibly beautiful woman, after all, who was all that any man could ask for in a wife. He must simply look at all women in that way, as if they were all created for his personal plucking. Before Isabelle, he might have thought so—his reputation said that he had—but surely that was in the past.

So she ignored his last suggestion and recalled him to the matter of her summons. "The hour is late, Your Highness. If you have aught to say to me, do you please say it now, so I may find my bed."

He glanced toward his own bed, then back at her. She stared at him blankly. He frowned.

"Are you as innocent as you seem, girl?"

She frowned as well. "Innocent in what way?"

"Do you love de Thorpe?"

This question was unexpected and opened an entire new line of thought. She had not considered bringing her grievances to him, but if he wanted to hear them, for whatever reason, she would not keep them to herself.

So she said, "Nay, I must confess I do not."

"Excellent." He confounded her by saying that with a smile most charming, and further baffled her when he added, "Then you will not mind overmuch if he repudiates you."

"I wish that he would, but he has resigned himself to our joining," she said with a sigh.

"He just has not been given a reason yet to

do so. But we can see to that most easily. I am pleased we shall both benefit by this solution."

"What solution?"

He stood up abruptly. "Come now, the answer is obvious," he replied as he put an arm around her shoulder to lead her to his bed.

The answer was indeed obvious by then, but Milisant was not willing to go *that* far to give Wulfric a valid reason to repudiate her. And she was a bit in shock. She had been summoned here so that he could bed her. That was why the queen was not present. And who but a king would think he could do so without any naysaying?

But he had underestimated his quarry. Milisant was not a timid creature to be cowed by his great power. That he was a king, and her king at that, might make all the difference to him, but it made none to her.

But keeping in mind Jhone's warning, she refrained from reacting as she would to any other who might have offended her as the king just had. She did dig in her feet to move no farther, causing him to stop as well. And although he didn't release her shoulder, he did turn a questioning look on her.

With a concerted effort, her tone was calm and quite reasonable, under the circumstances. "I thank you for the offer, Your Highness, but I must decline."

He seemed surprised. Then it seemed as if he might laugh. In the end, albeit with an amused tone, he asked simply, "Why must you?"

"Not to insult you, for you are a very attractive man, but I feel no attraction to you. 'Twould be like whoring to me, and I do not hold myself that cheaply."

"Nonsense," he scoffed. "You must trust my judgment in this. I do you a greater favor than you can realize. And your embarrassment will be minimal. I take the chance of losing a good friend in Shefford, but you will merely be found a different husband, mayhap one more to your liking. Is that not what you just implied you would prefer?"

"Aye," she answered. "But I will find another way to accomplish it."

"When I offer the means here and now? Bah, time is wasted in explanation. The decision is mine, not yours. *That* should ease your conscience." So saying, he pulled her more forcefully toward the bed.

Realizing that he meant to bed her anyway, despite her wishes, Milisant balked, yet did not try to pull away again. She had watched enough knights in training to know that tactics could make or break any skirmish, and she was fully prepared to test that theory.

He also expected resistance now, would merely tighten his hold on her if she began it, which was why she didn't pull back again. He was not nearly as tall as Wulfric, yet was he stocky of build like his father before him, and strong enough to keep her there if he used that strength on her.

So she did nothing for the moment, let him lead her right up to the bed, waiting until he turned more toward her to get her into it. He did so as she had guessed he would, and that was when she kicked him hard in the shin.

It was a loud sound even to her ears, for she hit the bone directly with the toe of her boot. His yelp was even louder, but was cut off in his surprise when she added a push that sent him onto the bed himself.

She had her boon, was not held for the moment, and took advantage of that right quickly, racing out of the room, down the stairs, across the hall to the tower that led to her own chamber, not stopping once until she had closed the door behind her and dropped the heavy locking bar across it. She didn't stop there, though, pushed several of her traveling chests up against the door as well. Still, her heart wouldn't stop pounding, nor her breath stop coming in great heaves.

Jhone was fast asleep, but had left a candle burning for Milisant. She used the meager light to fetch her bow and arrows, and sat there trembling on her bed with an arrow at the ready and a dozen more easy to hand. The first man to break through the barrier she had created at the door would not live to tell of it.

She sat there most of the night waiting, while Jhone slept blissfully on, unaware of Milisant's latest dilemma. And dilemma it was. John might not have sent his guards after her to slay her immediately for her treasonous attack upon his person, but one did not attack a king without paying dearly for it.

It was a long time before her breathing quieted. Her anxiety didn't lessen at all.

Thirty-one

"*Who were you* trying to keep out of here last eventide? Or were you just making sure I did not leave ere talking to you this morn?"

Jhone said it in a teasing manner as she shook Milisant awake. She hadn't noticed the bow yet, since the blanket had draped over it, hiding it from view. She had noticed only the chests piled against the door.

Milisant was surprised she had fallen asleep at all, but vaguely recalled getting beneath the covers because she had been chilled. She recalled also resting her head on the pillow for what she had thought would only be a few minutes, but remembered nothing after that.

She was wide-awake now, though, with everything recalled instantly, including her terror. She had actually kicked the king of England in the shin, *and* pushed him. She wondered which he would find the more insulting, and which the more deserving of his revenge?

She groaned inwardly before telling her sister, "I have to leave."

"Leave where?"

"Shefford."

Understandably, that brought a frown to Jhone's brow. "Did something happen with the king last eventide that I should know about?"

"Only that he means to kill me. Whether publicly or in secret is the only question."

"What did you do?" Jhone wailed.

Milisant threw back the covers, showing Jhone that she had not undressed for bed, had not even taken off her boots. Jhone also saw the bow now, and her eyes widened even further in trepidation.

" 'Tis not so much what I did, but what he did, that forced me to do what I did."

"*What did you do?*" Jhone repeated, even louder, all color drained from her face now.

"I did what I had to do to get away from him, Jhone," Milisant explained. "He might be the king, but that does not mean I wouldst allow him to bed me, which is what I had been summoned for."

Jhone stared, wide-eyed. "King *John* tried to bed you? *Our* King John?"

"Your skepticism is not misplaced. I still find it incredulous myself, especially when he is reputed to adore his own wife and she is here with him."

"Was he—taken by passion?" Jhone offered. "Unable to help himself?"

"Faugh, make no excuses for him. I do not delude myself to think that I am so irresistible as to cause him to be 'unable to help himself.' This was fully planned by him. 'Tis why he sent for me."

"Then—why?"

Milisant was still confused over that question herself. John had said they would both benefit. She had been sure at the time that he had meant that she would benefit by not having to marry Wulfric, and that he would benefit by the pleasure he would have in the bedding, yet . . . what if he had meant other than that? How else would he benefit from preventing the joining of the two families?

She could not see another reason herself, yet if there was one, could that mean that John had instigated disposing of her? Was behind the attacks on her? She could hardly see herself of such import that a king would want to be rid of her, yet in the greater scheme of things, a king would not hesitate to remove any obstacle in the path to a goal, however minor or great was that obstacle.

But whatever his motives had been previously, he now had new ones. And it was too much for her to grasp all at once, and too far-fetched, really, for her to want to repeat her thoughts to anyone, even Jhone.

So she said merely, "He spoke of it being a solution for us both, of giving Wulfric a reason to repudiate me, which it surely would have done. John is *not* approving of this wedding, Jhone, not by any means. Though why could he not have just said so, instead of resorting to despicable means to see the betrothal set aside?"

Jhone gave that a moment's thought. "Mayhap because his blessing was never needed for the match, when his brother had already given his."

"Or mayhap he is just too used to doing things in an underhanded way," Milisant added in disgust.

"Well, that, too. But I suppose he could have felt slighted, that he was never asked for permission, and so came here to put an end to it, without owning to the insult he felt, petty as it is."

Milisant nodded. That *was* another possibility. But did it really matter now that the damage was done? He could still order her death, could have already done so. She could meet up with one of his servants, just waiting to find her alone. Today. On the morrow. When she least expected it. She *had* to leave, to put herself out of his immediate reach. There was no other option now.

"Did you hurt him badly?" Jhone thought to ask.

"More his pride than his body, but that is enough for him to want revenge."

"But he would have to own up to what he attempted to do if he orders your death."

"Not if he does not make it public—which is why I must leave, to put myself out of his reach."

"But to where?"

"I will go to Clydon. I was thinking to do so anyway ere this happened, since Father has not arrived yet, nor even sent word, and I am beginning to suspect he does not intend to. So I will take Roland to him, and tell him also what has happened here. He cannot still insist on this betrothal once he knows the king is set against it."

"But that will not protect you from John's wrath for what you did."

"It might," Milisant replied, speculating. "He may forget what passed betwixt us if I marry elsewhere, as he wants. 'Tis my only hope now."

Jhone shook her head. "I think you should tell Lord Guy what happened instead."

"And put him at war with the king?"

Jhone paled. "You think it would come to that?"

"I am here under Guy's protection. What do *you* think he would do, does he learn that his sovereign tried to rape his son's betrothed, under his own roof? He wouldst be enraged, and rightly so."

"But John must have expected that ere he tried what he did. Mayhap that was what he wanted all along, for Guy to break his oath of fealty with him."

"Nay, what he *expected* was for me to comply and feel honored by his rape. No doubt when it came to light, he would have claimed that I was the instigator, that I threw myself at him, so only I would have been to blame. Verily, he probably would have brought it to light himself, rather than wait for the marriage bedding, for Wulfric to find out for himself that I was no longer pure. And who would take my word over John's—other than you, of course?"

"Lord Guy might."

"When it wouldst mean breaking with the king? You need only see it from John's point of view. The betrothal would have been ended, Guy and Father both would still be loyal to him, and I, in disgrace, would have been found another husband who would overlook that I had once dallied with the king. Ironically, I wish that all of that would occur—if only I did not have to bed the king to see it so."

"But you cannot just leave, Mili, not without Lord Guy's permission. And how will you gain that, without telling him what has occurred?"

"I said I had already thought of leaving. I did not say I was going to announce it."

"But you cannot get out of the keep without notice, much less the outer gates. How do you expect to just walk out of here?"

"With your help, of course."

Jhone groaned. "Mili, there must be another way. What if you confide in Wulfric instead of Guy—and wed him today, without further delay? *That* wouldst put an end to John's plot, would it not?"

"Not if what John really wants is a reason to brand Guy's family as treasonous outlaws, or our family for that matter, so he can confiscate both our lands. And not if he still wants revenge on me for attacking him. And not if—"

"Enough! *Jesu*, 'twas only a suggestion," Jhone complained, then scowled at Milisant. "And do not think I am not aware that you would *rather* leave than marry Wulfric. Verily, I doubt me not that you are secretly glad that this has happened."

To that Milisant sighed. "Nay, I am not glad to have made an enemy of King John, just to escape marriage to Wulfric. Even as a last resort, I would not have hoped for this."

Thirty-two

"*This will never* work," Jhone complained as she stared at the trunk that Milisant meant to climb into.

"It will as long as you remain with the trunk at all times, so the carriers aren't tempted to look inside to see why 'tis so heavy."

"Couldn't I just say 'tis a wedding gift for you that needs be hidden?" Jhone suggested. "Then I wouldn't have to pretend to be you."

"But you would not hide a gift in the stable, which is where I want the trunk delivered. Nay, it must contain special feed for Stomper so it can be placed near to his stall, which does not get much traffic since the stable folk do not like to get near him."

Jhone *tsk*ed. "You can't leave on Stomper, so why the stable?"

"Because it is close to the gate, and I can watch from there who leaves, to find a group I can blend with. 'Tis either that or I try to climb over the walls, which you pointed out would be much more likely to fail, with as many guards as are posted on them."

Jhone sighed. " 'Tis just much easier to be you when 'tis only a lark. When 'tis serious like this, I just know I will do or say something and give the pretense away."

"You will do fine, Jhone, I know you will. You need only deal with the guards at the door, my escort, and the two men you find to carry the trunk. You need not deal with anyone who *knows* you."

"Until you are gone," Jhone reminded her with a frown. *"Then* I must deal with your betrothed."

"I have told you how to do that. He made mention of it just the other night, that he tells the difference between us by the set of my mouth, the way I press my lips together when I am annoyed. You can copy that easy enough. Just keep your distance from him so you need not speak to him, and you will have no problems."

Jhone was not convinced. "But if he wants to speak to me—I mean you—then—"

"Fear not. I have been furious with him since we last spoke, and well he knows it. I have not spoken to him since, nor would he expect me to after what he did."

"Which was? You never did say why you have been killing him with your eyes these last few days."

Nor would Milisant have mentioned it, as embarrassed as she still was. But she could no longer keep it to herself if Jhone was going to take her place for the next few days, and do so successfully.

While she'd dressed in her old clothes, Milisant had repeated, as best she could recall, every conversation she had had with Wulfric. Jhone needed every detail just in case Wulfric did try to talk to her and brought up something that had been said between them.

She had left out only their last encounter, but realized now that she couldn't keep it to herself, not if Jhone was going to be successful for as long as possible. And the more time she was successful, the more time Milisant would have before she was pursued.

So she replied, albeit in a mumble, "Wulfric nearly bedded me."

"Nearly?" Jhone's brow shot up, then her expression altered to amazement when she concluded, "He tried to force you like John?"

Milisant blushed profusely, remembering. Then, not at all happy to be admitting to her own weakness, she muttered, "Nay, not exactly. I was rendered daft by his kissing again. I did not even think to tell him to stop. If Lord Guy had not come upon us, I doubt me not we would have sealed the joining ere the priest gives it his blessing."

Jhone opened her mouth to reply, then closed it, then shook her head. Lastly she sighed.

Her tone was reproving, though, when she finally said, "If this incident had not occurred with King John, I would have much to say about that. But with John obviously set against you wedding Wulfric—'tis better now for all involved if you do have Roland to husband instead, so let us hope all works out well with that."

Milisant smiled, now that Jhone was finally in

agreement with her. "It will, I am sure of it. I need merely reach Clydon, and my woes are sure to be ended."

"I wish I were as confident of that as you are," Jhone replied.

"You worry too much. You have been 'me' countless times. Never have you been discovered. You know how easy it is. If you can fool even Father—"

"He was always blurry with drink, Mili, whenever I did try it."

"Even so, he was always the ultimate test. No one else knows us as well."

"True," Jhone was forced to agree.

Milisant smiled now, to add to Jhone's confidence. "We *both* know you can do this. And this is the only way that will give me the time I need ere I am searched for. 'Tis all up to you, Jhone. Two days, longer if you can. That should be enough time for me to get to Clydon, even on foot, and then from there to Dunburh, as well as give me time to do any convincing that needs doing. As long as Lord Guy and Wulfric do not know I am gone, then no one will be searching for me. You *can* do this, I know you can."

" 'Twould seem I must," Jhone said, sighing again. "Then let us be quick about it, ere the sun is fully risen. 'Tis fortunate I woke so early this morn. The bailey is not full active yet, nor the hall below."

Milisant nodded, tying off her last cross garter. It was good to be in her own clothes again, rather than Jhone's borrowed bliauts. She felt almost free of the shackles that had been placed

on her with Wulfric's coming to collect her . . .
but she was too clean.

So while Jhone went to fetch two men to carry
the trunk down to the stable, Milisant began
looking about the room for dirt to smear on her,
and was soon cursing the castle maids for keeping the room so spotless—until she noticed the
window. Because the glass was murky to begin
with, letting in light but not offering a clear
view, it was overlooked as a gathering place for
dust and a buildup of smoke soot, which was
perfect for her needs.

Milisant had placed herself in the trunk along
with the few items she was taking with her: her
bow and one change of clothes. So she was hidden with the lid closed long before she heard
Jhone's loud chatter outside the chamber, which
warned of her approach.

There had been no nervousness—until then.
She might have discussed this escape fully with
Jhone, might have covered all aspects and possibilities of it, yet she knew she would not be
safe until she was actually behind Clydon's high
walls. And escaping Shefford was still her big-
gest obstacle, at least until she was out in the
countryside—on foot. But one worry at a time.

She found herself holding her breath more
than once on that long, jostling trek to the stable.
The trunk was nearly dropped once, causing her
heart to leap into her throat. Jhone should have
clouted the carriers. Milisant would have. She
wasn't *that* heavy.

But the nervousness didn't lessen any, even
after the trunk was finally set down in the stable, nor would it until she was finally out of

Shefford. There were still too many mishaps that could occur within the castle. And she couldn't even get out of the trunk until Jhone let her know it was safe to do so, which hadn't occurred yet.

Instead of the signal she was waiting for, she heard Jhone tell one of the servants she had fetched, "Find Henry for me. He is one of the lads who accompanied us here from Dunburh. He is easy to recognize, filthy as he keeps himself. He should be about the bailey somewhere, since he tends our horses. I had hoped to find him here . . ."

Milisant couldn't imagine what Jhone was talking about, since no Henry had traveled with them to Shefford. And it was still a while more before she could ask, with the four guards who had escorted Jhone to the stable still milling about, too near for her to get out of the trunk yet.

But as had been their habit, when Jhone showed no sign of leaving the stable soon, they dispersed a bit, two moving to the entrance to watch the doings in the bailey, one visiting a favored mount on the other end of the stable. The last, Jhone asked to fetch her a bucket, her own skirts hiding the bucket that was near to Stomper's stall.

At last, though, she kicked the trunk, the signal that it was safe for Milisant to get out of it unobserved, and she did that right quickly. She dashed into Stomper's stall to hide behind the planks there, in case one of the guards wandered near again. It allowed her to speak with her sister, for a few minutes at least.

"That was easy enough," she told Jhone. She wasn't going to mention how nervous she'd been. "Do you return to the keep now and take those shadows with you, I will be able to watch the gates—"

"Wait, I have thought of a better way. I just wish I had thought of it sooner."

"What? And who is this Henry you sent for?"

Jhone grinned. "You, of course. Not that the servant will find you, but the guards now know I am looking for you, so when *I* find you, they will think naught of it."

"To what end?"

"To getting you out of here on a horse."

"That would be wonderful, but we already agreed I cannot ride Stomper out of here or I will surely be stopped. He is not exactly an average-looking horse."

"Aye, but you are so used to riding no other mount that you did not consider another mount. Think you. If I was to send a message to Father, I would not send the messenger on foot, would I?"

Milisant began to smile and ended beaming. "Nay, of course you would not. But how will you find me when I am in here, yet the guards know Henry is not in here?"

"I will leave with them, yet pause just outside. If you can be quick about it, leave the stable through the back and come around to hail me. You can say you were told to find me. I will then tell you what I want, and we will get you a mount. I will also likely have to explain to the gate guards, to make sure you have no problems with them."

Milisant nodded. It could work very well, better than her own plan to try and blend with some other group leaving, especially since no group might be leaving that day, and she would have been forced in the end to try it alone.

"Let us do it then."

They did, and it did work perfectly. "Milisant's" escort didn't question Henry's presence, and she was soon mounted and following Jhone to the gate. There was a moment there of anxiety, since the gate guards took their jobs seriously and questioned everyone, coming and going.

After Jhone had explained Henry's duty, one guard questioned, "Will your father not be insulted by this filthy wretch?"

Jhone chuckled. "My father knows Henry well and his uncleanly habits. He was raised in our stables. Father would be more surprised to see the lad with a clean face, might not even recognize him."

Milisant made an appropriate mumbled complaint, which had the guards laughing at her—him. It worked, though. They waved her through. Jhone, bless her, had saved her a great deal of time with the change in plans. She was out of Shefford. Now she just had to deal with being alone in the country on the way to Clydon.

Thirty-three

The storm, thankfully, had traveled on to other regions, though the weather was still cold enough to freeze small bodies of water. The sun had made a few appearances, enough to melt the solid blanket of snow the storm had left behind, but there were still large patches of it remaining that were nigh blinding when the sun did appear.

Milisant had to shield her eyes often from the glare that morning. She followed the road toward Dunburh until she was beyond sight of Shefford. She then turned south to Clydon—at least, she thought Clydon was south. She had never actually been there, had only heard Roland speak of the location of his home a few times.

She had been loath to mention that to Jhone, though, that she didn't know exactly where it was. That would only have worried her sister further. And she felt no qualms about asking directions of whomever she came across, so she didn't doubt she would find it.

She was looking forward to seeing Roland again. She had missed the close friendship she had shared with him, and their many talks at Fulbray. She didn't consider that he might not be home at Clydon just now.

That would really put a serious dent in her plans, if he was not there when she arrived, especially when she had so little time to work with. She could speak with his parents, of course. Roland had never had aught but good things to say of them, and she had met Lord Ranulf that one time, and found him to be much like Roland, so she would not be *too* hesitant to speak with him instead, or his wife, the Lady Reina, for that matter. But that would certainly not be as easy as discussing her plans with Roland, and yet that, too, wasn't going to be *that* easy.

She had imagined many times what she would say to him, once she had made the decision to marry him. Never once, though, had she come up with the exact words that would be perfect. It was simply not something a lady did, making the proposal of marriage. That was usually left to the parents or guardians, or the lord interested in marriage. The bride-to-be was never asked for an opinion.

It should be otherwise. She wished it were otherwise. Yet another reason to rail against the body she'd been born into. However, Milisant *was* going to be the exception to the way it was traditionally done. She was forced to be, due to circumstances. There was no longer any time to have her father make the arrangements instead.

She had to do it herself, and *then* present it to her father for approval.

At least now, after what had happened with the king, she didn't doubt she would get Nigel's approval. Ironically, she actually had King John to thank for that.

Clydon was less than a day's ride from Shefford. She knew that much. And she soon found a road leading south, so she left the woods, knowing that she was more likely to come across others who might give her exact directions if she kept to a well-traveled road.

She was being followed. She had known it since she had left the woods. But she wasn't worried, assuming the three men to be a Shefford patrol who had spotted her in the woods and thus were doing their job, to make sure she wasn't poaching or anything else they might have to put a stop to. She expected them to double back the way they had come as soon as she was fully off Shefford lands.

She did get a bit uneasy, though, when they slowly but surely shortened the distance between them. They were not trying to be obvious, which was why she was getting nervous. If they wanted to have words with her, they were close enough now to get her to stop with a shout. They were instead being sneaky.

And that was when she recalled that in escaping one threat against her, the king's revenge, she was leaving herself open to that other threat—the men who had thrice tried to do her serious harm. If they had not given up, if they had been watching Shefford from afar . . . *Jesu,* why hadn't she once thought of them before she'd plotted her escape? Not that it would have stopped her. John had been the more immediate threat. But she could have been more cautious if she had recalled them sooner.

She had several choices. She could set her horse into a gallop and head back into the woods on either side of the road, to try to lose them. Not the best of choices since she wasn't familiar with these woods. Or she could stop beside the road on some pretext, to see if they would pass her by and continue on. Nay, she didn't like that idea either. It would let them get too close if they were indeed who she feared they might be.

There was one more choice. She could turn to confront them now, with drawn bow, which would get them to at least stop and explain themselves—or not. Yet if they were merely a Shefford patrol, they could likely convince her easily of that, find out that she was harmless herself, and go about their business. And if they were the Shefford patrol, they would also pursue her if she suddenly made an attempt to lose them, thinking she had something to fear of them in particular. So that would not let her know, really, who they were.

Either way, she would be better served to confront them, and hope she was being nervous over naught. But she needed to dismount to do so. If it was necessary to use her bow, her feet needed to be solidly planted. She couldn't take the chance that her horse might shift his weight or otherwise move to ruin her aim, when her aim was her only advantage.

It allowed them to draw closer when she stopped there in the middle of the road. But they did stop as well when she dismounted. She wasn't prepared, though, for their reaction to her bringing the bow off her shoulder to hand and reaching for an arrow.

They dispersed instantly, and in opposite directions, two galloping off to different sides of the road, and the third charging right toward her. It was a maneuver to confuse, expertly done, likely planned in advance. She couldn't keep her eye on all three of them if they were circling around her.

She had only moments to decide that the one charging directly at her was the one of immediate import, and only seconds to shout, "Desist and you can live!"

He didn't. She fired. Notching a second arrow was automatic and nigh instant for her, and she was turning toward the next target before the first hit the ground.

Two more arrows were released in quick succession. Whether she had done any serious damage through their heavy winter clothing was questionable, but she didn't stay to find out. One was slumped over his horse, the other two men were sprawled unmoving on the ground. She had disabled them for the moment, which was all she had really meant to do, in case they *were* Shefford men.

But those two who hadn't moved worried her as she galloped off. She prayed they hadn't been the Shefford patrol. She prayed that if they were, she hadn't killed them. She was sick at heart, fretting over it. Trying to convince herself that she had just saved her own life wasn't easy when she didn't know that for sure.

Thirty-four

Clydon was easier to find than Milisant had thought it would be, simply because it was much bigger than she had realized. Verily, the huge white castle with its high curtain walls spread out over many acres. It was a strong deterrence for the area, and that Shefford was its overlord made her realize just how powerful the Earl of Shefford was—and how powerful Wulfric would one day be.

Strangely, when she should have been thinking only of Roland and what she would say to him on that long ride, it was Wulfric who plagued her thoughts. She expected him to be relieved by what she was going to do. He would be able to marry as he wanted now, mayhap even that woman he was in love with. Despising him as she did, it was ironic that she was doing him this favor.

They would both benefit, and the king could go find someone else's life to meddle with. It was almost accomplished. She could be wed to Roland in a matter of days. She knew she could be happy with him. Well, she was sure. They were good friends, after all. So *why* wasn't she ecstatic? Why did she feel as if she had left something unfinished?

She was able to find a secluded spot in the woods to change clothes before she approached Clydon, and did so quickly. The sea green and gold bliaut went well with her light green eyes, which was likely why Jhone had picked it. Her attire had been the first thing Jhone had re-marked on when she'd seen her dressing in her old clothes.

"You cannot arrive at Clydon and expect them to believe who you are, dressed like that. You may not even get past the gates."

Thus she had brought the one change of clothes, to get her inside Clydon—and it did. The guards barely questioned her, though they did look at her strangely. Likely because she still had her bow slung over her shoulder. And her luck was holding true. Roland was in residence. One of the guards even went off to find him, while the other summoned a servant to take her to the keep.

She was impressed with Clydon Castle. Shefford was bigger, and with more people, always cluttered with activity. Dunburh was cluttered, too, though not just with people who lived there, but with the many travelers it offered hos-pitality to. But Clydon was clean, orderly. There was activity in the bailey, certainly, but it was more a homey atmosphere, with much friendliness.

And grass, rather than dirt, covered the large bailey. The mud left behind by the recent snow-

storm wasn't present here as it had been at Shefford, and always was at Dunburh as well. It
made for a much different appearance that Milisant, loving nature as she did, appreciated. She
was pleased, aware that she would not mind at
all living here.

Roland found her before she reached the keep.
She would have known him in any crowd, just
because of his height. Had he actually grown
even more since she had last seen him? *Jesu*, he
really was a giant, only a half foot short of seven
feet. And so handsome—well, how could she
forget that?

He had his father's light blond hair and violet
eyes, a remarkable combination. And he was not
slim of build for all that height, far from it. He
had one of the more perfectly proportioned bodies she had ever seen on a male, broad and thick
where he should be, tightly muscled where he
should be. It was why she had always enjoyed
watching him at arms practice. He was a perfect
example of his gender, what other men only
wished they could be.

In all fairness, she had to admit that Wulfric
was another example of a perfect physique, if a
few inches shorter. His perfectness ended there,
though. Roland had a wonderful disposition to
complement his strength: a teasing nature, kind-
ness, gentleness when called for. Wulfric, however, lacked all of that; he was brutish, of sour
disposition, argumentative, and . . . and why
was she *still* thinking of him, when Roland had
nigh reached her?

"*Jesu*, who rubbed your face in the dirt, Mili?"

was the first thing Roland said to her after he
lifted her high and bear-hugged her in greeting.

Milisant's cheeks burst with hot color. She
had remembered to change her clothes so she
would present a ladylike facade to enter Clydon,
yet she had forgotten about the sooty makeup
she had applied for her disguise. No wonder the
Clydon guards had looked at her funny. Faugh,
as if she cared what she looked like.

So why was she blushing? But she knew why,
if she cared to admit it. It was Wulfric's fault,
for making her aware of her appearance lately.
His blasted compliments. The way his eyes took
in every detail of her whenever he came near
her. She had actually found herself using a looking glass before she left her chamber in Shefford,
something she had never thought to do at home.

"Put me down, oaf," she grouched to Roland
in her embarrassment, and pointed out, "What
traveler ever arrives without a good deal of
road dust?"

"What road dust?" he countered, laughing.
"The recent snows washed it all away."

He set her down and immediately started
thumbing the dirt off her cheeks, an action very
familiar to her—Jhone always did the same. And
as was usually the case, she swatted the hands
away automatically. It did give her pause,
though, to realize that he was treating her as
her sister did, and she had just done the same
to him.

"The dirt was applied for a reason, to get me
here without much bother," she decided to tell
him. "I traveled not dressed as you see me, but
in my leggings."

"Why leggings? And who wouldst dare bother a lady under escort, which is the only way you . . . would . . . ?" His words trailed off because she was looking decidedly uncomfortable, and refusing to meet his gaze now. So it wasn't really surprising to hear him add, "Do you tell me you traveled here alone, I will beat you."

He would do no such thing, and they both knew it. He did know her well, though, which was why he had guessed accurately. And she did plan to tell him everything, so there was no reason for her to be embarrassed about it, other than the fact that she had never done anything so wildly dangerous before as travel so far from home—alone.

So she began, " 'Twas necessary for me to leave Shefford without permission."

That she had obviously arrived safely, in whatever manner, allowed him to set aside his concern long enough to tease her with a grin, "I know you think I need protection, Mili, but you did not need to come here to escort me personally to your wedding. My father always takes a large force along when my mother travels with him, and I will be with them . . . Forgive me. That expression you now wear says this is no matter to jest about."

She shook her head. "Nay, I love your teasing, so do not apologize. 'Tis just that much has happened, and none of it good. I do mean to explain fully, I just do not know where, exactly, to begin—nay, I do. The reason I had to leave Shefford in secret is I had an altercation with King John, who arrived early for the wedding."

Roland frowned. "What sort of altercation?"

"A serious one. 'Twould seem he is not pleased by the matter of my betrothal, and bethought himself a way to have it set aside—by bedding me. I objected—forcefully, for which he is like to want revenge, especially if I still join with Wulfric of Shefford. The only way I can think to appease John is to marry someone else."

"*Jesu*, Mili, you need not make such a sacrifice because of John's predilection for wenching. I can see why he would want to add you to his tally, but Shefford is too powerful for him to make an issue of this. He tried and failed. He is sure to leave it at that."

She shook her head once more. " 'Tis not what you are thinking. He did not just want to 'add me to his tally.' He wanted to give Wulfric a reason to repudiate me. He bespoke benefits for us both."

"Do you tell me he thinks so highly of himself that he accounts bedding him as a benefit for you?" Roland scoffed, then corrected himself with a measure of disgust. "On second thought, if anyone would esteem himself that highly, 'twould be John Lackland."

"But not in this case," she clarified. "I had let the king know I did not want to join with Wulfric in marriage. *That* was the benefit for me."

"Are you daft?" Roland asked, incredulous over her words. "How could you not want Wulfric de Thorpe? He will one day be my father's overlord, and mine after that. If his power is not enough to humble you with thanksgiving, the look of him should make you—"

"Not another word or I will clout you. Humble me with thanksgiving?" She snorted. "When did I give you the impression that I aspired to be a countess?"

"You did not have to. From birth you were destined to be Lord Wulfric's countess."

She sighed. "Not by *my* choice, Roland. We never spoke much of it at Fulbray, but I have despised Wulfric since we were children. He hurt me badly when we did first meet, caused me months of fear and agony when I thought I would be crippled for life. I can never forget or forgive that."

He gathered her close again, and his tone was soothingly sympathetic as he said, "I can see it causes you pain even to speak of it, so say no more. Come, let us find a warm hearth and a cup of mead, and you can tell me why you have told no one else of John's perfidy."

"What makes you think I told no one else?"

"Because you are here—alone—rather than letting your father or Lord Guy deal with this."

She blushed once again. He was too perceptive by half. And at least he had said no more about Wulfric, nor tried to excuse him by saying the doings of a child could not relate to the doings of a man. She knew better. But trying to convince anyone else of it was nigh impossible.

Thirty-five

It wasn't going to work, it wasn't. If it were not so important, if Milisant's future did not depend on it, then Jhone would likely have no problem with the pretense of taking her place. But that it was so important made her too nervous. Which was why she devised a new pretense. She herself became ill—no pretense, actually, since this whole situation was making her very ill to her stomach—and Milisant was staying with her to nurse her.

She would have pretended it in the reverse if she wasn't worried that Wulfric would demand to see Milisant if he thought her ill. He had done that when Mili had been hurt. He might also suspect any illness by her, as a means to avoid him. But with Jhone being the one "bedridden," there was no one who would insist upon seeing her, and as Milisant, she could turn others away at the door, without letting them into the room to see that there was no Jhone sick in the bed.

She had great hopes that this would work, and it did work for most of that first day, until late that afternoon. Then the very one she dreaded seeing came pounding on her door. She suspected it was he even before she opened the door, simply because of the loudness of the pounding.

So she had a moment to prepare herself to deal with him as she knew Milisant would, which was to snap as soon as she opened the door, "Did no one tell you my sister is ill? That I am tending to her? She was finally resting a bit peacefully—until you just made a racket."

"Aye, I was informed," he snapped back, not surprising, given her reception—not unexpected either, given his pounding. "But you do not need to attend her constantly. There are others here who can do that well enough."

"I trust no one else to see to my sister, any more than she does for me."

To which he scowled. "What is wrong with her?"

"She has been vomiting, profusely. Can you not smell the stench?"

Since Jhone had vomited at least once that afternoon in her anxiety, she was not lying. And she was beginning to feel like it again. She felt his anger strongly, and anger like that terrified her. She was only surprised that she had not dissolved into a puddle at his first scowl. If he did not leave soon . . .

With the intent of seeing him gone, she demanded, "Why do you come here? Just to disturb us?"

"To tell you to make an appearance at supper this eventide. Missing one meal when the king is in attendance, he might understand, but missing two formal gatherings in a row wouldst nigh be an insult. So whether your sister has improved or not, present yourself in the hall tonight."

" 'Tis not necessary for me to entertain the king."

"Is it not?" he countered. "When he is here expressly for *your* wedding?"

Jhone had to mentally keep her hands apart or they would be wringing. "Then of course I will appear, to pay my respects to him. But I will *not* stay long—unless Jhone is feeling better."

She had conceded, and most reasonably. How could he argue with that? He did.

"Methinks you are using your sister's malady as an excuse to avoid me. For how long do you intend to hold your voice from me?"

So that was what his visit was really about? He was feeling neglected? She considered saying, "Forever," which was likely what Milisant would have said. But that answer wouldn't get him to leave, would more like enrage him further. Yet she didn't want to say anything that Mili wouldn't say either, since that might cause him to give her a closer look and discover their ruse.

So she kept her lips pursed as Milisant had warned her to, and said as calmly as her nerves would allow, "I am speaking to you now, much to my regret. This *could* have waited until Jhone is well."

He took the hint, fortunately, yet with another scowl, ordered her on parting, "Be at supper tonight, and at both meals on the morrow as well, wench. Do *not* make me come and fetch you."

As soon as she closed the door on him, she collapsed back against it, her heart pounding with her fear. She had done it. Fooled him completely. But she couldn't do it again. She just didn't have Milisant's courage, to stand up to that man, not when she felt his anger so strongly. Yet his order rang in her mind. If he did not see Milisant in the hall tomorrow, he *would* come drag her down there.

She had to appear in the hall at least tonight. She could see no way around that now. Tomorrow, though, the first meal wouldn't be until midday, and that would have given Milisant the time she had asked for. Jhone could be herself again, and Milisant "missing." It would be another day again ere Milisant was looked for outside the castle walls. Plenty enough time for her to have gotten to Clydon, and then returned home from there as she'd planned to do.

Nay, tonight's gathering would be plenty. But to entertain the king? After what he'd done? *Jesu*, they hadn't even thought about Milisant having to face the king again. She had left so she wouldn't have to.

What if he was just waiting for that, to denounce her? But no, obviously he had said nothing of what had occurred between them to anyone, or Wulfric would have mentioned it. And with her absence today, he must have been thinking she was afraid to face him as well.

It might appease John if he thought she was afraid. It might appease him even more if she seemed afraid when they did meet this eventide. It would not be contrived. She was going to be terrified to get near him, after what he had tried to do to Milisant. And if he wanted to speak of it? *Jesu*, how had she let Mili talk her into this?

Thirty-six

She had delayed too long, the telling. Milisant fretted as the hour grew late and still she had found no opportunity to present her proposal of marriage to Roland. She could *not* let this day end without getting her future settled here. Yet one thing after another had occurred since her arrival, to keep her from being alone with Roland again.

He had taken her into the keep and presented her to his mother, who had promptly taken her off to a tower chamber for a bath and refreshments. She had not seen Roland again until the evening meal.

The Lady Reina was a surprise. Milisant knew Roland's father to be a giant just as he was, yet Lady Reina was a small, petite woman. She was not quite two score in years, her black hair as lustrous as it had been in her youth, her cerulean blue eyes just as clear and sharp. And she was outspoken, brutally frank actually.

She had felt no qualms about telling Milisant, "You stink, get in that tub," when Milisant had protested she had no time for bathing.

But she found she liked Reina Fitz Hugh. It was rare to meet a woman as outspoken as Milisant was herself. And there was a bawdy earthiness about her that either put one at ease or caused embarrassment. Milisant felt a little of both, which was amusing, after she thought about it.

She learned much more about Roland's family, during those hours she spent with Reina, than he had ever told her. There was an older brother, named after the Earl of Shefford, who was his godparent. There were two sisters, much younger than Roland. The youngest, Reina confessed, was the bane of her life. She could do naught with the child, who idolized her father and tried to emulate him in every way.

That had thoroughly embarrassed Milisant, when she realized that this youngest child was much like herself, wishing she had been born the opposite gender—and Reina found this to be a "bane." It made her feel more strange than ever, made her realize, also, that her own father likely thought the same of her.

She had not known, either, that Roland's family was related to the de Arcourts, another powerful family in the realm. Hugh de Arcourt, the head of that family, was in fact Roland's paternal grandfather, albeit from the wrong side of the blanket—another frankness of Reina's, to mention that as if it were naught out of the ordinary.

What she had found *most* interesting, though, was that Reina's father had been Roger de Champeney. 'Twas a name Milisant knew well, since Lord Roger had been with Nigel and Lord Guy when they had gone on Crusade with King Richard all those years ago. Roger had oft been mentioned by Nigel in his tales of those exciting campaigns that had occurred long before Milisant had been born.

It made her wonder if Nigel even knew that Roland was Roger's grandson, when he had discounted him out of hand as a choice for her husband, mentioning only that Roland's father was Guy's vassal. Roger had been Guy's vassal as well, yet a power to be reckoned with in his own right, Castle Clydon evidence of that, as well as the many other holdings in his possession. And Milisant was certain that her father knew nothing about Hugh de Arcourt.

Roland's family was suddenly a much better choice for an alliance than even she had realized. With wealth and power behind him, he lacked only being the heir to an earldom, as Wulfric was.

She felt better. Her father had to like this match. Of course, she was forgetting that she had not been betrothed for an alliance, but for the sake of friendship and life-saving debts of honor. Still, it would soften the blow when Nigel learned that John was against the joining of their two families, that to stay in his good graces—or at least get back in them, in her case—she would *have* to marry elsewhere. And who better now than Roland?

But she surely could have wrung Roland's neck by that evening when it seemed as if everyone, himself included, conspired to keep them from being alone for more than a minute. Even sitting next to him for the meal, she could not get his attention for any whispers, at least not keep his attention for more than a moment, when his father and brother both vied for it.

Finally, when the meal was finished, she was desperate enough to take his hand and drag him over to one of the window embrasures that Clydon's Great Hall possessed, replete with cushioned benches for comfortable seats. She was even bold enough to push him down onto the seat, which she managed only because he let her, huge giant that he was.

And she wasted no further time in amenities, saying immediately, "I have things to tell you, and ask of you, that require your full attention, which your family does not seem wont to share."

He chuckled at her pique. "We are a close family. When better to discuss each other's day than at supper when we are gathered?"

She couldn't argue that, said instead, "True, but you have a guest in dire straits! I have little time here, Roland. Verily, I should leave for Dunburh on the morrow. I had great hopes— that you would go with me."

"Certainly I will escort you there, Mili. You did not need to ask—"

She waved a dismissive hand as she took the seat across from him. "I need you to do more than that, Roland. I need you to marry me."

There, she had said it. Not very subtly, but she didn't have time to be subtle. She just wished that he didn't look so incredulous. And then worse, he must have decided she was joking, since he began to laugh.

His humor grated on her frazzled nerves. " 'Tis no jest, Roland."

He smiled at her gently. "Nay, I can see you are serious. But even were you not betrothed already, I could not contemplate wedding you."

She had hoped that the asking would have been the only hard part to get past. She had not counted on a flat refusal from him.

"Have you been promised to another?"

"Nay."

She frowned. "Then why will you not even consider my proposal?"

Rather than answering, he said, "Look you there at my youngest sister."

She followed his gaze to see only two young boys, mayhap ten summers old, grappling on the floor. She hadn't met his younger sister yet, at least she didn't think she had—she had been introduced to so many people today, she might have overlooked it.

"Where? I see only the two boys."

He grinned. "The, er, 'boy' on top, the one with the blond hair cut so short, that is Eleanor. 'Tis why I felt such an immediate closeness to you when we did meet at Fulbray—because you reminded me so much of my baby sister. Like you, she prefers to wear leggings, much to my mother's chagrin. But Eli does dress properly when we have guests. She only just arrived, though, so is unaware we have a guest. Notice my mother is furious with her, and my father, as usual, is quite amused?"

Why did this make her blush? Milisant wondered. She should be glad to see another girl much like herself, to know she was not so "strange" after all. Of course, young Eli made concessions, obviously, did indeed conform when she was required to, whereas Milisant had always stubbornly refused to bend even a little . . .

She sighed mentally. Was she so wrong? Was shaming her father worth the small freedoms she'd managed to gain? But she had let Roland distract her from her purpose. He hadn't answered her question.

She reminded him of that now. "What has your sister to do with this?"

He leaned forward to tenderly grasp her hands in his. "You were not listening. You reminded me of my sister then—you still do. I love you dearly, but you are *like* my sister, and the thought of bedding you . . . I am sorry, Mili, and truly, I mean not to insult you, but the thought leaves me—cold. Besides, 'twould be stealing my liege lord's bride. *Jesu*, he will be the Earl of Shefford, and I will one day hold one of Clydon's properties—through him."

She should have been devastated by his explanation. Instead, she realized, belatedly, how true it was, and that she felt the same way. That was why she had always felt so close to him, and why there had never been any sexual feelings where he was concerned—because he was like a brother to her. In fact, she couldn't imagine him kissing her, now that he was forcing her to think about it, at least not the way Wulfric kissed her. *Jesu*, *why* couldn't she have realized this years ago, when she had first thought of marrying him?

She nodded to let him know she accepted his

explanation, but then she sighed. "What am I to do then? I still must find a new husband."

He shook his head at her. "Nay, what you need to do, should have done to begin with, is leave this matter to those who can best handle it."

"*That* does not get me a new husband."

"You do not *need* a new husband," he countered.

To which she scowled. "You forget there are other reasons that I do not want Wulfric."

"I recall very well what you said about him. You have hated him since you were children, when he hurt you. But you said naught about what you feel for him now that he is a man."

"Aha! I *knew* that distinction would come up!"

"Is this where we are going to fight like siblings?" he inquired mildly.

She hit him in the shoulder. He grinned at her. She rolled her eyes. He came to her side of the embrasure and put his arm around her.

"Answer me truthfully, Mili. Have you even once set aside those childhood feelings long enough to see Wulfric as he is now? Or do you let those old feelings color your current perception of him?"

"He is still a brute," she mumbled.

"I find that *very* hard to believe," Roland said. "But even if he is, the question of more import would be, is he brutish to you?"

"He is a tyrant to me, ordering me about. Verily, he wouldst control my breathing if he could."

"Methinks you would think that *any* man who would dare to give you orders is a tyrant."

Milisant sighed once again. "Roland, I do see what you are getting at. But you cannot imagine what it is like to be around him. All we do is argue with each other. We cannot be in the same room but there is a tension between us that is thick enough to cut."

He appeared thoughtful for a moment, then said, "'Tis strange, but what you describe is what I felt when I desired a lady I *knew* I could not have. She was a guest here. I found that I argued with her constantly, every time I saw her actually, when what I really wanted—"

"Shush!" Milisant cut in, blushing. "This has naught to do with—that."

"Are you so sure?"

Thirty-seven

Are you so sure?

Milisant couldn't get that question out of her mind, even after she retired for the night. Her answer to Roland had been, "Certainly," but she wasn't really that certain—at least not in Wulfric's case. She could not know his mind, after all, and it was easy for a man to love in one direction, yet find desire rising in another direction. There were tales aplenty of men doing just that.

Wulfric *could* be frustrated in the wanting of her, now that he had fully accepted that she was going to be his wife, and that *could* have led to many of their arguments. If she considered that as a reason, then she would also have to consider that the arguments could well end once they were married—at least on his part.

Jhone had suggested the same thing. Keep him happy in bed and he would be more agreeable in nature and thus allow her more freedoms, had been her sister's recommendation. But what of herself? Keeping him happy was not going to make her happy with him.

It was a moot point. Once she told her father everything that had happened, he was like to agree that she should marry elsewhere now, if only because of King John's wishes. So it would not be with Roland, as she had long counted on. It still wouldn't be with Wulfric, and she should at least be happy about that.

So why didn't *that* thought give her some peace?

Milisant was glad to hear the soft knock on her door, unexpected as it was, simply because it interrupted her plaguing thoughts. It was the lady Reina who entered at her call to do so. She came to sit on the bed next to her. Her brow was knitted with concern.

"I knocked softly in case you were asleep," Reina said at first. "Yet I am not surprised that you are still awake, despite the lateness of the hour."

Milisant smiled crookedly. "I am, considering I slept very little last eventide. But why do you say so?"

"Roland sought me out."

"Ah."

"My son is worried that you are upset because he has disappointed you. Are you?"

"Did he tell you why?"

Reina nodded. "You amazed him, with your request. He is not sure you fully understood his reasons for declining, he was so addled when he gave them."

"I did, and I agree with them. When I thought of him as a man for me to marry, I only thought of our friendship, our closeness, and how ideal 'twould be to share my life with someone I enjoyed being with. I never once thought of the intimacy that we would have to share. Now that he has made me think of it, I know he is right. He sees me as a sister—and 'tis the same for me, I see him as a brother. We could never share the same bed.''

Reina nodded again, only to remind her, ''But you did not answer my question.''

Milisant frowned, not sure what Reina was talking about. ''But I did. I am not upset with him. 'Tis not his fault that I was foolish enough not to consider all the aspects of marriage before I put my proposal to him.''

''There was another thing you did not think to consider. Roland could not marry you without Ranulf's concurrence, but Ranulf would never agree to it. Even if your betrothal to Lord Guy's son was ended, for whatever reason, it would still be somewhat of an insult to our liege lord for us to seek an alliance with the Crispins through you, when the earl had himself sought that alliance through his son. Did you overlook those political ramifications?''

Milisant was blushing at the gentle scolding, and scolding it was. ''My father tried to point that out recently, but I confess, I was too distraught to let what he said penetrate deep enough to alter my course.''

''I suppose I need not have asked if you are still upset. That you are still awake in the middle of the night is answer enough.''

''But not because of Roland. You can assure him of that—or I will, on the morrow.''

''Is there aught that I can help you with, to relieve what else upsets you?''

It was apparent that Roland had not confided in his mother about everything. "Nay, 'tis just that I never wanted to marry Wulfric of Shefford. And now that I know King John does not want me to either—I wonder who my father will find for me instead. For many years I only had Roland in mind. I never once looked elsewhere."

"What makes you think John is against your marriage to Wulfric?"

"He told me so."

Reina shook her head and yet was smiling. "Mayhap I should have asked instead, what makes you think that John's preferences will come to bear here? 'Tis my understanding that your betrothal had King Richard's blessing. John's permission was not needed. And if he was going to forbid it, he would have done so. That he wouldst mention it to you, rather than to Lord Guy, says clearly that he has no intention of interfering directly. Verily, I would guess he does not dare to anger a vassal as loyal to him as Lord Guy is, when so many of his barons do now rail against him."

More reason for Milisant to be sure that if John intended to say naught of what she had done to him, then he also intended to place the entire blame on her if she dared to accuse him of aught, and claim full innocence. She should explain to Reina, but she hesitated. The more people who knew about John's attempt to end her betrothal by bedding her, even if *he* denied it, the more likely he was to want revenge for the way she had escaped it.

So she said only, "Mayhap you are right."

Reina nodded, then asked, "Now for the last part of your distress."

"The last part?"

"I mean not to pry, but that was quite an astonishing statement you made, that you never did want to marry Wulfric. I have known Wulfric de Thorpe since he was born. He has turned into a fine young man, a credit to his father. My own husband thrives on war and has been on campaign with Wulfric. He has had naught but good things to say of the lad. And I know that women find him attractive. My oldest daughter has made a fool of herself more than once when he did come to visit here. What is there not to like about Wulfric?"

Milisant really wished that were not the reaction of everyone. And rather than mention childhood grudges that she was sure the lady would try to discount, she mentioned yet another good reason why she didn't want him.

"He loves someone else."

"Ah," Reina replied, as if there were perfect understanding in that little word. "Well, that was not very wise of him, but may not be very serious, in which case it will not take much effort to overcome."

"How?"

Reina chuckled. "By giving him a reason to love you, too, then giving him reason to love you more."

"You must have met my sister," Milisant grouched. "You and she think much alike."

Reina laughed at that. " 'Tis merely common female logic, my dear."

And easy enough for any woman to suggest

who wasn't involved in such a situation. Much harder to get past serious dislike first—especially when both members of the couple shared that dislike.

"I should not have to fight for my husband's love," Milisant said, somewhat stiffly.

"Nay, ideally you should not have to. But realistically, most women do have to—that is, if they want that love. I am amazed myself how many women do not care. They have no expectation of love in a marriage that is arranged for political gain or alliance, and so have naught to be disappointed about when it is not involved. There are many things to determine a good marriage. Love is not usually amongst them. Ah, but when it is . . . you cannot imagine—"

"Giving away our secrets, Reina?"

It was amusing to see the older woman blush for a change, when with her own frankness she caused so many blushes. But blush she did as she turned to see her husband filling the doorway with his immense size.

"I was just coming back to bed," Reina told him as she stood up to leave.

"Were you indeed? Somehow I doubt it."

To that, Reina made a disgusted expression. Milisant didn't see it, was in fact worried that Ranulf Fitz Hugh was angry with his wife, and that it was her fault.

So when Reina said, "I was *not* meddling," Milisant was quick to support that with, "She really was not." And when Reina added, "Nor was I being a nuisance," Milisant added as well, "She could never be that. Verily, Lady Reina has been a great help to me."

At that point Reina glanced back at her and with a chuckle said, "Be at ease, child, he is not angry. Not that it would make a bit of difference to me if he was."

That was tacked on with a warning look toward Ranulf. The giant grinned, indicating he had heard the same thing, or something similar, many times before.

It was then that Roland pushed past his father to enter the room and said in exasperation, "I did not mean for you to keep Mili up all night, Mother."

To which Reina threw up her hands and huffed, "I am finding my bed posthaste," and she marched out of the room without another word.

"I will just make sure she finds it without any more detours," Ranulf said, then, "Do not be long, Roland. We all need at least a little sleep this night." And he, too, left the chamber.

Oddly, Roland and Milisant found they were both blushing after his parents' departure, perhaps because they had been left alone in a bedchamber, but more like because they both knew what had been discussed there. He was the first to make an effort to put them at ease, coming forward to sit on the side of the bed where his mother had sat.

"I am sorry," he told her, taking her hand in his. "I only wanted my mother to help if you were distraught. She is very good at that. I did not think she would keep you up half the night to do it, though."

"No need to apologize, Roland. I was not sleeping, or she would not have come in."

"Ah, so you *were* still distraught?"

Milisant rolled her eyes and pointedly changed the subject. "Does no one sleep around here at night?"

He chuckled. "I know not about everyone else, but my mother and I oft meet up in the kitchens in the wee hours, usually when some calamity keeps her from finishing supper. We have had many a pleasant talk there—at least until my father wakes to find her missing, and comes down to search her out, as he likely did tonight."

"And what is your excuse for not sleeping?"

" 'Tis not that I cannot sleep, but that I am *always* hungry, and cannot sleep when I am."

He said it with such chagrin that she had to laugh. "Aye, that is a big body you have there to keep fed."

Her amusement was broken abruptly by a noise at the door, which had been left open. They both looked to see what had caused it, for it had sounded very much like a sword being drawn from its sheath. It was indeed that.

Wulfric stood there filling the opening, his sword in hand, his eyes pinned not on Milisant, but on Roland. " 'Tis a shame that I am going to have to kill you."

Thirty-eight

Milisant blanched. Not because Wulfric was there when he shouldn't be. Not even because he had just calmly threatened to kill her friend. She paled because it occurred to her that the only way he could have known to find her at Clydon was through Jhone.

So the first thing she said to him was the accusation, "What did you do to my sister, to get her to tell you where I went? She would never have volunteered the information to you willingly."

That drew those sapphire eyes to her. The expression in them was chilling.

"Nor did she. She in fact collapsed in a faint at my feet when I merely did ask her."

"Merely?" she said suspiciously. "How angry were you when you asked her?"

"Very."

She sighed in relief. He hadn't tortured Jhone. He had simply frightened her to death. But then . . .

"How did you know to look for me here, if she did not tell you?"

"She inadvertently told my brother many days ago when she mentioned the endearment you had given your love. When you could not be found, I finally realized who your *gentle giant* must be, and that you would go to him."

His eyes had moved back to Roland as he said it. Hers did now, too, to find the "gentle giant" was grinning. Milisant decided Roland had to be daft to find aught amusing about this situation. Or did he think Wulfric had been jesting about killing him? Or that there was naught to fear because they were discussing this in reasonable tones, despite how furious Wulfric looked?

She wondered about that. There was no doubt that he was furious, yet it was a contained fury. The question was, what was he furious about? Her escape? Or where he'd found her—and with whom?

"You don't have to kill him," she said. "I discovered the feelings I have for Roland are only sisterly. Besides, he refuses to marry me, for the same reason. He's like a brother to me."

"You take me for a fool?" Wulfric replied. "The evidence is before my eyes."

With her relief had come the courage Milisant needed to argue with him, despite his rage. "What evidence?" she snorted. "If you mean because you found Roland in here with me, you should ask why ere you make conclusions. If you had appeared a few minutes sooner, you would have found both of his parents here as well. He came here to chase out his mother, who he suspected was keeping me awake. She was not, but she *was* here. I trust you will have the sense to verify that, Wulfric, ere you raise your sword."

"Mili, why do you deliberately provoke him?" Roland was finally heard from.

"I do no such thing," she denied.

"You do exactly that," he said, then to Wulfric, "my lord, what she says is true. Even were she not betrothed to you as she is, I could not marry her. 'Twould be like wedding my own sister, which, you must agree, would not be a desirable thing to do."

Roland was trying to ease the tension. It did not work with Wulfric, whose expression did not change. If anything, those dark blue eyes were smoldering a bit more as they turned back to her again.

"Do you say now that you lied to me when you said you loved him?"

Milisant could have wished he hadn't brought that up, but since he did, she was forced to admit, "I was not *in* love with him when I said it, nay, though at the time I did think it was possible. I always thought I *could* love him. I just never gave it enough thought to realize that I already did, but in a way that would not be compatible with marriage. We neither of us feel the least bit of desire for the other. How much more clearly must it be said?"

"You do it again, Mili," Roland complained, almost glowering at her.

"What?!" she snapped in exasperation.

"Provoke him. The explanation would have sufficed. You do not need to rub it in."

"Go to bed, Roland. You are not helping."

"I cannot." Roland sighed, as if he would like to do nothing better.

She realized then that he was afraid to leave her alone with Wulfric, but wise enough not to say so. She would prefer not to be left alone with him either, but she was more afraid for Roland at the moment than she was for herself, since Wulfric had yet to put away his sword.

Wulfric must have realized the same thing, or thought that Roland was too wary to try and pass by him when he was himself without weapon, because he did put his sword away now, before he said, "I am glad, for your father's sake, that I do not have to kill you after all. Do as she says." When Roland still hesitated to move, he added, "She has been mine since the day she was betrothed to me. Do not even think to interfere with what is mine."

They stared at each other for a long, tense moment. Roland finally nodded and left.

Milisant knew her friend wouldn't have budged from the room if he thought she was in any danger from Wulfric. She wished she could conclude, as he just had, that she wasn't. But she was not at all sure. In fact, she had an overwhelming urge to call him back, she was suddenly so nervous. That nervousness increased tenfold when Wulfric closed the door behind Roland—and dropped the bar across it to lock them inside the room together.

"What are you doing?" she asked him huskily, what little color she had gained back in her cheeks draining away again.

He didn't answer. He walked toward her until he stood next to the bed, looking down at her.

"We can discuss this in the morn—" she tried to suggest, but he cut her off most curtly.

"There is naught to discuss," he said, and when she started to leave the bed, "stay there!"

Which was when she began to really panic. His expression hadn't changed. He still looked so utterly furious. And whatever he was going to do, she knew she was going to hate it—if she survived it. She wasn't sure if she would. She wasn't sure, either, what he was going to do— yet. And then she was sure when he began to slowly remove his cloak, his eyes not once leaving her.

"Do not do this, Wulfric."

He didn't reply to that, he asked instead, "Did you really think you could marry Roland Fitz Hugh and that he would live to enjoy it?"

"If my father had agreed to it, you would have had naught to say about it."

He shook his head at her. "Think you that would have stopped me from killing him?"

She was beginning to realize what he meant. No matter what she did, he already considered her his. Even though he didn't really want her, she was *his*, and thus she could never marry anyone else, because he would see it as an adultery. Totally illogical. Utterly possessive. She didn't know whether to cry over that or laugh hysterically. She couldn't win. She had never had a chance to escape.

But she was forgetting about her unpleasant encounter with John Lackland. A king could make even the most powerful of men bend to his will. And Wulfric didn't know yet that John was opposed to their joining. Verily, he should be delighted when she told him. It would give him the excuse he had hoped to find, to not marry her. If *he* ended the betrothal, then he would no longer consider her his. She just didn't have the same option, apparently.

"You do not yet know what caused me to leave. It changed everything, Wulfric." His sheath and belt dropped to the floor atop his cloak. "Listen to me!"

"Has the betrothal been set aside?"

"Nay, but—"

"Then naught has changed."

"It has, I tell you! The king has involved himself. He is against our joining. This is the excuse you yourself needed to end the betrothal. We need only tell our parents."

"Even did I believe you, wench, which I do not, it would make no difference, since John has said naught about this to anyone—except you— has instead offered his approval quite publicly."

"I *am* telling you the truth!"

"Then let me be more clear why it does not matter. What John wants cannot be used unless he admits it, but he has not done that, nor is he like to. So we will make sure, here, now, that you know *who* you belong to, and do not attempt to deny it again. We are already joined by contract. We will put the final seal on it tonight." So saying, he pushed her back on the bed and made to join her on it.

She could not believe he had not jumped on the excuse she had just given him to get out of marrying her. But then she realized he was too angry right now to care.

It was that anger that made her desperate

enough to wail, "Nay! Do not do this, Wulfric. I will not try to escape again. I will marry you, I swear! Just do not take me like this—in anger."

There were tears in her eyes. She was so panicked, she didn't even know she had begun to cry. It was the only thing that stopped him, as angry as he was. He kissed her, hard, but then, with a foul oath, he left the bed, and immediately thereafter, the room.

Milisant collapsed back on the bed in trembling relief. Her own anger over the quivering mass he had reduced her to didn't come until much later—but it did come.

Thirty-nine

It only took moments after she awoke for Milisant to realize that she had slept half the day away. She was not surprised by that, though, not when the anger that had come upon her after Wulfric left her had kept her awake until nigh dawn. She was surprised only that no one had tried to wake her, Wulfric in particular. Or mayhap he did not intend to return to Shefford today as she had thought.

Then, too, he might still be abed himself, after riding half the night to reach Clydon, which would explain it. But whichever was the case, she had much to say to him, now she was no longer frightened out of her wits.

She still could not believe he had done that to her. Not only that, before she had fallen asleep, she had begun to suspect that he had not really meant to bed her, that his intent had only been to frighten her into giving her oath to him—which she had done right quickly.

Not that it mattered anymore, after what he had admitted to last night. Verily, did she marry someone else, 'twould be like signing his death warrant, as far as Wulfric was concerned, and she could not take the chance of that. So she *was* stuck with him as long as he continued to see her as "his," and she had run out of all options to alter that thinking when even the king's wishes had not swayed him.

Milisant dressed hurriedly, ignoring the bliaut she had worn yesterday in favor of her own clothes—just to spite Wulfric. He did not need to know she had brought along what he deemed "proper" garb. He would think she had naught else to wear. A small victory for her, too small to rid her of her anger, though.

That anger was obvious in her expression when she entered Clydon's Great Hall. The midday meal had finished. The trestle tables were being removed. Wulfric *was* there, near the hearth with Lord Ranulf. He had noticed her approach—and her expression.

"Get that look off your face, wench," was his first remark. "If you think I will put up with your temper after what you did, you are much mistaken."

She did not take that warning to heart, snapping, "After what *I* did? What of what *you* did?"

"What I *should* have done was not done, but we can rectify that right quickly if you insist."

She opened her mouth to retaliate, then shut it as swiftly when she realized he was talking now about beating her rather than bedding her. And she would not put that past him, oh, no, not him. So she was forced to swallow her bile and moved away from him to the dais table, which had yet to be dismantled, to snatch up a half-filled chalice of wine to help the bile go down easier.

Behind her she heard Roland's father laugh. *Jesu*, she had seen him standing there with Wulfric, yet had totally ignored him, her mind centered solely on the brute. It brought a blush to her cheeks, that she had been that rude. Her anger was no excuse; he was still her host.

By the time she turned back toward the hearth, Ranulf was gone. Wulfric was still there, alone now, standing with his arms crossed and his eyes narrowed on her. She lifted her chin defiantly. He raised a brow at her. She gritted her teeth, wondering if she could ever win where he was concerned. He no doubt was confident that she could not.

She knew, on a commonsense level, that the prudent thing to do would be to stay away from him until they had both had a chance to calm down. The trouble with that, though, was she didn't think she could calm down without venting, at least a little. Besides, she also needed to know what he intended to do about King John's machinations, especially now that she was going to be returned to Shefford where she would have to deal with John again herself.

So she did approach him a second time, though she managed to get the scowl off her face before doing so. And before he warned her again not to berate him, she introduced a subject that he couldn't ignore.

Without preamble, she asked, "Will you tell your father what John did?"

Wulfric didn't answer, questioned instead, "What, exactly, did the king do, other than give you the impression that he was against our joining?"

" 'Twas more than an impression. He wanted to give you a reason to repudiate me."

His frown was immediate. "The only way I might do that is if . . ."

"Exactly."

She was amazed to see the color leave his cheeks, then rush back in crimson streaks. "Are you saying John Plantagenet raped you?"

She was amazed again that she didn't want him thinking that, even for a moment, and quickly said, "Nay, he did not. Which is not to say that would not have happened, but I doubt me that he would view it as a rape. It did seem more like he felt that I should be flattered by his offer—and grateful. He did harp on benefits for us both."

"What—benefits?"

It seemed as if he had to force those words out. His anger was definitely back, though she wasn't at all sure who it was now centered on.

"He was not specific, Wulfric. I had assumed the benefit for himself would have been merely the pleasure of the bedding, though I later thought it could have been more than that. For myself, he had asked me directly if I loved you, and I answered him honestly. His response had been that I should not mind then if you repudiate me. He had seemed delighted and even said so. His words had been, 'I am pleased we shall both benefit by this solution.' "

"But you declined?"

She glared at him for even asking that. "Aye, but he was not inclined to accept my denial, was

going to 'ease my conscience' by making the decision for me, or so he said. I managed to get
away, but I was terrified he would want revenge
on me for thwarting him. 'Tis the main reason
I left, to put myself out of his reach, though I
will not try to pretend that was the *only* reason."

He snorted at that reminder, but kept to the
subject at hand, wanting to know, "This encounter with him happened the day of his arrival?"

"That night," she clarified. "One of his servants came to fetch me with the pretense that
the royal couple had summoned me. But only
John was present in the chamber I was taken to,
and he was alone. Nor did he waste much time
in trying to get me into his bed. When I declined
his offer, he made to force the issue—which is
when I kicked him to escape his clutches and
get out of there. I confess I spent the remainder
of the night behind a barricaded door with my
bow in hand. Jhone helped me to leave Shefford
the next morn."

"John was in great good spirits all the next
day. He did not even remark upon your absence."

"Absence? Did Jhone not . . . ? Never mind."

"What?" He raised a knowing brow at her.
"Did she not pretend to be you? Think you I
cannot tell the difference by now?"

Milisant ground her teeth together at the
smugness she detected in his tone. "You can*not*
be sure. At least not positively, and not every
time."

"I will concede that, which is why I am going
to warn you now—do not *ever* try to fool me in
that way again, Milisant, or I will ban your sister

from Shefford. Aye, I was fooled, until that eventide when I noticed a nervousness that was unlike you. 'Twas then I realized the ruse.''

She groaned inwardly. No wonder he had found her so soon. As for John's good spirits, she didn't doubt that he thought she was afraid to face him, and too afraid to tell anyone what had happened between them.

She said as much, adding, "If I had accused him of aught, I am sure he would have denied it. Just as I am sure now that he fully intended to place the blame on me, saying I seduced him or some silly thing like that, if he had succeeded. *Will* you tell your father?''

He gave that a moment's thought, then said, "Mayhap someday, when it might be useful. I see no reason to now, as long as John continues to offer the pretense of approval for the marriage.''

"Can you guess *why* John would be against it, other than his brother had approved, and he hated his brother?''

"Certainly. I had not known, until recently, just how rich your father is. To have such wealth combined with Shefford's holdings will make for an alliance of such power that even John would worry about it.''

"My father would never make war against his king—at least, I do not think he would.''

"Neither would mine, without serious provocation. But consider the army that could be raised with Shefford knights and Dunburh mercenaries. 'Tis a power that may never be utilized, but John would not see it that way. If he had the full backing of all his barons, it would not matter. But when so many have already broken with him, and been branded outlaws and traitors for it, he would be hard-pressed to raise a force as large. Verily, those same barons who despise him now would rally with Shefford."

"You make it sound not like a matter to merely worry about, but a matter to truly fear and stop before it comes to pass—by any means."

He guessed the direction of her thoughts. "Including killing you?"

She nodded, frowning in reflection. "He had said at one point, 'I do you a greater favor than you can realize.' At the time I thought he was implying 'twas an honor to be bedded by him— in his opinion. But the favor could have been that if you repudiated me, he would not have to have me killed."

"Mayhap," Wulfric replied thoughtfully. "But you must also consider there is a long-standing friendship involved, and that an alliance through marriage is not really needed to raise the huge army of which we spoke. That army is more like to be raised if it is known John has tried to interfere. Think you John would really risk that?"

"Did he not risk it when he tried to bed me?" Milisant countered.

He chuckled at her surly tone. "You already answered that yourself. He could easily claim the whole thing was your idea, not his, and that he was too weak to resist such an offer. No doubt that would have been his excuse had he succeeded, when I did learn of it and repudiate you . . . Did you really kick the king of England?"

She blushed, giving him only a curt nod. He chuckled again.

"Were it not for that, I would be tempted to— well, never mind. I doubt me the matter will ever come up with John. It might be wise to renew our oaths to him after the wedding, though, just to put his mind at ease somewhat. That is, if he is in attendance."

"Why would he not be, when he is already at Shefford?" she asked.

"Because if what you say is true, he may be too incensed to stay to see the joining made official. I am sure he has no lack of excuses he can draw from, to leave ere the wedding takes place."

She could hope. Actually, she hoped he had done so already, for she was *not* looking forward to any more dealings with John Lackland.

Forty

Before they departed Clydon, Milisant found out that Wulfric had arisen early after all, to spend time with his hosts. Also, it had been decided that the Fitz Hughs would leave for the wedding a day earlier than planned, to accompany them to Shefford.

Apparently Wulfric had ridden alone to come after her, and so was glad for the large escort for the return trip to Shefford. Whether he had come alone to save time, since a contingent of his men could have slowed him down, or to keep her attempt to escape a secret, she didn't know. Likely the latter. He would not like it if it became common knowledge that she would rather risk life and limb than marry him, and leaving on her own, with the recent attempts that had been made on her life, had definitely been risking life and limb.

She did attempt to ask him, very subtly, if all had been well at Shefford while she was gone. Specifically she was still worried about those three men who had followed her, who might have belonged to one of Shefford's patrols. If they did, she hoped for some assurance that she hadn't caused them serious hurt.

But Wulfric didn't take her inquiry seriously enough to give it more than a "Naught has happened that would concern you." That, of course, didn't tell her a single thing, since anything to do with Shefford's men-at-arms, Wulfric likely considered none of her business.

It was significant, to whatever had passed between Roland and Wulfric last night when they had stared so long at each other, that Roland was all smiles when he saw her today, and didn't even look her over in search of bruises. She wondered if Wulfric had spoken to him that morning and what he could have told him, because obviously he thought all was well with her now.

It was hardly that, but she didn't feel inclined to tell Roland. She had tried to involve him once, and had come close to costing him dearly for it. She would not do so again.

They were nigh ready to leave when Lady Reina appeared with her two daughters, the youngest dressed as one would expect of a daughter of the keep. Reina had done no more than raise a brow at Milisant when she'd seen her own attire, but that had been enough to have her blushing and rushing off to change into her only bliaut before they left. *Jesu*, it made her wonder, if her own mother were still alive, whether she really would hold even half of her stubborn preferences, or if she would indeed have been no different from other women, conforming to what was expected of her just as Eleanor Fitz Hugh did.

It had been easy, doing as she pleased when she was young, because her father had been either too intoxicated to notice, or unable to make her feel the shame that a mother could. How different would she be today if her mother had lived? Would she have accepted Wulfric without a single word against him, simply because she would have known that whatever she had to say wouldn't be taken into account?

As if her opinion had counted, she reminded herself. She *was* going to have to marry him. He had himself made sure of that with his dire threats to any other husband she might obtain, so even her father couldn't help her out of this marriage now. She should be utterly crushed, rather than just angry about it, and even her anger was more over Wulfric's attitude than having her last options gone. She wondered why that was so.

There was another brow raising, from Wulfric this time, when Milisant returned to the hall in the borrowed bliaut. She could have screamed in frustration at that point. Allowing others to dictate her actions as she'd just done, even if only by a look, went against the grain. Yet it was going to be so for the rest of her life, unless she did as Jhone had recommended and made an effort to cultivate Wulfric's goodwill, or at least his tolerance.

The trip back to Shefford took twice as long, with the large entourage that included a baggage wain. So it was just after dark when they arrived. Milisant counted that as a bonus, if her

absence was to be kept unknown for the most
part. And in fact she did manage to sneak up
to her chamber unnoticed, due to the fanfare of
the Fitz Hughs' arrival, and her own hooded
cloak.

Jhone had noticed her, however, and entered
the chamber right behind Milisant. Her face was
pale, her tone as distressed as she looked.

"How did Wulfric find you, and so soon? *Jesu*,
Mili, I am so sorry. When he figured out the
ruse that night, and started shouting at me to
tell him where you were, I crumpled at his feet.
He was truly furious. But I did not tell him—at
least, I do not think I did."

Milisant gave her sister a quick hug. "I know
you did not. Faugh, 'tis my own fault. I did the
telling myself, though inadvertently."

"How?"

"I pretended to be you one day last week, to
get out of the keep without that damn escort
that always followed me, yet I ran into Sir Raimund on the way, who wanted to talk to you
about the man I was 'in love' with. I did not
volunteer Roland's name, but because I was
supposed to be you, I could not just shrug him
off either, so I told him that you had never been
told the name, just that I called the man my
'gentle giant.' Wulfric, of course, knows the Fitz
Hughs, since Clydon is a vassalage of Shefford's,
and thus he was able to guess who I meant.
How many know I was gone?"

"Not many. Most still think that I was ill that
first day, and you were up here tending me,
then I let it be known you came down with the
same malady, to explain your absence today.

Whoever saw you in the hall just now might merely think you have recovered, if they even recognized you. I noticed the bliaut under your cloak, or I would not have realized it was you myself."

Milisant nodded. "I doubt me Wulfric wants it known that I was gone, so 'tis as well that you thought to use the excuse of sickness."

"I saw Sir Roland was with you. Did you not have time to put your proposal to him?"

Milisant sighed and explained briefly what had occurred with Roland, ending with, "I wish, I really do, that I had figured out my true feelings for him ere I went racing off to Clydon. I could have gone directly to Father instead and . . . Bah, it matters not. Wulfric has convinced me that as long as he feels that I belong to him already—and apparently he feels exactly that—even if Father agreed to break the contract and marry me to someone else, my new husband would not live very long."

Jhone's eyes widened. "He said that?"

"He threatened it."

"That sounds somewhat—romantic."

Milisant rolled her eyes before retorting, " 'Tis insane is what it is."

"Nay, what it proves is he now wants you, no matter what. *That* is what is romantic."

"I swear, Jhone, you would try to see a good side to a toad if given half a chance."

Jhone snorted. "His wanting you that much *is* a good thing."

" 'Tis possessiveness, plain and simple. It does not mean he has any tender regard for me."

"Nay, of course not, nor will it ever, as long as you stubbornly refuse to see it."

"Why are we arguing?"

Jhone sighed and dropped down to sit on the bed. "Because 'tis better than crying?" she said forlornly.

Milisant came over and sat next to her. " 'Tis not worth crying over. I know when to stop batting my head against the wall. My last options are gone, so I will marry him. But I will not let him crush me. I will be fine, Jhone—truly."

"That is not what you thought before."

"Nay, but I had other hopes then. Now, well, I will merely put the same effort I put into avoiding this joining into making sure Wulfric de Thorpe accepts me as I am, or at least does not try to change me too much."

Jhone smiled. "I would not have thought you would give in so gracefully."

Milisant abruptly pushed her sister off the bed, ignored her screech of surprised outrage, and snorted. "Faugh, who said aught about being graceful?"

Forty-one

It was not a surprise for Milisant to find King John in the Great Hall the next morning, just a terrible disappointment that he hadn't left as she had hoped. Jhone had confessed that she had been forced to speak with him during the ruse, and that as best she could tell, he had seemed amused by her nervousness.

Milisant was no longer fearful herself after hearing that. Her fear had been for immediate reprisal because she had dared to attack the king. But obviously John had no intention of letting that attack, and in particular her reasons for it, become public knowledge, if for no other reason than it would be an embarrassment.

If she'd had her wits about her that night, she would have realized that sooner. However, Jhone had not been left alone with the king either, where he could make a comment about what had happened between them, so they didn't know what he actually felt about it.

He noticed her entrance, but not with much apparent interest. At least, he did not break

from the conversation he was having with Lord
Guy and a few other important-looking men.
They were gathered around the table that had
been set out with bread, wine, and cheese for
those who wanted to break their morning fast.
There was much laughter amongst them, and
many smiles.

She was not hungry herself. Even if she were,
she would not approach that table. She held a
small hope that John would not wish to speak
with her again, if only to save them both embarrassment. And she would do her best to make
that easy for him, by keeping her distance from
him. So she didn't pause in the hall, heading
out of the keep to check on Stomper instead.
She barely noticed her silent escort who fell into
step behind her.

The weather was holding firm but cold, the
last of the snow on the ground nigh gone. Lady
Anne had fretted that the storm they had experienced would keep many of those she had invited for the wedding away, and so it might
have if the heavy snow and wind had continued.

But Milisant was not to be lucky enough to
have her wedding delayed by the weather. Most
weddings were planned for springtime or summer, for just that reason, because the many wit-
nesses required for a wedding could not all fit
in church, and thus it was typical for a large
crowd to be gathered outside the church during
the long wedding mass, which would not be a
pleasant prospect in the thick of winter.

On the way to the stable, the sound of swords
clashing drew Milisant's eyes toward the prac-

tice yard, as always. Today, however, her step slowed, then halted altogether when she recognized Wulfric there.

He and his brother were exercising with swords, though with the crowd gathered round, it was more like an exhibition. After watching them for a moment, she concluded that Wulfric would win hands down and without much effort, if he was serious about it. His sword seemed to be an extension of his hand, weightless, so easily did he wield it.

A cough behind her reminded her that she was not alone, and her escort was not dressed properly for standing about in the cold watching swordplay. Neither was she for that matter, wearing only a thin cloak. But she had been too mesmerized to notice the cold herself.

She didn't berate herself as she hurried on to the stable. She had never denied that Wulfric was a splendid specimen of manhood. Now she had to admit as well that his swordsmanship ranked among the best she had ever witnessed. She used to love to watch Roland in knightly practice. She had just experienced that same feeling watching Wulfric.

She smiled to herself as she entered the stable, then Stomper's stall. If she got nothing else out of her marriage, she would at least have that enjoyment, of watching her husband hone his knightly skills. She would just have to make sure Wulfric didn't realize she found it entertaining, or no doubt he would prohibit it, as he planned to prohibit everything else she found enjoyment in.

"Crispin's daughter—what was your first name?"

Milisant groaned to herself, so occupied with Stomper's grooming that she hadn't noticed John's approach. She was not really surprised, though, that he was suddenly there, and without his usual followers. He had obviously sought her out for a purpose, and she could think of one quite easily. He would want to know if she had told anyone about their encounter. She would have to convince him she had not.

"Milisant, Sire."

She accepted the subtle insult without rancor. She didn't doubt that John knew her name well enough, he just wanted her to think she was of such little import that he could easily forget it.

"I would not have thought to find you here, a foul-smelling place a lady would disdain to frequent," he said next, and with a good deal of that disdain he bespoke.

Another insult, however subtle. Was he deliberately trying to get a rise out of her?

She dealt with his remark, rather than the intent. After all, a stable did reek more in winter, when its doors were kept closed to keep out the worst of the cold. And most ladies did not attend to their own mounts, leaving that task to the stable lads whose job it specifically was.

So she said with a feigned sigh, "I am afraid no one will get near my horse, Your Highness, so I have no choice but to see to him myself."

It was unnerving to realize that he had not really noticed Stomper, big as he was, until just then, that his eyes had been only on her from the moment he entered the stable. Watching for her slightest reaction to him? Looking for the fear he had seen before, when Jhone had pretended to be her?

But he did look at the warhorse now, and after his green-gold eyes flared wide in his surprise, he actually forgot himself enough to say, "Are you mad, girl, to put yourself so near that animal?"

She managed to restrain herself from laughing. "He belongs to me, so is tame to me, though I cannot guarantee anyone else's safety, do they get near him."

His eyes started to narrow on her, as if he thought she had been subtly threatening him, but then he suddenly laughed instead. "True enough of any destrier."

"But hers in particular," Wulfric said as he came up behind the king.

Milisant was amazed to find herself actually relieved by Wulfric's sudden appearance—for once. Her escort, as usual, had not lingered near Stomper's stall, so John would have been free to say whatever he cared to and be assured no one would have heard him. Thankfully, he had not immediately done so, and now with Wulfric there, it was too late for him to mention what had passed between them.

John hid his disappointment well. He muttered something about thinking his own horse had been sheltered within, an effort to explain his being there in conversation with her, then abruptly left when Wulfric directed him to the stable where the royal mounts had been put.

Ah, how quickly relief could turn to dread,

now one nemesis had been replaced by another, or so Milisant found herself thinking. Ironic but true. Yet she *was* grateful that Wulfric had entered the stable when he had, for whatever reason, and so she would try, she really would, to not start an argument with him.

"Did you want to talk with me?" she asked him, keeping her tone neutral.

"Actually, I was bringing Stomper sugar ere I returned to the hall."

She watched in surprise as he did, indeed, produce a clump of sugar. Stomper quickly moved to the edge of the stall to take it from his open palm, as if they were old friends. She recalled that he had gotten the horse into his stall with sugar, but that one time would not account for how quickly the animal had just come to him.

"You have done that more than once." It wasn't a question, was in fact a bit accusing.

"Often," he replied with a shrug.

"Why?"

"Why not?"

Because it was a nice thing to do, and she had it set in her mind that he wasn't nice to animals. No doubt he did have an ulterior motive. She just couldn't figure out what it might be at the moment.

"Did he threaten you again?"

She was watching Stomper when he asked it. She continued to keep her eyes on the horse, rather than Wulfric. It was much easier to concentrate that way.

He had meant John, of course, and likewise, she answered without using his name. "He tossed some minor insults my way, mayhap intentional, mayhap merely thoughtless on his part. However, I doubt me his appearance here was coincidental, not when I know he saw me leave the keep, then he showed up here, alone, not long after."

"He followed you apurpose, then?"

"So it did seem. But whether he would have got around to discussing what happened that night . . ." She shrugged. "Your arrival kept him from revealing his purpose—if it was other than trying to make me feel like an insignificant gnat beneath his boot."

He ignored how sour her tone had just turned. "My father was going to have you restricted to the women's solar while we have so many unknown people coming and going who have arrived with the guests. I'm thinking now, 'tis not a bad idea and should already have been done."

Her eyes flared on him and her voice came out snarling. "That I be imprisoned?"

" 'Twould hardly be that, and only until after the wedding, when everyone here will be accounted for and known again. As it is now, your assassin could be standing right next to you, yet how would we know it, when he could as like be one of the guests' servants? It would also keep you from being found alone again—as you just were."

"I would as soon *know* what his intentions are now. I had hoped he would avoid me. But since that is not to be the case, would you rather not know if he can be appeased, or left to wonder? Or do you intend to speak with him about it yourself? I had thought you meant to avoid the subject with him as well. Would it not be better if I convince him that no one else knows, especially the de Thorpes? Would that not make it easier for him to back off?"

"Easier for him, aye, but I am not worried about making this easier for him, I am worried about you having to deal with him again on your own."

She snorted. "You think I will do more than kick him next time?"

"Nay, I just do not want there to *be* a next time. Is it so hard for you to understand, that I would protect you from his machinations?"

She was only used to motives like that from her father. It made her feel distinctly uncomfortable to hear him say it, since it suggested concern.

So she didn't address his question at all, changing the subject instead with the remark, "You never did say how you found me so quickly. Did you not even bother to search the castle for me?"

"I know you reasonably well, Milisant. You would not bother to hide, when you would eventually be found. What would be the point?"

She didn't mention that there were times when hiding was quite sufficient, as she knew from experience at home. Just this time, it wouldn't have been.

She liked it not, though, that he knew her 'reasonably well,' or thought he did. If he could predict her actions, even if only half the time, she would be at a distinct disadvantage, particularly when she was finding that she couldn't do the same with him.

He apparently didn't expect the new thread she had introduced to continue, since he opened the stall for her and said, "Come, I will return you to the hall."

"To lock me up?"

He sighed at that point. "Until I can recognize everyone who gathers in the Great Hall again, aye, I will not take the chance with you. You need not worry about your horse, I will see to him. You need not remain in the solar constantly, either. If you stay close to my mother, you may go where she goes. Likewise, if you are with me—"

She cut in angrily as she marched past him, "There is no way to make it palatable, so do not bother to try, Lord *Wulf*. A prisoner is a prisoner, no matter what small freedoms she is allowed."

Forty-two

It annoyed Wulfric that Milisant had made his nickname sound like an epithet. It annoyed him that John was not going to leave her alone. It annoyed him that she thought she could handle John on her own. But mostly it annoyed him that she was annoyed with him.

He had hoped to start anew with her after their return to Shefford. After the rage he had experienced upon realizing she had run off to Clydon, and recognizing it for the jealousy it had been, he had been forced to admit, at least to himself, that what he felt for her now was more than just the simple lust he had thought. His feelings had grown apace. The more he was in her presence, the more he wanted to be.

It was a new experience for him, the particular feelings she stirred in him, so he had no ready name for it. He knew only that he found her company very stimulating, both in mind and body. She amused him, frustrated him, provoked him by turns, and now, he realized, too, worried him. But she never, ever bored him.

Fortunately, or so it did seem to him, his mother was in the hall, so he didn't have to personally escort Milisant to the solar and call the guards to stand watch at the door to keep her there. He was able to leave her with Anne instead, not that it seemed to make much difference to her. She still glared at him in parting.

So be it. Her safety was more important to him than her animosity just now. Starting anew with her would obviously have to wait until after the wedding. For now . . . he went off to find his father and remind *him* to set Milisant's restrictions in place.

Guy knew that she had sneaked out of Shefford, but not about John's involvement in that. He thought only that she had panicked, with the wedding so close. Wulfric had told him last night about Roland Fitz Hugh and her mistaken feelings for him. Guy had actually found that amusing. Ironically, so had Roland's father, when Wulfric had discussed it with him before they left Clydon.

Neither parent saw it as a serious stumbling block for Wulfric. Yet he was finding it hard to ignore the fact that, even though young Roland had been taken off her list of likely husbands, she probably still had a list, since he knew she would *still* rather marry anyone other than him. The only consolation in all this was that she didn't actually love someone else as he'd thought, so he no longer had that to infuriate him as well. Ironically, he might never have learned that if she had not run off to Clydon.

When he returned to the hall later, it was to find everything almost back to normal. Servants were setting up the tables for the midday meal, and his mother and her ladies gathered at the hearth. The guests had all gone to watch an exhibition of archery that Guy had arranged for their entertainment. The ladies didn't find that of much interest, though he realized Milisant likely would, which was why he had come to fetch her.

His mother wanted his attention first, though, and hurried to meet him before he reached the hearth, pulling him aside so they would not be overheard by the passing servants. Yet it was those servants whom she apparently wanted to talk about, he found to his amusement—at least he was amused at first.

She nodded toward the tables with a frown. "Look you at that girl there with the dark hair."

"Which one? They mostly all have shades of dark hair, Mother."

"The trull."

Trull was a rather harsh name for a strumpet or prostitute, which amused him even more, since his mother rarely ever belittled anyone with name-calling. Yet the description did bring his eyes to one woman in particular whose manner of dress did suggest that profession, her bodice nigh full open to reveal a pair of very plump breasts, her girdle cinched in tighter than was likely natural, to emphasize her curves.

"What about her?"

"She does not belong here," Anne said stiffly.

That was true enough, if the girl actually was a prostitute. His mother didn't allow such to ply their trade in her hall, where her ladies would take offense at it. Yet the woman appeared to be one of the regular servants. After all, she was working in the hall, busy setting out trenchers of bread on the tables.

"Have you tried to correct her ways?"

Anne all but snorted. "Why would I do that when she is not one of ours?"

He frowned himself at that point. "Then what is she doing here?"

"I will leave that for you to find out. You *did* ask me to point out anyone I find suspicious. That is what I am doing. Of course, I questioned her immediately I saw her today. She *claims* to be a cousin to Gilbert in the village, who asked her to offer her help in the kitchens, since there is so much extra work needs doing while so many guests are here. But I know our villagers. Gilbert has never before mentioned relatives who live beyond Shefford."

"What did Gilbert have to say of it?"

"I have not had time to go to the village to question him. I only noticed the girl shortly ere you arrived. Now you are aware of it, you can do so. And while you are at it, take her with you. If she really is a relative of Gilbert's, you can explain to her that she is not welcome inside the keep. It has been many, many years since I have had to embarrass myself getting rid of someone like her. I would rather not have to resort to that again."

There were, of course, several whores among the castle wenches. It would be a strange demesne indeed that didn't have them, with the exception of religious holdings. But as they weren't conspicuous, Anne was able to ignore them for the most part. It was women who were blatantly obvious about the selling of their wares whom she objected to.

He nodded and approached the woman, who had, surprisingly, moved to the lord's table to distribute the last couple of trenchers she carried. That, frankly, amazed him, since the dais table had its own personal servants, those well trusted, and no one else saw to the care and serving of that table. Since it was common for poison to be used to get rid of one's enemies, no seneschal worth his salt allowed any servant unknown to him anywhere near his lord's table. It was no different here at Shefford.

He would allow the woman might be too dense to realize that. He would allow also that she might really be who she said she was and was only trying to help in a time when the castle could use additional hands. But he would find out for certain. And it was not his father he was worried about. Milisant's assailants were still out there, and were no doubt getting desperate, now she no longer ventured beyond castle walls where they could easily get at her.

Forty-three

"*Did you see* that?" Milisant asked her sister in a barely contained hiss.

Jhone glanced up from the robe she was sewing. It was a new vestment Lady Anne wanted made for the priest to wear for the wedding ceremony.

"What?" Jhone asked when she followed Milisant's gaze to find nothing untoward—at least, nothing that would cause the hot green ire now flashing in Milisant's eyes.

"Wulfric and that whore he just left with," Milisant clarified. "He does not even wait until after the wedding to openly dally."

Jhone stared incredulously at her for a moment, before remarking, "That is quite a conclusion you jump to, without knowing for certain—"

"I saw the whole thing," Milisant cut in sharply. "He stopped her to haggle over the price, then left with her—as if he could not see that I was here, and did not know that I watch him when he is near. He even put his arm around her shoulder to hold her close."

"Which means naught," Jhone reminded her. "He could have done so for any number of reasons that are unrelated to what you are thinking."

Milisant snorted. "You cannot defend him this time, Jhone. I have eyes."

"Then I must point out, what difference does it make who he goes off with, when he is not wed to you yet? What he does now has no bearing on you."

"What he does now shows me clearly what he will do later. If he had no hesitation in doing thus now, think you he would not keep his mistresses right under my nose?"

"Mili, why do you care? You sound about as jealous as a woman can be. Are you?"

Milisant blinked in surprise, but it was only a moment before her scowl returned and she denied hotly, "I am not annoyed because I care what he does. He can have all the women he likes. I just do not want to have my nose rubbed in it, nor be pitied by those around me, when it becomes obvious that he prefers other beds to mine."

Jhone chuckled. "Aye, pure jealousy—or you would be shrugging with indifference. Ere you rail at me further about it, think well on why you are jealous."

"I tell you I am not!"

Jhone merely nodded, though it was a condescending nod.

"Faugh, I do not know why I discuss aught with you anymore," Milisant complained in disgust. "You are so set on the thought that love is going to magically occur in this marriage of mine that you cannot see what is before you."

"And you are so set upon resisting it that it will take a sledgehammer knocking you on your head ere you admit the wolf is not as loathsome as you thought."

"I can admit that now," Milisant mumbled.

"What was that?" Jhone smirked.

Red-cheeked, Milisant retorted, "Just because I have not seen the worst yet does not mean it won't be brought forth once the vows are actually spoken."

Apparently done teasing her, Jhone said now with concern, "Mili, you need to stop worrying about it. What will be will be. If you but keep an open mind, and step softly, you might be pleasantly surprised at the results. Men *are* malleable. Whatever you still do not like about Wulfric, you can change. Just keep that in mind."

After mulling that over for a moment, Milisant didn't concede the issue, but she did remark, "You should have been an abbess. Your ability to guide, bolster, and teach with such calm self-assurance is amazing."

Jhone blushed and admitted, "I did consider it."

"Really?"

An embarrassed nod. "Aye, after Will died."

"Then why not?"

"Because although I did not want to remarry and still do not, I did enjoy being married. So I know I may not always feel as I do now."

For once, Milisant knew Jhone was speaking only for herself. Still, she saw the point. Life changed. Feelings changed. What she found so horrid today, she might tolerate or even like next year, and the opposite was also true. She could as well despise something tomorrow that she greatly enjoyed today.

Logically she understood that feelings could do this, completely change for many reasons. But she also knew she couldn't depend on that being so; feelings could stay the same as well. And what did one have to base one's outlook on except for current feelings? Thinking, even hoping, those feelings might change eventually didn't help to abate them.

She was still furious over what she had just witnessed, but she said no more about it, letting Jhone get back to her sewing. As far as she was concerned, her opinion had been reinforced that she and Wulfric would never get along. What was plain now was how little difference it would make for him. He had other outlets to see to his needs. He had just shown her that quite clearly, and no doubt intentionally.

He *could* have picked any one of the other serving women if he could not wait the two days more till they were wed. Not one of the women there was like to refuse him, just because of who he was. And many were certainly prettier than the slattern had been, and no doubt cleaner.

Milisant probably would have thought nothing of it had he walked out with someone else. Even putting his arm about her could have meant nothing more than a friendly gesture toward someone he had known for years. She wouldn't have noticed. She wouldn't have cared.

But he had instead picked the one woman there who was so blatantly obvious about what she was. Why else would he have done that except to point out to Milisant that he could, and there was nothing she could do or say about it?

Forty-four

Anger was an unpredictable emotion. Strange how it could ofttimes backfire on the one experiencing it, or cause more harm than the original occurrence that prompted it. Such had been the case when Wulfric returned to the hall that day he had gone off with the whore, and asked Milisant if she would like to accompany him to the bailey to watch the archery competitions.

Of course, she had told him no. She had still been too angry to tell him anything else. And yet afterward she had railed at herself for letting her fury interfere with something she knew she would have enjoyed.

That he invited her at all, she attributed to a guilty conscience. Assuredly he would not have done so otherwise, thoughtless brute that he was.

It was probably just as well that she had refused. Had she gone with him, she would likely have resented the fact that she couldn't join in the competition herself.

Her father would have let her do so, but then

all at Dunburh knew her skill with the bow and didn't question it. The de Thorpes, however, would see it as an embarrassment to have their *daughter-in-law* win in a male sport; thus she would be denied the chance to even try.

Milisant's new restrictions continued, though her time with Lady Anne did lessen the resentment of it. She still was forced to spend a goodly amount of time in the women's solar those next few days, though her mounting nervousness kept her somewhat distracted from the ignominy of it.

With it being no longer expected, at least by Milisant, it was a surprise when Nigel arrived at Shefford the day before the wedding, and with a ready excuse for being so tardy. He had been sick. His pallor and loss of weight attested that it was no lie.

She was forced to admit she had been wrong in thinking he meant not to come at all, just to avoid hearing her present opinion of Wulfric. On the contrary, it was the first thing he questioned her about, as soon as they found a moment alone together that night.

She and Jhone had put him to bed early, sending his squires away so they could see to him themselves. He had not been well enough, really, to travel yet. That was obvious. Yet he had come anyway.

Milisant loved him dearly for that, though she had scolded him profusely for it. So had Jhone for that matter, and Lord Guy as well. Her poor father had been quite grouchy after all that scolding, but now he was merely tired.

However, he asked her to stay for a moment,

after Jhone bid him good night and left them. "What have you decided about young Wulfric? Confess, he's a damn good choice for a husband, is he not?"

She wasn't going to distress her father with the truth. Not because he was ill, but because it would simply do her no good. Even if the contract *could* still be broken at this late date, now that Wulfric had promised to interfere, she didn't dare look elsewhere.

So she said merely, "He will do."

That made Nigel laugh. It obviously pleased him greatly that he had been right and she wrong. She saw no reason to disabuse him of that notion. At least someone was happy about her wedding.

"Are you nervous?" he asked next.

"Only a little," she lied.

She was in fact so nervous, she had been unable to eat anything all day, afeared if she did, it would come right back up. And she was not even sure what she was nervous about. The bedding? Or finally being completely and utterly under Wulfric's control?

"That is to be expected," he said, patting her hand encouragingly. "How is your shoulder?"

"What? Oh, that. 'Twas so minor, it has long been forgotten."

"And you would not tell me even if it still pained you, would you?"

She grinned. "Likely not."

He chuckled. "Just like your mother, always trying to keep me from worrying about her."

"I wish I had known her—better—longer—"

She broke off, sighing. "I am sorry. I know it still hurts you to think of her passing."

He smiled at her to make light of it. There *was* pain in his eyes, though. "I wish you had known her better as well. Actually, I wish she could have known you longer. She would have been so proud of you, daughter."

Tears came to her eyes. "Nay, she would not. She would feel as you do and be ashamed—"

"Hush! Sweet, *Jesu*, what have I done to you? Never think I am not proud of you, Mili. Verily, you are the one who is so like your mother in nigh every way. She was as stubborn, she was as willful, she was as fiery, and I loved her for all of that, not despite of it. There are women born to be different, though not all realize it or try to be. You and your mother were not meant to be as others are. Young Wulfric will appreciate that, once he gets used to it. I know I would not have had your mother be any other way."

It was wonderful to hear him say it, yet she didn't believe him—not completely anyway. How could she when she had all the times he had railed at her and bemoaned her behavior to recall, as well as the times he had specifically mentioned her shaming him? And yet . . .

"If you felt I was born to be different, as she was, then why did you try to curb my independence?"

He sighed. "When you were younger, Mili, you needed to *see* the difference, be made aware of it. You needed to understand that there would be others of less tolerance who would *not* accept the path you choose for yourself, and to save yourself grief, you should have learned to adapt to such circumstances. Your mother *did* know when to give in gracefully, and likewise, she also knew when she did not need to. I had hoped to teach you that lesson at least, but . . ."

He didn't finish, looked uncomfortable. She smiled. "But I failed to learn it."

" 'Tis not that you failed, you just—refused. You have a strong desire to do things you know you are capable of doing, yet are some of those things not appropriate for you to be doing. You choose to do them anyway, and bedamn any opinion to the contrary."

"Is that *so* wrong?"

"Nay, not at all. What is wrong is the 'bedamn' part, and not accepting that *some* things are just so unnatural for you in particular to do that they require compromise, or at least restraint. Did you know that I sew?"

She blinked, then after a moment, chuckled. "Was that a trick?"

"Nay, I do sew, Mili. I find it relaxing. I love doing it. And even with these old, gnarled hands, I can turn a finer stitch than some women."

She blinked again. "You are not jesting?"

He shook his head. "I made many of your mother's clothes, though no one knew it besides us. I did it in the privacy of our chamber. I never would have considered sewing in the Great Hall where anyone could have seen me at it. Why? For the same reason that you just laughed. 'Tis not something you would expect to see an old warrior doing—unless he had no one else to do it for him, which certainly is not the case for me, and even then he would only repair his own raiments, not make clothes for women. 'Twould cause snide comments and snickering, likely make of him a laughingstock."

Milisant nodded, aware of how hypocritical she had just been, or rather, self-centered. She had always railed at the unfairness of it, that she couldn't do all that she wanted to do, because much of what she wanted to do was in the strictly male domain, not to be breached by a lowly, incompetent female. She had never thought that a man might find himself faced with the same restrictions.

" 'Tis just horrid," she remarked, with years worth of resentment in her tone, "that we must change and make compromises because no one else is willing to accept that some people are different. You do not resent that you must hide to do something you enjoy doing?"

"Nay, it does not lessen the enjoyment, that I sew in private, it merely avoids the ridicule. And I know that what *you* enjoy doing is not so easily concealed. I was not trying to show you that our difficulties are similar, just somewhat the same. But that is where compromises come into play. If you could just accept that what you like doing could be done some of the time, just not all of the time, I think you would be much happier, Mili."

"I think I have finally come to see this, ironically, by witnessing another girl similar to myself make such compromises and yet still enjoy certain—restricted—freedoms. And since coming here, I have not really minded so much, the wearing of these cumbersome bliauts. Verily, 'tis that I don't want to see the lady Anne's frowns

over my garb that I readily give it up—for now.
I have become quite fond of her, and don't want
to disappoint her."

He gave her a brilliant smile. "You cannot
imagine how I have longed to hear you—"

"Faugh, I did not say I was completely re-
formed," she cut in with a grumble.

He chuckled. She gave in and smiled back,
grateful that for a short time he had taken her
mind off of tomorrow—and the joining.

Forty-five

Thone had personally made Milisant's raiments
for the wedding, allowing no one else to aid her.
The result was a grand, beautiful bliaut of jade
velvet worthy of a queen, richly detailed, en-
crusted with gems and thickly embroidered
with gold thread. Along with the matching mantle, gold satin undertunic, and heavy gold-
linked girdle, the whole ensemble likely weighed
as much as Milisant did, which was why she
was not looking forward to wearing it. However, she would never tell that to her sister, who
had put much loving care into its creation.

But then another gown arrived that morning,
just before Anne's ladies presented themselves
to help with the formal dressing. It was
wrapped in lace ribbons, sitting on a tasseled
satin pillow, delivered by a young, turbaned
page with a cheeky grin.

He said merely, "A gift from yer papa."

When she unwrapped it, a bliaut of silver was
revealed, of a strange glimmering material Milisant knew to have been in her father's treasure

trove from the Holy Land, for she had been fascinated, having discovered it there as a child. Soft as silk, light as down, it sparkled in the morning light. No other embellishment was needed on a material that unusually beautiful, yet two rows of tiny seed pearls did adorn the neckline. The undertunic was a pristine white silk with silver thread that made it sparkle as well.

Jhone, of course, was disappointed, staring at the two gowns laid out side by side over their bed. "I cannot imagine why Papa would have this made for you, when he should have known I would not let you appear at your wedding in leggings. And 'tis too thin to wear for winter."

"Not with an appropriate, thick mantle," Milisant pointed out, then whispered a bit in awe, "Do not laugh, but I think Papa made it himself."

Jhone looked at her askance and said merely, "I did not hear you aright."

"You did. I said nigh the same thing to him last eventide when he told me he enjoys sewing. He admitted he even used to make clothes for our mother."

"Now I *know* you are jesting," Jhone retorted. "I am glad that your nervousness has abated long enough for you to make light of this, but—"

"Look at me," Milisant cut in. "Do I look like I am jesting? And I really do think he made this gown. Look at the stitching. Who do you know at Dunburh who can ply a needle this fine— other than yourself, of course? For that matter, who do you know whom he would trust to work with this particular cloth, which has been in his keeping all these years since his return from the Crusades—again, other than you?"

Jhone picked up an edge of the silver cloth to examine it more closely. "No one, at least at Dunburh. But then he could have found someone outside of Dunburh to make it. Not that it matters. You still must wear his gift, because he gave it."

Milisant chuckled. "You have been taking stubbornness lessons from me, eh? 'Tis not as if I will not have plenty of opportunities to wear the one you made me. These de Thorpes entertain royalty, after all."

Jhone was appeased somewhat and poked her in the ribs with a bit of teasing. "I still think you will freeze on the way to the village church."

Milisant smiled in amusement. "Nay, you would not allow that. I trust you will force on me the very heaviest of your cloaks."

Jhone nodded. "Aye, and I know just the one that will match perfectly, the double-sided white velvet one trimmed in silver fox."

It was another brief interlude of distraction for which Milisant was grateful, for too quickly her nervousness returned in full measure, and too quickly she was dressed and on her way to the church. And *much* too quickly, she was joined to Wulfric de Thorpe.

She would remember very little about this day, so deep was the daze of her anxiety. It was the culmination of everything she had dreaded, and that dread was full upon her. The slow procession to the church, the long mass, the priest's intonements, none of that could be recalled with any clarity. Even the celebration that followed in the Great Hall and lasted the rest of the day was no more than a haze of loud revelry enjoyed by all—except her.

The painfully embarrassing bedding ceremony, in which she must be presented to the groom—and anyone else who managed to crowd into the room—for the supposed search for hidden imperfections that could, if desired, allow repudiation, must have elicited none, since she had been left alone with the groom. Her only consolation to having missed most of her wedding was that she had missed that as well.

"Did I tell you how beautiful you looked today?" Wulfric asked her.

It was the first thing that Milisant actually heard clearly, after hearing naught but indistinguishable babble all day. "Not that I recall."

"Actually, I was jesting, since I must have told you at least a half dozen times," Wulfric said, then, "You really do not recall?"

"Certainly, I was jesting as well," she lied, and had to wonder what else had been said to her in the last hours that she had no memory of.

She realized she was a bit intoxicated, though she did not remember drinking any wine. But despite the relaxing benefit of the wine, it was still disconcerting to become suddenly aware that nigh the entire day had passed as if she had not been there. To find herself in bed with a husband, both of them completely naked. To wonder—*Jesu*, had she missed the bedding as well? Was it over? And finally, to wish that she could go back to being—not there.

"Have we—finished here?" she asked.

He laughed. She scowled. It had been a reasonable question, she thought.

"I find I want to wait until your mind is cleared of the wine haze, but I find also that I cannot wait any longer, when it does seem like I have already waited forever. A fine dilemma, wouldst you not agree?"

"Nay, seems easily decided to me," she said with an emphatic nod. "You wait."

He chuckled. She scowled again. *What* did he find so amusing?

Unfortunately, with her awareness returned, so, too, were her feelings for him fully remembered, including her most recent rage over that incident with the whore. She almost scrambled from the bed, she was suddenly so furious again, would have if, in doing so, she would not have lost the sheet that presently covered them both.

It was impossible for him not to notice the change in her, which prompted a sigh and, "What now?"

He was *not* going to know that she couldn't stand it, the thought of him touching that woman, or any other woman for that matter, so she said merely, if quite rudely, "Did you clean yourself thoroughly after bedding that whore?"

His new expression said she had baffled him completely. "What whore?"

"There have been that many for you not to remember?" she fairly growled, then, "The one you left the hall with the other day."

He stared at her blankly for an extended moment, but then he burst out laughing. "You thought I bedded her?" He laughed yet again.

Milisant had no trouble understanding his humor this time. As Jhone had warned her might be the case, she had apparently jumped to the wrong conclusion that day, and he found that hilarious.

Despite her embarrassment, she still asked, "Then why did you leave with her?"

"Mayhap to find out who she was and why she was working in the hall that day, particularly in readying the tables for the meal, when she was not a Shefford servant and thus had no business being there."

"She came not with one of the guests?"

"Nay, and she gave my mother an excuse which she doubted, which was why she had asked me to question her, Milisant. She was worried that the woman was there to cause mischief, or more to the point, serious harm—to *you*."

Jesu, his reason had to involve her? But she was forgetting one other matter.

" 'Twas necessary for you to put your arm around her to find that out?"

He shrugged. "I felt her unease as I was taking her from the hall. I wanted to make sure she did not bolt from me. Alas, she did just that as soon as we reached the crowded bailey, nor was she found again. That she ran proves she was up to no good, so 'tis unlikely she will try again, now we are aware of that, and I have men watching for her."

"How did she manage to enter the castle if

she is not of Shefford, nor came with the guests?"

"She had claimed to be a cousin of one of the villeins. He had agreed to say she was a relative in return for her favors, but he had had no intention of supporting the lie, other than with his neighbors. When I put the question to him, he immediately admitted the truth."

She had no further questions herself to ask on the matter, just the embarrassment remaining, of accusing him of something he had not done. She ought to apologize, was about to, but he had more to say.

"I will allow you your fits and rages, but not here," he told her.

"Fits?" she sputtered.

"Whatever you wish to call your unreasonable temper. You will not bring it to our bed. Here you will have only good feelings, and think only of pleasing me. I will likewise think only of the pleasure I want to visit on you in full measure. Can you agree to that? And keep in mind ere you answer that I could forbid you your anger at any time."

She gave him an incredulous look. "You cannot control another's anger."

"True, but I can make it very unpleasant for you to reveal yours."

The conclusion that statement prompted had her retorting, "You think to beat it out of me?"

"Nay, but a time spent in the solar every time you raise your voice in anger—I think eventually you will be very soft-spoken and wear naught but smiles. Actually, 'tis not a bad idea."

He sounded like he was teasing, he really did,

yet *Jesu*, he was talking about locking her up, and *often*. She could not take the chance.

"I agree," she mumbled.

"What was that?"

"I said I agree to your terms!" she snapped.

"Hmm, when do you intend to start then?"

She blushed. She closed her eyes against his smile. She was still amusing him, apparently, while she had to make unreasonable *compromises*. It was so blasted unfair. Not even wed a full day, yet already he was asserting his new power over her.

Forty-six

When *Milisant's silence* continued and her eyes stayed closed, Wulfric's finger came to her brow and she heard in a soft tone, "Is it so hard for you to not be angry with me for a little while?"

She groaned inwardly. She wanted to say aye just on principle, but that would be a lie. There had been times when she had not been angry with him for one reason or another, times even when he had made her laugh, and certainly times when he—well, when he confused her so much she didn't know what to think or feel.

At the moment he had defused her real anger by explaining about the whore. She was only annoyed now that he was laying down rules for her already, but she supposed she *could* leave that annoyance for another time.

She opened her eyes again. She found a new warmth in his. He had been staring at her all the while she wasn't looking, and possibly thinking of that pleasure he had mentioned earlier. She had not listened clearly to those words when said, because of what he had added about her anger, but she recalled them now. *I will like-wise think only of the pleasure I want to visit on you in full measure.*

Her stomach swirled unexpectedly. *Jesu*, he *wanted* to give her pleasure? And she knew that he could, for he had done it before.

She had tried so hard not to think of that plea-sure after that night, or want it again. Mostly she had managed to force it far from her thoughts, yet it was so hard. It had been so nice, so worthy of repeating. He could also send all her thoughts flying, and she did fear that, but 'twas a small price to pay for the pleasure she remembered—which she could now experience again.

A shyness came upon her. He was patiently awaiting an answer. But concessions were not easy by any means. And her stubbornness wouldn't let her make them outright—if she didn't have to.

So she said finally, "Hard, aye." But before he could take exception to that truth, she added a slight smile to make it more palatable for him, as well as, "But not impossible."

He chuckled. "Verily, I would have expected no other answer from you. And I *will* appreciate whatever effort it costs you to keep peace in here. I will also make every effort on my part to assure that you do not regret it."

"That sounds—promising."

"Mayhap you need a demonstration?"

It occurred to her suddenly that from the mo-ment the daze left her enough so that she be-came aware of him next to her in the bed, possibly before that, he had not been his usual self. As before, his behavior toward her was completely different when he was in this seducing frame of mind, which was all she could think to call his present behavior. And amazingly enough, she liked him when he was like this.

She had a suspicion that it would not be so hard, after all, to set any anger she might be feeling aside whenever they did share a bed. She had a feeling, also, that she was about to find that out for sure, when the fingers at her brow moved slowly down to her chin to angle her face just right to receive his kiss.

And it was an amazing kiss—tender, then hard, then tender, then so heated she thought her lips might combust under his. What made it amazing, though, was how quickly she responded to each nuance of it. Now that she was willing, or rather, accepting, even—anticipating, that they were finally going to get to the bedding part of the joining, she was more relaxed about it, her fear forgotten for the moment. And that left all of her senses unencumbered so she could experience it more fully. And she did.

Slowly, tentatively, she even participated in the kissing. Actually, she was not being daring about it, she simply couldn't seem to help herself. She suddenly *needed* to know the taste of him, the exact texture of his lips, just how hot his tongue was. It was incredible. The more she kissed him back, the more she wanted to.

She had been sitting with her back against the pillows, the sheet clutched to her breasts. The sheet had fallen now as her arms wrapped about Wulfric's neck. She didn't notice that. She didn't

notice either that he was slowly moving her
down until she was lying there, with him leaning over her.

His hair tickled her neck as it fell against her.
His breath fanned hotly against her face as his
lips moved about in further exploration. His
tongue licked at her ear. Shivers raced down her
spine just before she gasped in delight. His teeth
nipped at her neck. She moaned softly. She
heard an answering groan from him, felt his
body strain to contain what he was himself
feeling.

Her thoughts fast deserted her. It was all feeling now, all exquisite sensation, the taste and
scent of him, and then the caressing . . . In combination with the kissing, it was nigh too much.
The hand at her breast was kneading, gently
pulling, then suddenly his mouth was there,
closing around the turgid nipple, drawing it
deeper into his mouth while his tongue laved
against it.

Scorching heat. Coils unwinding in her belly.
And then his hand went there, too, as if he
sensed the turmoil and meant to soothe it, but
there was nothing soothing about his touch, far
from it. The rage of passion his hands and lips
provoked had her holding her breath and gasping by turns, had her thrashing about, arching
against him . . . pulling him. It did no good. He
was unmovable. He was determined to drive
her wild. He was on fire himself and his hands
were the brands that brought not pain, but the
sweetest pleasure.

Onward he caressed, endlessly, his fingers
magically finding each area that would give her

pleasure. The anticipation was incredible, the memory of the ultimate pleasure he had released on her before ever present in the back of her mind, waiting, wanting, impatient, and then finally within reach as his fingers went there.

She became hot and weak inside as the heat flushed through her. He teased. He parted her legs for easier access, yet only touched her lightly. She writhed, not knowing how to tell him what she wanted. His tongue delved into the indent on her belly, then left a wet trail up over her breasts, up her neck, and reaching her mouth, plunged inside . . . just as his fingers entered her deeply.

Her body slammed up against his, demanding greater contact. He finally relented and her flesh quivered as he molded her against him. Yet still that pulsing pleasure she remembered wouldn't come. It was close, so very close, yet each time she thought it would be upon her, he stilled his movements, until she felt like screaming.

She didn't scream, but her frustration reached such a point that she did retaliate by hitting him, first on his back, then his shoulder. She was aiming for his head when he caught her wrist and, with a chuckle, moved his body over hers and gave her what she wanted and yet . . . not what she was expecting.

Swiftly he entered her, deeply and easily, she was so ready for him. Instantly, too, did her mind clear and her thoughts return.

Amazing, that she had forgotten there was to be pain involved with this first bedding. Even more amazing, though, was it had been so minor that it really only startled her, rather than seriously hurt. But the frustration was only halted for a few moments. It rushed back with a vengeance, but now his body was so fully pressed to hers that she couldn't move, she couldn't think of a way to end it.

He knew how . . .

"Wrap your legs about my waist and lock your feet there, imprisoning me against you," he told her in a voice tight with constraint. "Do not let go. No matter how rough the ride, Mili, do not let go of me."

"Nay, I will not," she promised, more to herself than to him.

Instinct and raw passion guided her as he began that ride. Here was the greater pressure she had clamored for, the fullness and heat. Here, too, was the remembered pleasure, come upon her nigh instantly after his first few thrusts, and yet it was not at all the same. It was deeper, more satisfying, infinitely longer and much more exquisite. She was still feeling the pulsing aftershocks when, with a low groan, he pressed even deeper into her and then collapsed against her, motionless except for his deep breathing.

She realized she was still holding him to her very tightly, with both her arms and her legs. She did not feel like letting go, but supposed she must.

When she started to unwrap her legs from his waist he stirred enough to say, "Not yet."

She smiled to herself. Had he read her mind? Or like her, did he just not want to lose such pleasant contact yet?

Forty-seven

It was the first good sleep Milisant had had in weeks. She woke with a smile on her lips, but didn't realize it until Wulfric remarked on it.

"You must have had pleasant dreams."

Such a shock, to find him still there in bed with her. She hadn't expected, well, hadn't thought . . . She groaned inwardly. She had spent all her recent time worrying about the bedding and the expected restrictions that would be placed on her after the joining. The simple things that went along with marriage, like waking up next to Wulfric, had not once occurred to her.

"My dreams were—actually, I do not recall any, I slept so deeply."

"Ah, then I will be so bold as to take credit for that smile. You should have seen my own, wife. 'Tis like to have lit up this room brighter than the sunrise."

She realized several things at once. He was teasing her. He was well pleased with her. He was bragging—with good reason, but still . . .

And he had just called her wife. All of which made her blush, which in turn made him chuckle and rub his shoulder. To her horror, she realized he was reminding her that in her passion, she had hit him.

She buried her head under her pillow. He laughed and swatted her backside.

"Come, we have guests to be rid of. Most will be leaving today."

She sat up, thankful for the neutral subject. "The king as well?" She could hope.

"Aye, there is no reason for him to stay longer. He has not bothered you again?"

When would he have had the chance, as locked up and guarded as she had been these last few days? But she didn't point that out to him, merely shook her head in answer. She realized she did not want to start an argument with him so recently after—last night.

She flushed yet again, just remembering. He noticed and grinned at her, then leaned forward to brush his lips softly against hers.

"You are so funny when you do that," he teased. " 'Tis so unlike you."

"I will be sure to never do so again," she retorted, and managed to thrust aside her embarrassment—for the moment.

"Truly?"

His gaze dropped to her breasts, bare before him. She did it again.

Actually, to her complete discomfort and dismay, Milisant spent most of that day blushing. Now that she no longer had the protection of her dazed stupor, she heard every single ribald jest uttered near her, sat mortified through the traditional parading of the sheets by the older ladies, listened to the sexual prowess of men, and her husband in particular, discussed in thorough detail.

Wulfric seemed to take it all in stride and even joined in, but then it was hard to imagine that his good mood could be dented, it was so exuberant. She did wonder why he seemed so— happy. He did love someone else, after all, and his last chance to marry that other woman instead of Milisant was now gone for good. Given that, he should be as miserable today as she . . . should be.

Jesu, why *wasn't* she miserable? She should be. Just because she had thoroughly enjoyed his lovemaking was no reason to think everything between them would be wonderful now. How could it be when he was still, basically, a brute? She need only try to leave her bedchamber in leggings to find out what a tyrant he really was. Or fetch her bow and attempt to go hunting, which she sorely missed doing.

It was almost mandatory that all be present to send the king's party on their way with good wishes. Milisant watched Wulfric as he bid John a safe journey. Strictly formal, in no way did he by deed or word give away that he knew John's sordid secrets.

She wondered if she could be as circumspect. She was forced to find out, for after John was mounted, when it looked like he would ride out, he instead dropped his gaze to her in the crowd and unmistakably—at least she did not mistake it—bid her approach him.

Was that another blush coming on? Undoubtedly, for everyone gathered there was now looking curiously at her as she approached the king, and she hated being so centered in attention.

Not Wulfric, though; at least, he wouldn't wonder why John might want to single her out for words. He had been standing behind her, his hands on her shoulders, and had seen the summons as well. And had held her back to whisper to her before she stepped forward.

"You need not, if you do not want to. He would not make an issue of it."

His tension had been palpable. He must hate it, that he had so little control where the king was involved. Anyone else, he could call to account for doing what John had done, but not John—not unless he wanted to be branded a traitor.

She whispered back, "Nay, but then we—I at least—wouldst die of curiosity, to know what is now on his mind. Let me find out, Wulfric. 'Tis to our benefit."

She gave Wulfric no other chance to stop her, stepped quickly across the short span in the bailey to where John waited. He didn't dismount, merely leaned forward so his voice wouldn't have to carry far, since what he had to say was obviously for her ears only.

"I know 'tis unnecessary," John began, looking only slightly uncomfortable with what he had to say, "but we offer apologies, Milisant de Thorpe, for any misunderstanding that has passed between us. I had several talks with Guy after our—encounter. I am satisfied that he is mine and will remain faithful unto me. Your father has likewise reassured me. So guard well what bears no relevance."

He was telling her, in his way, that he was no longer against her marriage to Wulfric. She knew, also, that his last remark was a subtle warning for her to keep silent about their encounter.

He was guessing that she had told no one thus far, or hoping, since no one had brought it up to him. There was no reason to correct that assumption.

"Certainly, Highness," she assured him, and gave him a convincing smile. "I would not have it known by anyone that I had kicked the king of England."

It was a daring risk; mentioning her attack could bring on the famous Angevin temper. It didn't. He burst out laughing instead.

"I like your spirit, girl. 'Tis what I told my man when I sent him to—put an end to certain deluded grand schemes. Spirit like yours should not be crushed."

So saying, he nodded and sent his horse into a canter, his large entourage falling in behind him. She watched them for a moment, then sensed, more than felt, Wulfric at her back again. This was proven when he put his arm around her shoulder to lead her back into the keep.

He said nothing yet, nor was he like to, with so many people around them. But they were the first to reach the Great Hearth, everyone else still lingering in the bailey. And he was not going to let the matter pass.

His "Well?" was quite to the point.

"I think that whatever was involved in those attempts against me—and I am not so sure now that 'twas just John's doing, though he *was* aware of it—has been called off," she told him, warming her hands before the fire. "He said as much, in a roundabout way."

"You are sure?"

"I suppose I could have misunderstood, but I doubt it, since he also warned me not to speak to anyone about it. 'Tis over, as far as he is concerned."

He sighed. She heard relief in it. She knew why she was relieved, but she wondered about him and looked at him curiously. The question formed in her mind and wouldn't leave her. She never would have thought to ask it before, but after last night—after that sigh—she had to know . . .

She asked him, "Would it not have been to your benefit if John, or whoever else was involved, had succeeded ere we wed? Why did you protect me so judiciously? If they had succeeded, you could . . . have . . ."

She couldn't finish, he was now looking at her in such utter fury. "Where in the name of all the saints do you get these wild notions of yours? Do you actually think I could wish you harm, for *any* reason? And what possible reason could there be . . . ?"

"There was one very obvious one," she cut in stiffly, annoyed that he should take offense over a very logical question—all things considered. "That you would have preferred to wed with another, in particular the woman you love."

He looked—confused. There was no better

way to describe what briefly took the place of his anger. And then the confusion was gone, leaving the anger again, just not as strong, or at least his tone wasn't as harsh, merely scathing enough to scald her.

"If you are referring to that silly remark of mine that was made in response to your own declaration of love for someone *else*, then you are even more dense than I was, since for you, mere common sense would have told you by now that there was no substance behind that remark. Or do I behave like a man pining for another woman? Verily, if I do, I wish you would point out how, so I can correct such behavior, since there *is* no other woman."

So saying, he walked stiffly away from her. Milisant barely noticed him leave, she was so bemused.

He *didn't* love someone else? That had merely been a rejoinder because *she* had said it first? But—what was she to think now? His loving someone else had been high in her objections to him. It had prevented her from even considering her sister's suggestions concerning ways to get rid of her *other* objections. If he didn't love another, then he was free to love—her.

A warmth passed over her that had nothing at all to do with the nearby fire. It left her smiling.

Forty-eight

Milisant watched Wulfric closely that night at the evening meal, and afterward as well. He was still insulted, though it wasn't all that discernible to the average observer, since he made the effort to appear otherwise.

Yet Milisant knew, sensed it easily. He was still stewing. She, likewise, was still somewhat bemused, or at least she had been unable to stop thinking all day about what had been revealed by him, and the new possibilities that were now open to her.

She had spent much of the afternoon visiting with Roland and reminiscing about their fostering days at Fulbray. He and his parents would be leaving on the morrow, so she didn't have much time left to spend with her old friend and took advantage while she could.

She didn't discuss with him, of course, what was most on her mind right now, but she did manage to find Jhone alone for a few minutes that afternoon. And with her sister, she could talk of anything.

There was no reason to discuss what Jhone was most concerned about, though. One of those constant blushes that Milisant had been experiencing today, when Jhone had asked, "Well, did you like it?" was enough to satisfy and delight Jhone without explicit detail.

But her sister had other concerns as well and also wanted to know, "Think you that you can live here now without constant despair?"

"I think it will depend upon what room I am in," Milisant replied with a chuckle.

"Why would that . . . ?"

"Never mind, I was only jesting, since 'constant despair' sounded so—constant. Actually, I have learned a thing that *may* make it better here."

"What?"

"He does not love anyone else."

"But that is wonderful news!" Jhone exclaimed with delight. "Verily, it means Wulfric will soon love you—if he does not already."

"Already?" Milisant snorted over that farfetched possibility. "There is something else he does not like about me, or do you forget how many years it took him to fetch me? And he arrived at Dunburh most aggrieved to be there, even admitting that he had also tried to have the betrothal broken. If 'twas not because he loved someone else, then why was he furious at the idea of marrying me?"

"That was before and so should not matter. Now is much different, Mili, since he has come to know you. I watched him yesterday. He seemed a most happy groom."

"He is good at giving false impressions that have naught to do with his true feelings."

"You know him to be unhappy still?"

Milisant fidgeted somewhat. "Nay, not exactly, though he *is* presently wroth with me."

Jhone rolled her eyes. "What did you do now?"

Milisant rolled her eyes right back. "Asked him a simple question about his true love. He growled at me that he never had one, and that I *should* have realized that for myself, based on his behavior, as if I could guess that he only said it because I had said it."

"Did I not tell you nigh the same thing, that 'twas possible he had lied, just as you did? I *knew* he did not seem like a man pining for another."

Milisant winced at that choice of words, so similar to his, but pointed out, "*Seem* does not suffice where he is concerned, when he deliberately conceals. You have not been present for our many heated arguments. I have had *no* evidence that what he claimed was in fact a lie, other than he likes kissing me. Our constant fights supported his lie."

But Jhone was becoming as stubborn as Milisant was, and offered yet another contrary view. "Or they supported, as you say, whatever it is that he objects to about you. Have you asked him what that is?"

"Nay."

"You should. It might be naught of import, might be a misconception, might be easily set aside. And then what will you have left to object to yourself?"

"You know the answer to that," Milisant grumbled. "He still means to control my every action."

"Of course he does," Jhone agreed. "He *is* your husband now, after all. But *you* have the choice of accepting that or tempering it with love. As I pointed out before, which do you think would gain you more freedoms?"

They were interrupted after that and did not get a chance to talk privately again. But it had given Milisant more to think about. And imagining Wulfric in love with her was not an—unpleasant thought. But . . . there was still his original fury that he must marry her.

She still didn't know what had caused that, yet was now curious enough about it to broach the subject that night in their bedchamber. Theirs . . .

Aye, all of her belongings, without warning, had been moved that day into Wulfric's chamber—except for her pets. The animals had been left behind with Jhone—by Wulfric's order? Or had his servants merely been too hesitant to try to move her pets themselves? Rhiska could be intimidating, after all, especially to a servant not used to handling falcons, and Growls could make anyone leery if he started growling.

Wulfric wasn't there yet when she went up to retire that night. She *was* keeping his latest order in mind, though it was unnecessary. She was not the one who was presently angry, he was. And he still was. That was obvious when he walked in stiffly, frowning, and said no word to her as he started to disrobe.

She gave a mental snort. He thought to ignore

her? To take his own anger to bed with him? Well then, she might as well get her last question out of the way now, in case it annoyed him as much as the last one had.

She walked up behind him, tapped him on the shoulder, waited for him to turn around. He did so with raised brow. She got the distinct feeling then that he was expecting an apology. For making him admit that he had lied to her? She kept her second snort to herself as well.

"I wouldst finish our discussion begun earlier," she told him.

"It was finished."

"For you, mayhap, but I still have a question that needs answering. If there was no other woman—nay, do not interrupt me, hear me out," she said when he started to cut in. "If there was no other, then why did you come to Dunburh in such fury? And do not try to deny it. You *would* have preferred to marry another."

"Mayhap because the only memory I had of you, wench, was that you were a veritable termagant, and what man wants naught but temper tantrums from a wife? I may even have had another in mind. But I was not in love with her."

She should have been satisfied with that answer. It was not even high in the way of import, as far as she was concerned. But his description of her was unsettling and sparked her own temper. However, she still had not forgotten what she had agreed to last night.

So she did what anyone so constrained in a certain room would do. She took his hand and tried to drag him out of the bedchamber.

He wasn't cooperating, however, so she didn't get very far, only a few steps, actually, before he asked, "What do you think you are doing?"

"Taking us out of *here*, to finish this—discussion," she retorted.

After realizing what she meant, he chuckled and pulled her to him. "Nay, I think not."

She pushed against his chest, though not with much effort. She didn't really want to break the contact, flush as it was, and reminiscent of last night.

" 'Tis to be one-sided then, this setting aside of anger?" she asked.

He smiled wryly. "Nay, and thank you for pointing that out. 'Twas a silly annoyance anyway, not even worth saving for another day." His hands cupped her cheeks, his lips hovering just above hers. "I hope you feel the same."

"About what?" she asked breathlessly.

"If you do not know—far be it from me to be so misguided as to remind you."

Forty-nine

Two days after the wedding, all of the guests had departed, except for one earl who had made mention that he would be staying for at least another sennight. That would not have concerned Milisant in the least were it not that her restrictions had yet to be lifted, even though she was now married, even though she and Wulfric, at least, had determined that the threat against her had been "called off" by John himself.

Or so she had thought, that they had both determined that. She found out differently, however, when she brought the subject up to Wulfric that day. He had been discussing how much he had liked the window embrasures in Clydon's Great Hall, and added that he meant to put the suggestion to his father that they build the same here.

She was barely listening to him, afraid she already knew the answer to what she meant to ask. She had found out that morning that if Anne or Wulfric was not available, she was *still* to be locked in the solar. Worse, she had found it out when she'd arrived late to the hall to say good-bye to Roland and had tried to leave the keep to catch him in the bailey.

Wulfric was already out in the bailey, and possibly Anne was as well, since she was nowhere to be found either. But Milisant had *not* been allowed out herself, had in fact been escorted straightaway to the solar when she'd been discovered alone in the hall, and locked away just as she had been before the wedding.

'Twas midafternoon now. They both stood next to the Great Hearth, far enough away from Anne and her ladies to speak in private if they spoke at a normal level.

Milisant waited until Wulfric seemed done with his subject. She had restrained her anger well. She was trying, after all, to keep the peace between them, since she had actually been enjoying that peace. But her present grievance was too great to not mention it, which she finally did.

"You did not think I would want to bid Roland good-bye this morn?"

He raised a brow at her. "After you spent so much time with him yesterday?"

There was the tiniest bit of resentment in that question, which she chose to ignore for the moment. "What has that to do with common courtesy?"

"You had ample time to bid him farewell ere the Fitz Hughs left the hall," he pointed out.

She gritted her teeth, since he was obviously ignoring the meat of her complaint. "Even if that were so, which it was not, since I arrived too late for that, I still would have liked to be present when they rode out. Yet did I find that was impossible. I found instead that I am still to be locked in that blasted solar if neither you or your mother is around. Why did those guards throw me—"

"Throw you?" he interrupted in a near choking tone, his expression just as incredulous.

"Shove me inside," she corrected.

"Shove you? They laid hands on you?"

She was snarling by now. "Nay, I am making a point here, Wulfric. Stop jumping on each little word. They insisted! There, does that sound better to you? Which is beside the point. Why am I still to be locked up? We are wed now. The threat is gone."

"The threat is not gone until I am assured 'tis gone," he said in stiff response to her angry tone. "And as long as we still have guests here who come with a full entourage of their own servants, as many do, there will be folk here not easily identified."

"And what happens when a new guest arrives, or have you bothered to think that far ahead? Am I forever, then, to be shut away like an errant child?"

"Why do you persist in viewing it that way? 'Tis for your own protection."

"Mayhap because I do not need protection any longer! Mayhap because at least I am smart enough to realize that the threat is over."

That last was a direct insult, deliberate as well, she was suddenly so angry. And it struck true. His blue eyes became more intense. A muscle ticked in his cheek. And his tone, well, that turned downright menacing.

"I sometimes think you provoke me in hopes that I will beat you, just so you can then hate me more. Methinks 'tis time you got what you deserve."

So saying, he took her hand, dragged her out of the hall, up the stairs, straight into their bed-chamber, where he then slammed shut the door. She had not once tried to stop him, too shocked that this was to be the result of a few harsh words between them. But then she had known it would come to this eventually, and that she would despise him for it. She had expected no less from a brute such as he, had *known* to expect it, which was why she hadn't wanted to marry him. *But so soon after the wedding?!*

When she felt no blows yet, she forced herself to look at him. They were standing in the center of the room. He still held her hand. He was staring at her, but his expression was now inscrutable. She was herself so tense now, she could have shattered in a strong breeze.

"What are you waiting for?" she demanded, but got no answer. "Will you beat me or not?"

Wulfric still didn't answer for a moment, but then he sighed. " 'Tis not a matter of 'will,' but of 'can,' and I cannot."

"Why?"

"I would rather cut off my own hand than cause you the least little harm, Milisant."

She stared at him wide-eyed, and then she started to cry, those words having gone deep to wrench at her heart. She had never heard anything so—so nonbrutish in her life. And coming from him?

"Would that you could have felt that way

when you were younger," she whispered in a small, quavering voice.

"And how were my feelings then any different? I have never hurt you, Milisant. I even once took a great deal of punishment just so I would *not* hurt you."

She frowned now, swiping at her eyes, embarrassed to realize she had been crying, yet too bemused by his new statement not to ask, "When was this? I do not recall meeting you other than one time when we were young."

He smiled sadly. "Aye, and you must admit, 'twas a time neither of us has ever forgot. I wouldst apologize, belatedly, for killing your falcon that day. I only just learned of it recently from my mother. I had not known the bird died. That was certainly not my intention. Merely did I want to get it off of me when you sent it to attack."

He was apologizing for the first Rhiska, but not for nearly crippling her during the same incident? But of course, he hadn't known of her broken foot. No one had known about it. Yet he had viciously pushed her, which had caused it. And he considered that *not* hurting her?

She was unable to keep the old bitterness from her tone when she corrected at least one part of his statement. "I did not send Rhiska at you."

"You most certainly did."

"Nay, I moved to put her back on her perch so I could summon a guard to get rid of you, since you did not leave at my bidding. She did the attacking herself, having sensed my anger. She had only just been tamed, she was not trained yet, so I could not call her off of you. I stepped to you to get her *away* from you, but you were too quick to throw her off and kill her instead."

"I did not think I had killed her, Milisant, or I would have made amends then and there. I assume 'twas your grief that sent you at me tooth and nail? Or was it still your other rage, in hearing that we wouldst marry? And why *did* that enrage you so?"

These memories were not pleasant, but his last question dealt with the least of them, so she answered that at least, explaining, "One of the villagers had beat his wife to death just that week. The reactions to this were that she must have deserved it, that it was not of great import, that he would have to worry now about who would cook his dinner. She was dead, but he must now cook for himself, poor man."

"Villeins do not have the same concerns that we do," he pointed out. "Their priorities in matters of import wouldst not be the same as yours or mine."

"Mayhap, but I was so appalled by these reactions, I swore then and there that I would never marry myself. I had yet to be told about the betrothal, so did not know the decision had already been made for me. Then there you were, telling me that you were going to be my husband."

"Verily, that does indeed explain your original anger. I was unaware you had yet to be told of the betrothal. I knew of it, so I assumed you did."

"My father was still so grief-stricken over my

mother's death that he did not even think to discuss such things with me yet. 'Twas another two years ere he did, another two years ere I even knew *who* you were. That day you were no more than a stranger intruding where you did not belong, a complete stranger telling me he wouldst be marrying me, a stranger who had killed my falcon and caused me such—"

She didn't finish, couldn't. She was about to cry again and hated that she had so little control over her emotions now—just as then.

"Caused you such—what?"

It was the wrong time to be asked. She was choking on the memory, couldn't hold it back any longer.

"Pain! And for three months, the horror of thinking I wouldst be a cripple!"

"*Cripple?!*"

"When you shoved me away, you did not look to see the result. You just left."

"*What* result?"

"I fell on my foot. It broke. I put the bone back in place myself. I have no idea why I did that, other than the thought of being a cripple so terrified me that I was unaware of what I was doing. I could not cry, could not scream, could make no sound at all."

He yanked her to him, put his arms around her, squeezed hard. His face had gone pale. She saw that just before she was buried in his arms.

"*Jesu,*" he whispered hoarsely. "No wonder you have hated me. But I had no choice that day, Milisant. 'Twas the only way I could think to get you off of me. 'Twas done to *save* you harm, not cause it!"

"Do you tell me a small girl child was threatening you? Giving you no choice? I may have been insane with grief and barely aware of what I was doing, but you were big even then, Wulfric, big and sturdy. How was I giving you no choice but to shove me violently away?"

"Would you like to see the teeth marks you left on my inner thigh? You bit deep enough to leave scars, though I did not know that at the time, since you had also unmanned me with a blow to my groin that caused any other pain to be insignificant in comparison. Your falcon had also taken a chunk out of my hand. Would you like to see that scar, too? So I could not use that hand to restrain you. You had me on my knees from the blow you landed. You were rending my face bloody as well with your nails. Aye, I felt I *had* to get you off of me. You were giving me no choice. But instead of hitting you to make you stop, which would have been the quickest way to end it, I tried to save you injury by pushing you back. God, I am sorry my action had the opposite result instead."

She said nothing. She was trying to take in all he had just said, to picture it in her mind from his perspective, to set it beside everything else she knew about him now—and finally knew, without a doubt, that he was telling her the truth. He had not meant to hurt her. It had been no more than bad luck that she should fall just so, a horrible accident, but an accident nonetheless.

He was still squeezing her so tightly she could barely breathe, let alone speak. At the moment he was more upset than she was. Oddly, she wanted to soothe him now. That was out of the question, but . . .

"I did all of that?" she said at last.

"You did."

"Good."

He stilled. He set her back from him and looked at her mulish expression and then—he started to chuckle. For some reason, she started to laugh as well.

It felt so good to have that tightness in her chest ease away. As it left her, she realized the memory of that day was never going to cause her pain again, and she had Wulfric to thank for that. How incredibly ironic.

Fifty

"Fetch your bow."

Milisant turned to Wulfric to see who he was speaking to, certain it could not be herself, yet he *was* staring at her, and she *had* heard him aright—which left her suspicious enough to question him, "Why? 'Twould not make good firewood, I promise you."

He laughed. "Because I feel like hunting, and I thought mayhap you would like to join me."

She stared at him in utter amazement now. They had just finished the midday meal, were still sitting at the high table, long after most everyone else had left. His mood had been jovial all day, well, had been since yesterday afternoon, when they had cleared up so many misconceptions between them. He had barely left her side since then, and she found she did not mind that at all.

She had yet to fully dissect the conclusions she had reached yesterday, was still so amazed that she had no further serious objections to Wulfric that she hadn't figured out all the ramifications of that yet. There were still a few things she was not overjoyed with, but they were too minor to mention, and besides, she was enjoying, for a change, not being angry about anything, enjoying his company, enjoying the way he teased her, the way he . . .

With that thought passing through her mind, she had to ask now, "You are not teasing me, are you? You actually know how to hunt with a bow?"

"Why would I not know how?"

"Because hawking has been considered the elite way to hunt for so long that many lords would not know what to do with a bow if it was handed to them."

He chuckled. "I assure you I am not one of those, Mili. Verily, like you, I actually prefer using my own skills, and do possess a few of them that do not require the lifting of a sword."

"Including archery?"

"Aye. Now, what are you waiting for? And wear something . . . appropriate for hunting."

He was *telling* her to wear her leggings? She could not believe this—yet she wasn't going to give him a chance to change his mind about it. In fact, she threw her legs over the bench so quickly that her skirts got left behind and she nigh fell on her face on the floor as she lost her balance. Wulfric's hand was quickly there to steady her until she could yank her skirts across the bench.

He didn't laugh as she might have expected, but she heard her father chuckle nearby and wondered if he had given Wulfric the suggestion to take her hunting. She did not care where the idea came from; that he was willing to do so was what she found so amazing.

She ran into Jhone on the stairs, nearly knocked her over in her haste. She grabbed her hand, pulled her along behind her, unwilling to stop for even a moment to talk, yet wanted to share with her how excited she was.

"*What* is your hurry?" Jhone huffed once she was inside Milisant's chamber, then seeing her go straight to her coffer and start tossing clothes out of it said, "You have finally taken leave of your senses, aye?"

"Wulfric is taking me hunting."

That should have explained it all, did so in Milisant's mind, yet Jhone said, "So?"

"So I had feared I wouldst never be able to hunt again—at least as I prefer to. Now here he is, only two days after we have joined, taking me hunting. You see no significance in that?"

"I do, of course," Jhone replied smugly. "The question is, do you?"

Milisant chuckled as she shrugged out of her cumbersome bliaut and chemise. "Is this where you are going to tell me, I told you so? That is a bad habit you have, Jhone, of always being right—*and* gloating over it."

Jhone snorted. "I do not gloat—are you sure you should wear those?"

Milisant had reached for her leggings. She paused long enough to grin at her sister. "Aye, he ordered me to."

Jhone rolled her eyes. But she came over to help Milisant tie up her cross garters and find a loose tunic to wear with them.

After a moment Jhone wondered aloud, "Has he told you he loves you yet?"

"Not yet."

"Mayhap today then."

"You think?"

"Me?" Jhone snorted again. "What do I know, since I am so rarely right?"

Milisant laughed, hugged her sister, snatched up her bow and quiver of arrows, and ran out the door.

Jhone yelled after her, "Wait! You forgot a cloak. It *is* still winter, if you have not noticed!" Then with a smile to herself, since Milisant didn't come back, "Never mind, I doubt me he will let you get cold."

Milisant hadn't felt so exhilarated in years—and happy. Aye, happy. It was in her expression. She couldn't hide it. And the man beside her wore a constant grin as well, as if he knew he was responsible for her jubilation—and so he was. Imagine that.

When he had come for her last month at Dunburh, she had thought her world was ending. Nothing was ever going to be right for her again, unless she could somehow avoid wedding Wulfric de Thorpe altogether. Now, wedded and bedded by him, she could suddenly find no fault with anything. Just the opposite. She was *happy!* She was delighted to *be* with him. He seemed to be going out of his way to please her, and she was indeed pleased, in so many ways.

Did he love her then? Like Jhone, she was now inclined to think so. She had only to hear it from him to be sure. And if she did hear it? Should she lie and tell him the same, if that would make him happy?

His love was needed, as Jhone had pointed out, to allow her the freedoms she so craved. Today was sure proof of that. But her own feelings . . . She *was* happy; there was no denying that. She *was* pleased with him now. Would that be enough for him? Or would he demand her love in return? Would it even matter to him, as long as they continued to get along so splendidly, as they presently were?

She moved ahead of him through the woods. They had left the horses a ways back. She had feared that Wulfric would make too much noise because of his size, and frighten any game away. But he surprised her. She could barely hear his footsteps behind her. And then she heard an arrow fly.

She turned, saw him lowering his bow. She looked in the direction he faced, and saw the dove on the ground. She beamed at him, wondering if he'd shot it out of the air, and joined him to collect it.

"Do you pluck?" she asked when she got there and saw that it was a nice, medium-sized bird. "Roasted sounds good about now."

"Me?" He looked down at the bird and laughed, which was answer enough. "What about you? Do you pluck?"

"I never have," she admitted. "I always brought my kills home for the table."

He nodded and stuffed his kill in a sack he had tied to his belt. "We will have to bring one of the kitchen helpers along with us next time, if you want to eat as you hunt. I agree, fresh roasted over a campfire does sound rather tempting at the moment."

Next time . . .

She was so pleased, hearing there would be a next time, that she could have kissed him. Then she went very still, staring at him, as she realized that there was nothing to stop her from doing so. She did so.

His reaction was swift as he pulled her to him, taking over the kiss. The sack had dropped to the ground, as did his bow. After a moment, though, he paused to gaze at her, his eyes filled with tenderness, one hand just as tender on her cheek.

She gazed back at him in wonder, and said with the same wonder in her tone, "You love me?"

"It took you this long to figure that out?"

"Aye." She blushed slightly. "My mind had been on other things."

He nodded, smiled. "Let us hope those other things bother you no more, and from now on your mind dwells more on things like . . . this."

He kissed her again. The contrasts were noticeable, his nose cold against hers, his hands warm, though, and his lips downright hot, because the rest of their exposed skin was chilled—but quickly warming. She imagined that if they continued, they would soon be giving off steam . . .

She heard the blow, a solid thwack, then felt Wulfric tilting toward her, actually falling. He did fall, taking her with him, landed on top of her, then—utter stillness. She was still herself, having had the breath knocked out of her, but when she regained it, she could still barely breathe because of his weight.

The realization came suddenly that he was too still, unnaturally still. At the same time, she felt warm blood drip on her neck from the back of his head.

The scream gathered in her throat just as he was shoved off of her. She was yanked to her feet before she got the sound out. She stared down in horror at Wulfric, bleeding, more pale than she had ever seen him, not breathing that she could see, then at the man holding her wrist in an iron grip, a thick branch nigh the size of a small log in his other hand, which he had clubbed Wulfric with.

"*Jesu*, are you mad?" she gasped in horror.

"Nay," the man said, and he was actually grinning at her. "Just lucky." She didn't understand, not at all—and then she did when he added, "Come along, lady. Our meeting is long overdue."

Fifty-one

Milisant had not been able to see where she had been taken. Tears had blinded her, and with her hands restrained behind her back, she had been unable to wipe the tears away. By the time she could see again with any clarity, she was inside a thatch-roofed hut.

The dwelling could be right in the village, near it, or sit alone in the woods—she couldn't be sure. An old couple lived there. The woman had been severely beaten, lay half dead in the corner. The old man sat beside her on the rush-covered floor, unharmed but looking terrified.

From a remark she heard, she gathered that he was being used to get rid of anyone who might come to visit. His wife had been beaten to get him to cooperate and give a good performance, pretending that nothing was wrong.

It wasn't a large hut, was only the one room, and so was crowded since there were others there as well. Aside from the man who had brought her, there were two other men—and that woman whom she had thought a whore, the one she'd thought Wulfric had dallied with.

Hers was the first voice Milisant heard when she was roughly shoved into the hut. "Finally! *Now* can I return to London? I have been of little use here, since that lord got suspicious of me."

"You belittle yourself, Nel. You have talents other than poisoning," the man at Milisant's back replied.

"Aye, Ellery, but you have not wanted them," she sniffed resentfully.

Ellery chuckled at her. "Alger and Cuthred are much appreciative, though. You have kept them most happy during the wait."

"Indeed," one of the other men said from his seat at the table, and tried to pull Nel onto his lap, only to get his hand slapped away.

"But aye," Ellery continued. "You can leave now. Just make sure you are not seen doing so."

"As if I want that lord breathing down my neck again. I had had a good cover, had worked that villager well to get it, but soon as that lord started questioning me, 'twas all over. I was lucky to escape with my skin. They are too watchful by half around here."

"But to no avail," Ellery said, and there was a great deal of smug triumph in his voice. "Since they have lost their pretty treasure, and now we have it."

"Patience does pay off," one of the other men said. "You said it would, and seems you were right as usual."

"And vigilance," the other man piped in, then added, "Where did you find her? Out hunting again?" The last was asked with a snicker.

"Actually, she was."

An amazed whistle. "I had not thought she could be that foolish again."

"To give credit, she was not alone this time," Ellery corrected.

"Ah, so not *that* foolish—just too foolish for you, eh?" was said with a laugh.

"Exactly," Ellery agreed. "I expected another journey, though, like her last one. If she could escape once, she could again—which was why I continued to keep watch on the gates. I found them on the way to my usual perch."

It was telling, that no one asked what had happened to the one who had been with her, telling that the others took it for granted that Ellery had seen to him, which to them meant he was dead.

The tears started again. Was he dead? If only she had been given time to find out. But she feared the worst. She had been unable to see if he breathed. He had been too pale—deathly pale.

It was killing her inside, how little hope she had that Wulfric might have survived the vicious blow to his head that Ellery had dealt him. And to realize too late that she loved him. He hadn't asked to hear it from her, but oh, God, she wished she had said it, wished he had heard it before he . . . The tears wouldn't stop, were running into the gag that bit into her cheeks.

"If you scream, I will hurt you bad, might even cut out your tongue. I would rather not have to do that, would rather hear your voice, just not a loud one. Do we understand each other?"

Ellery said this to her, whispered it softly near her ear as he untied the gag from her mouth. The rope that he had wrapped about her wrists before he had tossed her up on his horse he had removed as he spoke with his cohorts. With so many of them there and the door closed, he must feel restraints were no longer needed.

She didn't answer, hoped that would be answer enough for him. If she felt it would be useful to scream, she would scream, despite his threats. But it would serve her no purpose whatsoever to tell him that.

She turned to face him now. She had not gotten a good look at him before, had been too horrified to see other than Wulfric lying there in his own blood, then she'd seen nothing at all, she had cried so hard.

She was surprised that he was a big, handsome man, but surprised only for a brief moment. Killers came in all varieties, after all.

The other two men, stocky, bearded, had the look of typical mercenaries for hire. They laughed, they joked with each other, they might question their task, they might not. This one, though, this Ellery, he had a different look, a more menacing quality.

She had a feeling he would feel no different swatting a fly or slitting a baby's throat. Neither would engender an emotion in him that might stop him from doing so. A man without conscience, able to kill, maim, rape, and thumb his nose at the laws of the land, simply because he could. That made him more dangerous than the average mercenary for hire, much more dangerous than his two cohorts.

Cuthred and Alger were watching her with interest from where they sat at a rickety table in the center of the room. The old man in the corner seemed afraid to look at her. Nel was stuffing a few scattered things into a sack. She was leaving, and quickly. So she was to have poisoned her? Wulfric had been right about that.

Yet Milisant didn't understand why these people were still here, why they still wanted her captured—dead. And she had to assume she was to be killed if Nel had been brought here to try to poison her.

Had she completely misunderstood King John's innuendos? If these were not the ones who were to be called off, then who? Or had John's man simply been unable to find them yet to tell them? *Jesu*, had Wulfric been killed for nothing, because of a messenger's tardiness?

"You have erred," she said in a voice hoarse with choking emotion.

"Have I?" Ellery smiled at her. "When I do not make mistakes?"

"But you have," she insisted. "Whatever you do here, were you not told that the king has called this off? He no longer wishes me harm."

To that, Ellery shrugged and said simply, "We do not work for the king."

"Who then?"

A new voice, heard as the door opened again. "They work for me."

Fifty-two

He was a lord or a rich merchant, or so his raiments declared him. Rings and chains of gold, fine woolen hose, a tunic of thick velvet. He stood proudly, arrogantly, as if he expected everyone there to bow down to him. The look he turned on Milisant was gloating.

But Ellery put a dent in the man's apparent triumph when he said with such obvious disgust, "De Roghton, *how* do you keep finding us?"

The lord stiffened. "That implies you have been hiding from me?"

"Aye, it does, does it not?"

Hot color suffused de Roghton's face, hotter still when he saw Milisant's surprise, that he would be spoken to like that. "How do you expect to get paid if you cannot be found?" he bit out.

Ellery snorted. "Mayhap by going to you instead? But how is it you come here now, *just* as she is found?"

"Mayhap as you have been watching for her,

I have been watching for your success—belated as it is."

Ellery colored slightly now. The lord's tone had been insulting, but Milisant could not detect an insult in the words. Ellery had heard it, though, whatever it was. Then it occurred to her . . .

"Was there a time constraint on my capture?" she asked, though she did not really expect an answer. "You can at least tell me what this is about."

The lord was going to ignore her. She was to die. Explanations did not need to be wasted on her.

But Ellery said, "Aye, she does deserve to know why. I would like to hear that answer myself, so answer her, Lord Walter."

She knew of no noble who would take such orders from a common mercenary, nor would this lord have. But he heard what she heard, the very real menace in Ellery's tone, a subtle threat.

De Roghton still tried to ignore it, demanding, "Why is she still alive?"

Ellery took out his dagger. Milisant felt the blood leave her face. But the weapon was not for her—not yet anyway. He very calmly, very slowly, cleaned a fingernail with the tip of the blade. And then he looked back at de Roghton, stared at him, and continued to stare at him.

After several tense moments of this, the lord answered her question, glaring at her as he did. "You should have died ere you were married. The joining of the Crispins and de Thorpes should not have occurred."

"Because King John was against it? 'Twas his idea then? You are merely his lackey?"

She should not have tried to insult him. Her words caused Ellery to laugh, which in turn enraged Walter de Roghton all the more. He could not hide it either as he glared at Ellery. The hate between these two men was palpable. Yet the one worked for the other?

Despite his new rage, Walter de Roghton still answered her. "Nay, 'twas my idea, but I had John's tacit approval. He would have then recommended my daughter to Shefford for his son to marry."

"But the joining has occurred," she pointed out. "You are too late."

"Nay, all is not lost, just not as ideal as it could have been. But young de Thorpe will still need another wife—when you are dead. John may still be benevolent enough to make the recommendation, since the solidity of the alliance will not be as firm with you dead."

She shook her head, incredulous over such reasoning. And besides, John had changed his mind.

She pointed that out, telling him, "You delude yourself. You will find that John has withdrawn his approval. He has reaffirmed with both the earl and my father, and thus approves of my marriage now. He has sent his man to find those who have tried to harm me and tell them to desist. So it is you his man seeks but has yet to find?"

"You lie," Walter snarled, but she saw doubt in his eyes and pressed her point.

"Do I? And what will be John's reaction when

he learns you have directly disobeyed him? Think you that you will live much longer than I will? And for what? I had to die just so your daughter could marry Wulfric. 'Twas so hard to find her a husband, you had to kill to do so?"

He took the insult to heart. "It goes much deeper than that, vixen. Anne should have been mine. I spent months courting her. Her wealth should have been mine. But de Thorpe was chosen over me."

"Ah, I see now. This was merely another bid for that wealth, since you yourself cannot manage to make your own fortune."

It was one insult too many for him. He took a step forward and slapped her. She had expected it, provoked it. What did she care, anyway, now that Wulfric was dead? And therein was the joke. The arrogant lord didn't even know that the one he had hired to kill her had also killed the man he hoped would be his son-in-law.

She *was* going to tell him, was going to throw it in his face, that every foul thing he had worked for had been destroyed by the swing of a sturdy branch. She would tell him just as soon as the truth could get past her choked emotions, caused by thinking of it again.

But she didn't get a chance to tell him. Ellery, for some reason, took exception to the lord hitting her. He swung him around, backhanded him once just for the pleasure of it, then stuffed his dagger into his gut. And she had been right. Not a single emotion crossed his handsome face as he killed a noble of the realm.

His cohorts were less blasé about it, quite the

opposite. They both jumped to their feet, one incredulous, the other horrified.

"Are you mad?!" was asked nearly in unison.

"Hardly," Ellery said with little concern as he bent to wipe his dagger clean on the dead man's tunic, then slipped it back into his boot.

"You just killed our employer!"

"And a lord!"

"Who is going to pay us now?"

"Aye, you could have at least waited until he paid us first."

"Ellery, a lord?" This from Nel. "They will hunt you down for this."

He looked at Nel and chuckled. "And how will anyone know what happened to this arrogant bastard? Think you someone here will be carrying tales of it?"

That was so telling a remark, Milisant's hands broke out in a sweat. It meant the old couple would not be left alive here. It meant she wouldn't either. His friends were the ones who wouldn't be carrying any tales, which he was quite confident of, and with good reason. They were likely as afraid of him as Milisant was.

"But what of our pay?" one of the men repeated in a sour grumble. "We have been at this job for over a month. For naught?"

Ellery made a sound of disgust himself. "Enough whining, Cuthred. I will pay you myself. In fact, you are no longer needed here, so return to London. Take Nel with you, and take the body, too. Dump it along the way."

That seemed to ease the two men's minds. Nel was already heading out the door. One of the men hefted de Roghton's feet and dragged him out.

The other stared at Milisant for a moment before asking Ellery, "Can I at least hit her once, for that wound she gave me?"

"Nay, I want no blood on her ere I cause it myself. Go on. I will finish here and meet you in London. She will pay for the wounds, never fear."

The man seemed satisfied with that, and it was not long before the door closed again and Ellery turned to give Milisant his full attention. The old man was huddled against his wife, hiding his face against her, trembling. Clearly he expected to die right then. But obviously Ellery found him so insignificant, he didn't even look at him. His eyes fixed on Milisant and didn't leave her.

Milisant's blood turned cold, her breath caught in her throat. It would not be so bad if she thought she could reason with him. But one could not reason with a man without conscience, a man who killed for hire, who did so without emotion, and there was not a speck of emotion in those cold eyes that stared at her now . . . There was no hope whatsoever.

Fifty-three

The silence that continued was nerve-racking. Ellery remained standing by the door, staring. As soon as he moved, Milisant knew she was going to scream. If he didn't move soon, she was going to scream. She was so tense, she was going to scream anyway . . .

"I have waited a long time for this."

The satisfaction in his tone was thick enough to cut. It was almost a relief that he was finally ready to end this. Almost.

"You take such pleasure in killing then?" Milisant asked him.

"Killing?" He seemed a bit surprised. "Nay, the killing could have been done many times over. I have kept you alive instead."

"Why?"

"Why else, m'lady? Because I want a taste of you first. That is the only reason you still live, when there were so many opportunities to kill you ere now."

She was going to be sick. That "first" meant he was still going to kill her, *after* he raped her.

But his reason for killing her had just been dragged out of the hut, dead. Hadn't that occurred to him yet?

"I would have killed that deluded bastard myself, am grateful that you did, so I will not be telling anyone of his demise. Why then must I still die?"

"I will have to think on that. I pride myself on finishing a job I start, and I was hired to kill you. Of course, with de Roghton unable to pay me now . . . aye, I will have to think on it. But there will be time aplenty for that. I have thought of you and having you for too long now. I have a feeling one taste may not be enough."

That might have given her hope if the thought of his touching her were not just as bad as his killing her. She would rather he just killed her. He might be a handsome man, but after Wulfric and his tender touch, she could not bear it, to have anyone else touch her, and in particular this cold-blooded killer.

He took the first step toward her. She didn't scream. She had him talking now and wanted to keep him talking. Not to delay the inevitable, but to find the key that might change his mind. She couldn't imagine what that might be; a word, a phrase, she had no idea. But she had to try.

"Your man said I wounded him. How?"

He rubbed his shoulder. He smiled. It was hard to see the murderer in him when he smiled.

"You wounded us all with your arrows. How is it you do not remember?"

"Oh, that."

He chuckled. "You are possessed of either a terrible skill with the bow or an excellent one. I am inclined to believe 'tis the latter, so why did you try only to wound, rather than kill? That was foolish of you."

More foolish than she could have realized. "I thought you might be the Shefford patrol."

"Ah, then I must be glad of that, since we were not expecting you to attack, were unprepared for it. Some wounds are deserved."

Resentment filled her tone. "But you want to punish me for that as well?"

"Nay, wounds heal, dead bodies do not. I am grateful for your foolishness."

Was this the cord she had hoped to find? She grasped it with both hands, telling him, "If you are grateful, return the favor. Let me go."

He chuckled at the request, dashing that small spark of hope. "I have already returned the favor. You are still alive, are you not?"

Bitterly she said, "Verily, I wish I were not. You killed my husband! I have no reason now to continue living, so just be done with it."

He had reached her. He trailed a finger along her cold cheek. He smiled again, was completely unaffected by her impassioned speech.

" 'Tis warm flesh I want to feel, lady. Take off your clothes for me."

She slapped his hand away from her. "Cooperation, you will not have from me."

He shrugged, withdrew his dagger from his boot again. "So be it," he said. "It hardly matters how I have you, as long as I have you."

She should have stepped back from him when

she'd had the chance. He was too close, and too swift. In a second, his dagger tip was pressing against her throat and his lips smashed over hers, swallowing her scream. She tried to lean into the metal point, but the dagger was not there to hurt her, was there to cut away her tunic.

The material ripped open easily under such a sharp blade. The sound of the tearing was like a death knell to her ears. She barely heard the scratching that followed.

He did. He released her, staring at the door. She heard it clearly then, a scratching against the wood, like an animal's nails . . .

The door burst open with such force, it seemed to rock the entire hut when it hit the wall. The wolf bounded in before the man who stood there, filling the opening. The animal could smell the fear in the room, reacted to it, and went right to its cause. Fangs bared, snarling, he moved into a position to leap and shred.

"Call him off, Mili!" Wulfric shouted from the doorway. "I want him for myself."

"Growls!"

The wolf came to her, but half whining, half growling. His instinct to kill had risen, was hard for him to give up immediately. The same instinct was in the man, and he wasn't giving it up.

Wulfric was not dressed for battle. He had fetched his sword and Growls to track her, but nothing else. He had not even stopped long enough to bandage his head. Blood trailed down his neck, some dry, some still wet, adding to that which soaked his tunic. But oh, God, she had never been so pleased to see anyone in her life. He was alive!

Ellery was not pleased by the interruption, but clearly he didn't count it too much of an inconvenience, his confidence was so great. He threw the dagger in his hand first, but didn't seem surprised when Wulfric dodged it. His sword was drawn next. Wulfric's was already in hand.

"So we meet again, m'lord," Ellery said so casually, they could have been sharing mugs of ale in a hostelry.

"Aye, but for the last time."

Ellery chuckled. "My thoughts exactly. And I will take the advantage of fighting in these close quarters, which I am quite used to, whereas you are used to fighting on an open battlefield."

"Take it," Wulfric replied, "though I will warrant, the only advantage you will have is the time it takes me to reach you."

As this was said as he charged forward, it was no advantage at all, since their weapons clanged together mere seconds later. The sound made Wulfric wince. Milisant realized his head was hurting him, mayhap severely, and that was the advantage Ellery would have, that and that he was wearing the thick leather of a mercenary.

Otherwise, they were nigh the same size, had much the same strength, so it would be an equal fight—or so Milisant had thought. She was forgetting, though, having watched Wulfric that day in the bailey when he had practiced with his brother. She had thought at the time that his skill was vastly superior. He proved it now, and she knew the very second that Ellery realized it, too.

He was capable of emotion after all—fear, like the fear she had felt, like what Wulfric must have felt when he'd awakened in the woods to find her gone. Ellery obviously felt it now, when his every thrust and swing was repelled, when he couldn't manage to do the same and started bleeding here, there, a half dozen different places, and his own blood slackened his grip. And he felt it most strongly when his guard slipped and he saw the sword coming at him, and knew it would not be stopped this time . . .

Fifty-four

The hut was not so far from the village after all. It had been moved, by general insistence, off into the woods just a bit, because the old man snored so loudly, he had actually disturbed his neighbors with it. It was close enough to see, but enough brush had grown up around it over the years that it was also concealed adequately for Ellery's purpose of coming and going from it unnoticed.

Wulfric carried the old lady into the village to her daughter, who would be able to tend her. The way back to the castle took much longer, though, because Wulfric's head was hurting too much now to ride to it, so they walked. Hand in hand. And stopped quite frequently to hug— at least Milisant did.

She was still so incredulous that he was actually alive, that she was, too, for that matter, that she just had to share her joy over that with him, again and again. But he didn't seem to mind.

At the castle, though, she made haste to get him the help he needed, sending for Jhone and her needles, sending for water and bandages, posting one burly guard at the bottom of the stairs to make sure the castle leech did *not* come up to their bedchamber. She fretted that she could do so little for him herself, but she did carefully get his tunic off, sat him on a stool near the fire, plied him with wine, and got most of the blood off him before Jhone arrived.

Their bedchamber became a gathering place while Wulfric was being fixed up. His parents came to fuss over him. His brother and a half dozen others, wandering in and out, came to make sure he was all right. Anne didn't stay long, hated the sight of blood herself. Guy hovered nearby, listening to Wulfric's account of what had happened.

And Milisant was wringing her hands because of the pain he was feeling with each dip of Jhone's needle. She repeatedly admonished her to be more careful, repeatedly asked for reassurance that he would be all right.

She was making such a nuisance of herself that Jhone finally stopped what she was doing, pointed a finger at the door, and told her sister, "Get out!"

Milisant did leave, huffed out, but was back in less than a minute and making a nuisance of herself again. But each of his winces was driving her mad. She finally knelt before him, put her head on his chest and her arms around him. It was the only way she could offer comfort at the moment.

Nigel found them like that when he arrived, with Wulfric's cheek resting on the top of Milisant's head. Jhone rolled her eyes at Nigel as he raised a questioning brow at her. Milisant hadn't heard him come in, so wasn't aware that he was now standing there, watching Jhone work.

Until he said in all seriousness, "I could probably sew a much straighter line—if I could manage to ply a needle around all that blood and gore."

Jhone's mouth dropped open. She simply stared at her father. She really hadn't believed Milisant's account of his sewing abilities, but now . . .

Milisant, however, hearing only the description he'd just given, wailed, "I am going to be sick."

"So am I," Wulfric agreed.

Which had Milisant bristling, "There! You see what you are doing to him? Stop it!"

"Making him forget to notice the pain, if you ask me," Nigel said, and chuckled, moving over to stand out of the way with Guy.

The two fathers smiled at each other as they watched their children. A remark or two was made, but didn't carry far enough for everyone to hear other than a word or two, words like "knew" and "stubborn" and "just a matter of time."

Finally Jhone was finished, the bandages applied. Wulfric was dressed again and refusing to go to bed in the middle of the day just because he had a few stitches. He did agree to sit back in the bed, though, if Milisant would join him there. She shooed everyone else out, barred the door, and did just that, even snuggled next to him, an arm across his waist, her head on his shoulder.

She didn't want to talk of what had happened anymore, even though he didn't know the whole of it yet. He had given his account of it to his father, but it was from his point of view, which didn't include Walter de Roghton, since he had been dragged away before Wulfric arrived.

But there would be time and enough to tell him the rest later, when he was feeling better. And she was sure he would agree with her, too, that there would be no need to tell his mother that an old, jealous suitor of hers had nigh wrecked all their lives with his far-fetched ambitions.

"Did I tell you yet that I love you?" she asked after a while of comfortable silence.

She had wound down herself, finally, was relaxed now, leaning there against him. The room was warm, quiet, and she had been thinking only vaguely about bringing his dinner to him in bed. *He* might not think he needed bed rest, but *she* disagreed with that. And she was confident that she would be winning at least half of their disagreements from now on, if they even had any more that pertained to other than health.

"I think you told me about a hundred times on our walk back to Shefford—aye, I think you told me already."

She smiled at his teasing. "You will have to forgive me. 'Tis just very new to me, this feeling."

"Aye, for myself as well, but we can muddle through the intricacies of it together."

She kissed him lightly on the chest, snuggled

closer, then said out of the blue, "I want to have a baby."

He burst out laughing, then moaned because it hurt. After a moment he said, "I trust you can wait the requisite time for such things to occur naturally?"

She sighed. "If I must."

He glanced down at her closer then. "You were not jesting? You really want a baby?"

"Aye—if he looks like you."

"We can throw him back if he does not, I suppose, but I would rather *she* look like you."

She grinned at him. "We can always have one of each."

He stared, then rolled his eyes and chuckled. "*Jesu*, I had not once thought of that, that twins will now be a possibility in my children." And then tenderly, "You have brought more to this marriage than I bargained for."

"Twins are a surprise and a handful," she remarked. "Never a bargain."

"I was referring to love."

"Oh."

She blushed. She beamed inwardly. She hugged him tighter. If she got any happier, she was afraid she was going to burst with it.

"We could begin now," he said after a while more.

"Begin what?"

"Making that baby."

She sat forward, smiled, but shook her head at him. "Oh, no, you will be having your healing time first. Do not even think of doing a single thing that is strenuous until your stitches are removed."

"I find naught strenuous about making babies."

She almost giggled, he said that so indignantly. She did lean back into him.

"Mayhap when your pain is gone then," she conceded.

"What pain?" he asked, straight-faced.

She did giggle this time. And kissed him lightly, gently, but with infinite feeling. And then got out of there posthaste before this became one of the times that he won the disagreement. She *would* see to his health. But mayhap later tonight he would be feeling better . . .